CHASING THE DOLLAR

MIRANDA VAUGHN MYSTERIES #1

ELLIE ASHE

PRAISE FOR ELLIE ASHE

"Smart, sexy, and so suspenseful! The Miranda Vaughn Mysteries take you on a wild ride through the world of big-money crime, and you won't believe whodunit!" –*Traci Andrighetti, USA Today bestselling author of the Franki Amato Mysteries.*

"High stakes, high energy, and a highly humorous good time! From Belize to Macau, this is one globe-trotting adventure you don't want to miss!" —*Gemma Haliday, New York Times bestselling author.*

Winner of the 2015 HOLT Medallion awards from the Virginia Romance Writers for best first novel and novel with romantic elements.

CHASING THE DOLLAR
by
ELLIE ASHE

Cover design by Qamber Designs and Media

Ellie Ashe

http://www.ellieashe.com

❀ Created with Vellum

CHAPTER ONE

"Not guilty."

The two words sliced through the thick atmosphere in the courtroom, and my heart leapt. The boa constrictor of stress that had been wound around my body for the last year and a half eased a tiny bit. Next to me, my attorney, Robert Fogg, tensed. We weren't remotely done, his body language warned.

"As to Count Two, wire fraud, the jury finds the defendant—"

A pause. Why was the clerk pausing?

"Not guilty."

The breath escaped my lungs, but Rob put a cautious hand on my arm warning me not to get too excited yet. He'd spent much of the last fourteen months explaining the odds, explaining the process that I'd face if I insisted on going to trial, comparing the risk I'd face with the known quantity of the plea offer—a mere four years in prison if I agreed to a plea deal and admitted to defrauding clients of the investment bank where I'd been an analyst, compared to ten years or more I risked if I was convicted at trial. And I'd almost certainly be convicted, Rob had assured me. Even if the witnesses against me were convicted felons, liars, conmen who would say anything to get a break on their own prison sentences. The documents were undeniable, incontrovertible evidence of my guilt.

"As to Count Three, wire fraud, the jury finds the defendant—"

Damn her, why the dramatic pause?

"Not guilty," she finished.

This time I glanced over at the jury and made eye contact with several of them, my heart still in my throat. Instead of the impassive expressions they'd worn in the last two weeks, they looked relaxed. Friendlier. Less scary. And they were looking at me. That was one of the signs Rob told me might signal a favorable verdict. If the jury walked in and wouldn't look at me, they probably had convicted me. When they had filed in with their completed verdict forms, I was too nervous to look in their direction.

"As to Count Four, wire fraud, the jury finds the defendant not guilty."

No waiting this time. The clerk flipped the page to the next form and continued reading, her pace picking up. She must have realized that if she kept pausing before the big reveal on each charge, we'd be here until dark.

"As to Count Five, wire fraud, the jury finds the defendant not guilty."

I couldn't relax yet, not quite yet. There were still ten more opportunities to hear I was going to prison.

Fifteen fraud charges. Fifteen chances to hear the clerk announce that the jury had believed my former boss, his former boss, and the government's accountants and investigators who had testified that I, Miranda Vaughn, participated in a conspiracy to defraud banks and investors. That I, with my business degree from a state school still freshly inked, managed to find a way to outwit regulators for the entire six years I worked at Patterson Tinker Investment Strategies to reap huge profits at the expense of the most established investment advisors in the industry.

Rob's hand gripped my arm, and I realized that the clerk was done reading the verdicts. The room was blurry, and I felt the wet tears running down my cheeks for the first time. The stress of holding those tears back in the last year had caused me to lose sleep, lose hair, and develop a nasty habit of grinding my teeth when I finally managed to close my eyes at night. But I knew that if I had let loose those emotions, I'd never be able to rein them back in and would have ended up in a stark white room with no interior door knobs where I'd spend my days rocking back and forth and waiting for my next round of pills.

"We did it, Miranda," Rob whispered, putting an arm around me in an awkward hug.

I looked up to see the judge watching me. Instead of the stern glare I had grown accustomed to, he was almost smiling at me. I blinked. It must have been the tears in the way. But when I wiped my eyes, there it was—Judge Smith's softening expression, looking like someone's granddad instead of the dour arbiter of my fate.

The judge addressed the jury, thanked them for their service, directed them to the jury commissioner's office to turn in their parking passes, and then looked back at me.

"The bond is exonerated. You're free to go, Ms. Vaughn. Court is recessed."

He stood, and everyone in the room followed suit. The jurors filed back into their room off the side of the courtroom to collect their belongings. Several of them smiled at me, and I smiled back but could feel my lips start to tremble. I swallowed hard and tried to pull myself together. Rob began gathering the legal pads that littered the defense counsel table.

I stood next to the table, still stunned and unsure what I

was supposed to do now. Part of me expected to be found guilty, even knowing that I hadn't done what the prosecutor accused me of. I had prepared myself for that. Studied the post-conviction proceedings, the deadline for filing a notice of appeal, researched sentencing procedures and even federal prisons. I hadn't planned what would happen if I were acquitted of all the charges, and I was at a loss as to what to do now.

Turning to the nearly empty courtroom, I saw my lone supporter. The entirety of my cheering section was blowing her nose noisily into a hankie. She came toward me, pulling me into a warm hug over the low railing that separated the gallery from the attorneys and defendants.

"Aunt Marie, when did you get here?"

She gripped me harder. "Somewhere around count seven," she said. "Rob sent me a text when the jury came back. I hot-footed it right down here."

I relaxed into her embrace. The familiar scent of Chanel and baked goods that always permeated her clothing soothed me and took me back to the safety of my childhood. She had come straight from work because she was still wearing her apron with the Sugar Plum Bakery logo.

"Miranda, I'll take care of the bond paperwork," Rob said, interrupting our family reunion.

I pulled away from Aunt Marie and nodded. Rob's face was flushed, and he looked two decades younger than his sixty-three years. He seemed incapable of suppressing the huge grin on his face. Suddenly I felt awkward, unsure how to tell him how grateful I was.

"I don't know what to say," I said. "Thank you, Rob. Thank you so much."

The words were inadequate. During the fourteen months since my arrest, I always felt that he believed I was guilty of *something*, but despite that, he had done an admirable job defending me. He gave me a crooked smile.

"You're welcome," he said. "We'll talk soon. I'm going to see if I can catch a few of the jurors and talk to them. Come by the office later. We'll celebrate."

He leaned across the railing to shake Marie's hand and was pulled into a tight embrace. When she finally released him, he gave her a kiss on the cheek and smiled as he gently wiped a tear from her face. Then he turned back to the counsel table and continued clearing it of folders and notepads and his laptop computer, sliding the whole mess into the large black case that he'd been wheeling into court every day of the trial. He zipped the case, gave me another quick hug, and walked over to the other counsel table.

I turned to see how the prosecutors were handling the news. My tormentors—an older, brittle veteran prosecuting attorney named Donna Grayson and Matthew Reese, her younger co-counsel, a clean-cut young man who looked like he was my age. Neither of them would look at me, and their expressions were grim as they shook Rob's hand. Finally, Matthew Reese made eye contact with me and gave me a nod.

"Good luck to you, Ms. Vaughn," he said.

I almost believed his words were sincere, but then I remembered three days earlier when he called me a thief in his closing argument. I returned the nod without a word, not trusting myself to hold back if I spoke to him—something I'd been forbidden to do for well over a year.

I slipped through the low swinging gate and took Aunt Marie's arm, leading her out of the dark courtroom into the bright, wide and empty hallway. When I had been arraigned on the fraud charges in this courthouse, the hallway had been packed with reporters clamoring for a comment. But since then, they had lost interest. The prosecutor's office wouldn't be putting out a press release on the loss, and I wondered if anyone would even care that I had won. That the woman the government had called "a slick con artist and one of the masterminds of the greatest financial fraud ever seen in this state" was walking out of court and not heading to prison.

I was free to go. No longer facing a decade in prison. Not under a cloud of allegations that had cost me my career, my good name, and my peace of mind. That had driven off friends. Led to the break-up of a five-year relationship. Cost me every last dime of savings and most of Aunt Marie's retirement as well.

I walked up to the wall of windows and looked down on the city, the busy intersection by the federal courthouse, the people jaywalking to get to the Starbucks across the street. A normal day, with everyone bustling about in the bright afternoon sunlight, enjoying a typical California summer day.

I was free to go.

Free.

To go where?

CHAPTER TWO

The temperature in the bakery was stifling, hotter even than the record hot temperatures outside. The ovens heated up the commercial kitchen early in the day, and the temperature never really dissipated. I fanned my face with a menu and checked the supply of muffins and pastries in the racks.

"Miranda, sweetie, can you bring out the apple turnovers?"

Aunt Marie poked her head through the swinging door, letting some of the cooler air from the front of the bakery into the steaming hot kitchen.

"Be right there," I said, grabbing the tray from the rack.

Marie pulled out the empty tray, and I slid in the full one as a crowd of hungry office workers watched. Sugar Plum Bakery was in the heart of Sacramento's downtown and did a brisk business starting before seven o'clock when office workers stopped by for their coffee and breakfast. The bakery was hopping through the busy lunch hour, even though the menu was limited to soup and sandwiches, and into the late afternoon, when many of those same workers returned for a second blast of caffeine to keep them going into the evening.

That had been my schedule for six years when I worked at

Patterson Tinker Investments, just two blocks away from the Sugar Plum Bakery. Now I was waking up at four in the morning to start work in the kitchen and get the store ready to open at six o'clock. My arms and back were sore and aching by mid-morning, but it felt good to be working hard.

Good thing I liked it, since I wasn't having any luck finding a job in my field. I had degrees in economics and finance, but the best job offer—oh, hell, the only job offer I'd had was as a bookkeeper at an auto body shop. The owner called later and said his daughter was going to do the books after school. After I was beaten out by a teenager for my only promising employment lead, I decided to stop looking for a little while and just focus on helping Marie at the bakery. Two employees had retired recently, and she needed someone to fill in until she could hire replacements.

It had been nearly two months since the verdict, and I was still there, rolling out dough in the morning and hiding in the kitchen during the lunch rush to avoid seeing anyone I knew in my former life.

"Oh my God, Miranda?"

And so much for that plan. I stood up and dusted my hands on my apron and found myself facing Katrina Lore, the receptionist at Patterson Tinker. Though she was certainly popular with most of the investment bankers, I had never been a fan. Maybe because her fan base included my former fiancé, Dylan Holland. I'd heard that they'd been seeing each other for about a year now.

"Hello, Katrina. How are you?"

She tilted her head and smiled in a condescending manner not normally seen outside of country clubs. Her hair was pulled up in a smooth French knot, and her makeup was toned down from the gloss-and-glam style I remembered. Her wardrobe, too, had been upgraded. Gone were the tight, short dresses and 4-inch heels. The new, more refined Katrina was wearing a silk sheath in a lovely shade of coral and a pair of diamond earrings that practically screamed for attention. Even her blond hair had been subtly improved, lightened a couple of shades to a pale corn silk. More the color of my hair than her former brassy golden shade. I noted with some satisfaction that the darker blond at the roots was starting to show, something I didn't have to worry about.

"I'm fine, Miranda, thank you. How are *you*?"

As if she cared. *Not chasing after your boyfriend, so don't worry*, I wanted to say. "I'm doing well, thank you."

The bakery was too busy to give a truthful answer.

"Well, it's really good to see you," she said, her voice taking on a higher pitch that made her sound even less sincere.

"You, too. Take care," I said, bagging the apple turnover and handing her the bag.

She was already holding a cup of coffee in her right hand, so she reached up with her left, and as she did, I saw it.

An engagement ring.

My engagement ring.

The engagement ring I had been wearing before the legal nightmare began. When Dylan called off our engagement, I had done the right thing and returned the ring. I didn't want it anyway. I didn't want any reminder of the man who said he'd love me through good times and bad, but who then fled when put to the test. Plus, it had belonged to his grandmother, and I would have felt funny keeping his family's heirloom. Even though his family was a bunch of tight-assed, boring snobs who could have bought the country where the diamond had been mined.

I must have let out a gasp because Aunt Marie turned from the espresso machine and gave me a quizzical look. I shook my head and turned back to Katrina, whose smirk made me doubt it was coincidence that led her to the bakery.

"Deb will ring you up," I said, ignoring the giant, sparkling elephant in the room. I wouldn't give her the satisfaction of addressing her engagement. I forced a smile, or at least an expression that I hoped didn't look like the snarl I felt on the inside.

I started to turn back to the kitchen, but not before seeing a tall, silhouetted figure enter the bakery. The broad shoulders, the close-cut hair, his ears pink from the sun shining behind him. At one time, I thought those teacup ears were cute. Now I gritted my teeth and continued back to the kitchen, before I did something that I would regret later.

I fought the impulse to slam the metal tray on the wood top work surface because I didn't want to alarm Sheldon, my kitchen coworker. Instead, I pressed my lips together and put the tray in the dishwashing stack with the others.

"Shel, I need you to handle the counter for a few minutes," Marie said, coming into the kitchen.

Sheldon looked at us and then slipped out of the kitchen without comment. He was a man of few words anyway and seemed to know better than to argue with Marie at that moment.

"That woman," Marie said. "Are you all right, sweetheart?"

I smiled. "I'm fine."

She shook her head. "You're not. I should have spit in her half-caf cappuccino."

"Probably so, but that would be bad for business," I said.

She sighed. "Well, I thought she'd have the good sense to stay out of here. Did you see him?"

I nodded. The vision of Dylan Holland, even in silhouette, had caused my stomach to do a flip. Not because I loved him still. I didn't. I pretty much hated him, and I certainly didn't want to see him. Or his girlfriend—or rather, his new fiancée. It was a reminder of what I dearly hoped was the low point of my life. I wanted to start over now, rebuild my life. And seeing him made the last year feel too recent, like I was still scrabbling around at the low point and hadn't moved up at all.

"I'll be fine, Aunt Marie," I said, taking her soft hands in mine.

Her lips were pursed and her head tilted, but unlike Katrina's pose, Marie's concern was sincere. She loved me like no one else—not my parents who left me on her doorstep twenty-seven years earlier, not my untrustworthy former fiancé.

"But here you are, hiding back in the kitchen," she said. "There's nothing to be ashamed of working here. This place raised you up."

I closed my eyes and took a deep breath. She was right. There was nothing shameful about working in the bakery. Marie had done it her entire adult life and provided me with a wonderful childhood. We hadn't been rich, but I hadn't wanted for anything. Or at least my wants had been modest enough that Aunt Marie could indulge me. I hadn't meant to insult her and struggled to explain how I felt.

"That's not why I'm not comfortable out front," I said.

But it was. I was embarrassed to be working here. I had been working in a prestigious investment bank, in a responsible position, in line for a promotion, engaged to a handsome and accomplished man. And I had lost it all. No matter that I knew I hadn't done anything illegal. Others would think that I had, and that made me want to hide my head under the covers. Or hide in the kitchen.

Marie clasped my hands tight in hers.

"You should be holding your head up high. You're a survivor!"

"I just don't want to see anyone," I said. "The ones who talk to me would just ask about the trial, and the ones who won't talk to me..."

Marie's lips tightened, and I felt a knot grow in my throat. I swallowed hard and exhaled. I still had the lunch rush to get through. I couldn't lose it now.

There was a slight knock on the swinging door, and it opened slowly. I gripped Aunt Marie's hands tighter when I saw Dylan's face peer around the edge of the rubber stripping.

"I keep knives back here," Aunt Marie said by way of a greeting, her eyes narrowing.

"Hello, Marie," Dylan said.

"Sharp knives."

"I'd like to speak with Miranda," he said. An uncomfortable expression crossed his boyishly handsome face. "Please."

I squeezed her hands until Marie looked at me then gave her a nod. She frowned but nodded.

"I'll be right on the other side of that door," she said, picking up a cleaver on her way.

Dylan scooted out of her way and stood near the center island in the kitchen. I moved to stand on the other side of it from him, not entirely trusting myself to be within knife's reach of him. In his tailored light grey suit, Dylan looked out of place in the middle of the bakery kitchen after a sustained morning rush.

"How are you doing?" Dylan asked, his voice low and concerned.

He also tilted his head as he looked at me. It was hard to tell if he was concerned about me, or if he was concerned that I'd make a scene in public with his new bride-to-be. That wouldn't do for the newest vice president of the newly reconstituted Patterson Investment Company. The company had dropped any mention of founding partner Ralph Tinker after his arrest and seemed to be thriving, despite the unfortunate scandal.

I shrugged and hefted a block of dough onto the floured surface in front of me. "I'm fine, thank you," I said, grabbing a wooden rolling pin.

He gave me a half-smile. "You look beautiful."

I closed my eyes. That used to turn me inside out. He'd tell me how beautiful I looked, and it made me feel loved and worthy of this man, this beautiful man who was privileged and was wealthy enough to have whatever, and whomever, he wanted. I'd have done anything for him, walked through fire. He was my prince charming.

I opened my eyes and saw him now as he really was, as he probably always had been. He was weak and spoiled. And he had replaced me with the receptionist within weeks of our breakup. And he owed me—big time.

"Thank you," I said, turning back to the dough.

"I was happy to hear about the verdict," Dylan said. "Are you doing all right?"

"I've been better." I laughed and died a little inside at how bitter I sounded. "I told you I didn't do it."

He gave me a long stare and I was caught in his cool blue-grey eyes. "I never thought you did."

"You just didn't want to stick around to be sure of that," I said.

He gave me a reproachful look.

"You know that's not the full story," he said softly. He sighed and ran a hand through his carefully combed hair. "I'm sorry that Katrina came in. I didn't know you'd be here. I wanted to tell you myself, but well, I wasn't sure how to."

"Oh, right. Where are my manners? Congratulations," I said. "I hope you two will be very happy together."

In hell.

He nodded and studied me as if he were going to take a test later. His scrutiny made me hyper-conscious of my jeans, t-shirt and flour-dusted apron. My face was no doubt shiny from the heat in the kitchen. I had been working for five hours without much of a break and hadn't bothered with make-up. I wasn't entirely sure I'd brushed my hair before I had pulled it up into a messy knot.

"I've missed you," Dylan said, moving around the center island. His hand reached up, and he touched my cheek. "You really are beautiful, Miranda. You look amazing."

The touch sparked something, but it was a memory, not an emotion. His gaze moved over me from my feet to my face and reflected the approval I no longer sought. The ten pounds I constantly battled and stressed over when I was with Dylan had melted away after I was arrested, along with another ten that I didn't need to lose. The unjustly- accused diet was good for unnatural and unhealthy weight loss.

"You should go. Your fiancée is waiting."

His hand dropped. "Sorry," he said, giving me a smile. "You're right. Is there anything—Can I—Do you need anything?"

Dylan's stammered offer threw me off balance. He was always so poised and polite. He truly seemed at a loss about what to do with me.

"Yes," I said, before I could change my mind and talk myself out of it. "I need a job. I can't even get a call back."

"Where have you applied?"

I listed several banks and investment houses, and Dylan nodded. "I'll see what I can find. I'll make some calls."

He walked to the kitchen door and paused. "Take care," he said. "I'll call you soon and let you know if I hear of any openings."

"Thanks, Dylan."

He disappeared behind the door, and the breath left my

body. I hadn't realized how tense it was being around him until he was out of sight.

Marie burst through the door and stood, her hands on her hips.

"What did that little bastard want?"

I didn't know how to answer that. It was difficult to believe that he had an attack of conscience for how he treated me, since he rebounded so quickly. It was the first time I'd seen him in more than a year. In that time, I had only spoken to him once, and that was to arrange to pick up my things from his house. He'd already packed them and made arrangements to have them delivered to me, so even that was a quick phone call.

Why had he bothered to apologize for Katrina? Was it an inherent need to avoid ugly unpleasantness, drilled into him by his mother? Not that I cared, if he could help me get back to a real job and start earning the money I needed to repay Aunt Marie for my legal bills.

"He's going to help me find a job."

CHAPTER THREE

The courtyard at Robert Fogg's office was quiet except for the crunch of leaves under my boots. The red leaves from the Japanese maple trees littered the grey stone walkway and fell into the low dark green hedge that lined the square entry to the building. I had seen this courtyard through all the seasons—summer, fall, winter, spring—then summer again. During the year leading up to my trial, I trudged in nearly every day to work in the conference room and study the documents the government had seized from Patterson Tinker.

When the FBI raided the office the previous spring and arrested me, my boss, Tim Norquist, and his boss, Ralph Tinker, Aunt Marie insisted that I retain the best criminal defense attorney in the city. But that guy was too expensive, and Ralph hired him right away. So I drained all my accounts, sold my car, gave up my expensive condo, and moved into the apartment over Aunt Marie's garage. And was still short of funds to retain a lawyer.

Fortunately, Rob was a long-time friend of Aunt Marie's, and he practiced criminal defense. He hadn't done a white-collar criminal case before, though. His career had been built on defending bank robbers, drug traffickers, and gunrunners. He knew how to try a case in federal court. And I knew my way around the investment firm's files, so I could help him understand the voluminous records the government had seized. Even with my promise to act as my own paralegal, I still had to borrow money from Aunt Marie to pay Rob. He had expenses—rent, insurance, and payroll for his small staff—Sarah Girard, his paralegal; Theresa McFarren, his secretary; and Burton Worthington, the investigator.

I'd just been fired and was under indictment in a federal fraud case. Employers weren't beating my door down to offer me jobs. So I had time on my hands.

I let myself into the office and found it unnaturally quiet. Theresa's desk was empty and tidy, which was a good sign that she was gone for the day.

"Miranda? That you? I'm in the back."

Rob was working in the large conference room, an open book on his lap and his boots propped up on the long table. He gave me a friendly wave and motioned for me to join him. As I walked in, I heard the soft thumping of a dog's tail from under the table. I reached down to pet Basil, Rob's oversized Golden Retriever. He raised his head and gave my hand a sloppy wet greeting, sighed and returned to his nap.

The office was quiet and Rob was alone. His staff kept their own hours, though, so Sarah and Burton could have been out in the field or working at home.

"Have a seat," Rob said, waving me toward a seat at the conference table. "How have you been?"

I sat and shrugged. "I've been fine."

He put his feet on the ground and the book on the table. "Is that true? Your aunt says you're still looking for work."

His kind eyes were studying me intently, and I squirmed. Before I hired him as my lawyer, I'd seen him around the bakery for years and knew he and Aunt Marie were friends. Rob was a tall, rangy man. He looked like he'd spent his youth on a ranch, which was the case. Before he went to law school, he'd been a farrier and a roper on the rodeo circuit. He looked a little ill at ease in a suit, but he knew how to do his job. He waited patiently for me to answer his question, and I knew he'd wait forever, and that I'd eventually give in.

With a sigh, I nodded. "Yeah, I'm having some problems getting back into the workforce. I've sent in dozens of resumes and can't even get a call back from most of them."

Rob's face softened. "It's going to be hard to brush off the scandal for a while. Have you considered doing something else, besides finance?"

I frowned. My education didn't make me qualified to do much other than work in investment banking.

"I hadn't really thought about it. What would I do?"

"You were a damn good paralegal," Rob said. "Have you considered going to law school? Becoming a lawyer?"

I tilted my head. "I don't know if I'm cut out for that, Rob. I mean, maybe it's because it's still so soon after my experience with the justice system, but I think it would be too stressful."

He nodded and looked thoughtful. "I may be getting a new fraud case soon. If you're interested, I could use your help sorting through the discovery and making sense of it. If you think you'd want to do that."

The thought of burying myself in paperwork in Rob's small conference room, dubbed the "War Room," and looking for ways to fight against the federal government's narrative made me want to throw myself out the window. It wouldn't do any good, though. Rob's office was on the ground floor. Plus, I really needed the money.

"I guess I could do that," I said.

Rob threw back his head and laughed. "Don't get too excited.

It won't be as hard as working on your own case—you can keep your distance. It's not going to be your own life on the line. Plus, since you figured out all the fancy new software, you can take the laptop and work from home if you'd like."

That fancy new software had been bought and paid for by my retainer. The FBI had seized a huge trove of paper and electronic records from Patterson Tinker in its raid, and all of that was made available to Rob and his staff for preparing my defense. Because the federal agents weren't sure how deep or wide the fraud scheme was, they grabbed everything they could, sweeping in vast quantities of client information, banking records, computer hard drives, email servers, phone logs, you name it. A portion of the information—about 110,000 pages worth—was culled out by the government, scanned, and provided to Rob as evidence related to the charges against me. The rest was in a warehouse, where we could go review it. Or rather, where Rob, Sarah, and Burton could review it. I wasn't allowed. I guess they were afraid that I might eat something vital.

I was afraid that there was something in there that I needed to prove my innocence, so I sold the last asset I had—a mountain cabin with a sliver of a view of Lake Tahoe. It had been in my dad's family for sixty years and was the only thing I'd ever gotten from anyone with the last name of Vaughn. If any of the Vaughns could have been bothered to write a will, I wouldn't have inherited it. But thanks to their laziness and the laws of *intestate* succession, I became the owner of the rustic one-bedroom cabin with single-pane windows, leaky pipes, a roof made of papier-mâché, and a charm that bears found irresistible.

But I wasn't going to enjoy the cabin while spending a decade in federal prison, so it went on the market, and I used the proceeds to pay for a service to come in and scan the rest of the documents in the warehouse and convert them to electronic versions that we could search, and the software to manage that much electronic data. It wasn't cheap. But it was worth it. I learned more about Patterson Tinker than I had ever thought possible.

"Think about it, anyway," Rob said. "I can't use that high-tech software for my usual clientele. It would be good to put it to use, and if this new client decides to retain me, I'll probably need it."

"What about Sarah? She knows how to use it."

He waved a hand. "She's already busy with the usual research and writing. It would be easier to have one person devoted to this job."

"I'll think about it," I said, though I wondered if he was just taking pity on me.

He must have heard his former clients complain a thousand times that they couldn't find work, but most of his clients were busted for drugs or bank robbery or identity theft. That narrowed one's employment options. I'd been cleared of the charges—at least in court.

"So you're here to pack up the War Room today?" Rob asked, leaning forward and resting his elbows on the table.

"Yeah, Theresa said you're going to need to prepare for another trial soon. I know I should have come by sooner, but I guess I was putting it off."

He smiled and patted my hand. "No problem. I could have done it myself, but I thought you'd probably be better at keeping it organized. Not that I'll need to return to it, since we don't have an appeal to worry about. But the state bar says I have to keep all my records for five years. Or is it seven years? Anyway, I put a stack of boxes in there, but just give a holler if you need more."

I left him in the large conference room with Basil and went down the hall to the windowless room with the "authorized personnel only" sign on the door. The tiny room was lit with fluorescent lights and lined with banker boxes, labeled with tags that read "United States v. Vaughn." I'd spent about nine months in this room, sorting through the boxes and staring at the laptop screen until my eyes were dry. Just being back here made my heart beat faster and my stomach fill with dread—a Pavlovian response.

Rob had thrown a couple of empty boxes on top of the table dominating the middle of the room and had scribbled out the old labels with a black felt-tip pen. They lay haphazardly on stacks of papers and folders that would need to be organized before they went to storage. I started at the far end of the table and worked my way to the open door.

I had nearly cleared the table when Rob and Basil appeared in the doorway.

"I'm heading out for the night. You're welcome to stay as late as you want, or you can come back on Monday—your choice." He leaned on the doorframe and rested his hand on Basil's head, stroking the dog's ears.

"I'm close to finishing. If you don't mind, I'd like to get it all done tonight," I said.

"No problem. You still have a key?"

I wondered how many criminal defense attorneys gave their clients keys to the office.

"Of course. The alarm code still the same?"

"It is," he said and started to turn away. "Oh, and I almost forgot. Can you check the laptop for any electronic files? I know the external hard drives have all the discovery on them, but we had pulled copies to the laptop for trial. I want to make sure our only electronic copies are on the external drives in storage so we're not violating the protective order."

"Sure, I can do that," I said. "But how would that be violating the protective order?"

"We're not supposed to copy the files except as needed for the case, and now that we're done with your case, I don't want any extra copies floating around. I want to be sure that all of the evidence in your case is in these boxes or on those external drives. Any extra copies of documents put in the shredder."

"Got it," I said, wiping my hands on my jeans and standing up. "Thanks for giving me some extra time to get this cleaned up."

He gave me a wink, and I could see the young charming cowboy in his eyes. "Don't stay too late. It's Friday night. Go have some fun."

He locked the office door behind him as he left, and I returned to my task. Before long, my stomach was protesting the lack of dinner. The boxes were labeled. I entered each container's label and content into a chart for Theresa, in case she ever needed to order something from storage. All that was left was the laptop.

As I waited for the computer to turn on, the cell phone in my pocket buzzed. It was such a rare occasion anymore, the sound startled me. The caller's number was blocked, and I expected a telemarketer when I answered.

"Miranda? It's me, Dylan."

The sound of his voice over the phone made my heart skip. That, too, was only a memory, though. I had missed him for a long time, and then I had hated him. But now, I needed him. Which made me hate him a little more.

"Hi, Dylan."

"How are you?"

Annoyed with having to make small talk with you.

"I'm fine, thank you. What's going on?"

He cleared his throat, and my heart sank. It was a nervous tic of his—a way of avoiding giving bad news. When he dumped me, he had sounded like he was in the later stages of tuberculosis.

"I, uh, made some calls, like I said I would. You know, about any job openings."

He really didn't even need to continue. I knew what was coming.

"Here's the thing. The industry, you know, it's still rebounding from the recession."

Bullshit. Corporate profits for banks were as obscenely huge as they'd been at the height of the market. Did he think I didn't still read the *Wall Street Journal*?

"So, there's that. Plus, you know, you've been out of the game for a year."

You're so full of shit. I was falsely accused of a crime. Set up by someone at Patterson Tinker to take the fall.

"And the thing is, well, you're sort of radioactive right now. Given some time, that will probably change. But right now? Well, it's going to be a tough sell to get you in the door."

My face flushed. *Radioactive?* That's not what I expected to hear. I mean, I knew it was going to be tough, but I figured there was a chance. I wasn't going in without credentials or experience. I graduated near the top of my class. I did excellent work, knew what I was doing. Sure, my best references were en route to federal prison, but I had been cleared of all charges.

I tried to talk, but my throat was closed up like a fist.

"Listen, Miranda, if I hear of anything, I'll let you know." He cleared his throat again in the uncomfortable silence that followed.

"Thanks, Dylan."

I didn't know what else to say. I wanted to rage, wanted to scream at him. But it wasn't his fault and I couldn't burn that bridge. As much as I hated to admit it, Dylan was the only person in the banking industry who would return my calls.

He said a hasty goodbye and hung up, and I sat in the small airless conference room, surrounded by the proof that I hadn't done what they said I did. That I wasn't a swindler, a con artist, a fraudster.

Or was it proof? I remembered one of the jurors quoted in the local newspaper after the acquittal had said that she wasn't convinced that I didn't know what Ralph and Tim were doing, but the government hadn't proved it beyond a reasonable doubt. The jury had deliberated for four days, and the testimony of the victims who lost their life savings had almost swayed them. Almost, but not quite. At the time I read it, I didn't care about that nuance because I was so happy to not be going to prison. Now I understood that the gulf between being cleared and being found not guilty was going to haunt me. Maybe forever.

I leaned forward and put my forehead on the smooth wood surface of the table, trying to quiet the roaring in my head. All my years of working crappy waitressing jobs to put myself through college, all my hard work at Patterson Tinker, everything that Aunt Marie had sacrificed for me—it was all swirling down the drain. I'd be stuck making apple turnovers at the Sugar Plum Bakery and dodging my former colleagues until everyone forgot that I was the woman who was arrested on fraud charges. Which was approximately never.

The laptop sitting next to my head beeped, and I sat up and reluctantly opened the electronic discovery software. It looked like I had no choice. I'd be working for Rob, reliving my past in his new white-collar criminal cases. I was going to get reacquainted with the computer I'd spent so much time with. I navigated to the folders that contained my case, and my finger hovered over the delete command.

I paused for a moment, my earlier discussion with Dylan echoing in my head.

I *had* been set up. I had known it as soon as I saw the

evidence against me. Someone knew that I was in charge of transferring client funds and had set up an account in my name and used it to siphon off investments. I knew I hadn't done it. But it was someone with access to my computer, my information, my passwords. Ralph and Tim would have known enough to do it, and Rob had been successful in convincing the jury that they certainly had motive to set up an underling and lie on the stand about it.

My finger still inches above the delete key, I looked up at the rows of boxes.

Maybe the answers I wanted were in here. The FBI was convinced that I was guilty and was only looking for evidence to corroborate Tim and Ralph's stories. But what if there was something here, something that would finally prove that I was innocent, instead of merely "not guilty."

A plan began to percolate through the haze of self-pity I'd been wallowing in for the past several weeks. I could clear my name. I could find the money stolen from the investors.

No one knew the ins and outs of Patterson Tinker like I did. Not only had I worked there for six years, I had studied it thoroughly in the past year. And no one knew the evidence in the case like I did. I knew where the bodies were buried, so to speak.

I just needed some time. And the computer. And those hard drives sitting in a box waiting to get shipped off to Rob's storage unit.

I stood up and dug through the stack of boxes, ripping the lid off the one I was looking for before good sense could catch up with me. From between folders stuffed with papers, I pulled out the two external hard drives, their cords trailing behind them. Between them, they contained every page of evidence from that government warehouse. I stuffed them in my messenger bag and resealed the box. I turned off the computer and slid it into the bag, too, along with the cords and a binder that I had compiled months earlier as a directory of the volumes of evidence.

The bag weighed heavily on my shoulder as I composed a quick note to Rob, agreeing to work on the financial fraud case and letting him know that I had taken the laptop home to review the software before I started using it again. Then I turned off the light in the War Room and shut the door behind me.

I left the note on Rob's desk, locked the office, and turned on the alarm, flooded with an unfamiliar energy. Something I hadn't felt in nearly two months.

It was a sense of purpose. I finally had a plan.

CHAPTER FOUR

I heard the sound of Sarah's motorcycle as she turned down the alley behind my apartment and I closed the laptop, sliding it into a backpack and under my lounge chair. A moment later, her hand reached over the fence and unlatched the gate.

"I hope you have enough beer to share," she said, trotting toward the pool.

I kicked the lid off the cooler near my feet to expose the five remaining beers submerged in ice.

"Oooh, good stuff," Sarah said, tossing her helmet onto a chair and dropping her backpack onto the grass. She grabbed a bottle and raised an eyebrow at the craft beer's label. "Russian River Brewing? Are we celebrating something?"

"Isn't everyday a celebration, really?"

She laughed and caught the bottle opener I tossed her. When she drank the icy brew, she closed her eyes and let out a sigh of contentedness. "That is good IPA."

"Make yourself comfortable," I said.

She stripped off the black jacket and then unzipped her padded pants and pulled her long-sleeved t-shirt off, revealing a red-and-white striped bikini underneath. From her backpack, she pulled a bottle of sunscreen and applied the goo liberally to her skin.

"To what do I owe the honor of your presence?" I asked, opening my second bottle of the Blind Pig IPA.

Sarah had called that morning and wanted to stop by after work. It was my day off from the bakery, so I told her she'd find me by the pool. It was a perk of living over Aunt Marie's garage —I got to share the backyard swimming pool.

"Nothing really, I just wanted to catch up. Oh, and I brought your last invoice from Rob. There's nothing due, but there's also nothing left in the trust from your retainer."

I suspected as much and wasn't expecting that there would be a balance. Rob had probably paid for some of the last expenses out of his own pocket before the trial was over.

"Rob says you're going to come back and work on the new case," Sarah said, settling into the padded lounge next to mine. Her chair was in the sun. Mine was shaded because I'd been working on the computer. Also because I'm a fair-haired girl of Nordic descent who burns at the first glimpse of sun.

I nodded and took a drink. "It's been hard finding a job."

Rob had probably already told Sarah the whole story. The office was small, and news traveled fast. That's how Sarah and I became friends, working in close proximity and on the same case for months on end. Plus, we're the same age and had a lot of the same interests. Except that she's a bad ass and I'm scared to death of motorcycles. Officially, Sarah was Rob's paralegal, but her duties often went beyond researching and drafting documents. She was the office fixer—able to find information from public records, deep social media searches, or even a little undercover work. And when Burton had trouble serving subpoenas on reluctant witnesses, he often turned the job over to Sarah.

Sarah leaned forward, brushed her shiny black hair out of

her face, and then dug into her bag and pulled out the envelope from Rob. I stuck it unopened in my backpack.

"It will be good to have you back at the office. We're getting a ton of calls for fraud cases now. Your acquittal was the best advertisement Rob could have hoped for."

"Rob was hoping to retire."

She waved her hand. "He'll never retire. He enjoys what he does too much."

"I'll probably be working at home most of the time, since I just need the computer and the electronic files to review," I said.

"That's cool," Sarah said, adjusting the top of her swimsuit. "Hey, did you hear Burton's got a new girlfriend?"

I raised an eyebrow. Burton Worthington, the investigator who rented an office from Rob, was a notorious ladies' man. And it was easy to see why. Towering over six feet tall, smooth mocha-colored skin, a rogue's smile—the man was a wall of muscles and sin. "Is he giving up the life of a player?"

Sarah shrugged. "Don't know about that, but I did meet this one."

"And?"

Another shrug. "She's okay. Looks like a stripper."

I laughed, and she shot me a steely glare. There was something going on between Sarah and Burton, though neither would admit or even acknowledge it.

"So, since you're not working full-time and the new case won't pick up for a couple months, what are you going to do?" she asked, and I let her change the subject.

I stretched so my feet were in the sun and wondered how much to tell Sarah of my new plans. I'd spent every free minute in the last week going over the electronic evidence I'd swiped from Rob's files. It was enough time to get an overview of the discovery and reacquaint myself with the volumes of files. I had broken my research into chunks and started the night before on bank records, looking for transfers that were out of the ordinary.

And it hadn't taken long to find that—and more.

Had the FBI been looking for evidence of criminal activity, they had only to dig into their own warehouse. But they had been investigating me and my role in fleecing the hundreds of investors in the Sahara Fund, a mutual fund Ralph and Tim managed. So the agents must have focused on just that one investment fund and missed a much larger problem. I couldn't yet tell exactly what the scheme was, but there was something odd—huge sums were being transferred to accounts for Patterson Tinker offices overseas, mostly in Macau and Geneva. But when I cross-referenced those transfers, I couldn't figure out why the money was flowing to those accounts.

It would be natural to bounce this question off Sarah, who was super smart and savvy about criminal enterprises. But if I told her, she'd be obligated to let Rob know that I had taken the evidence from the office, possibly violating the court's protective order.

So instead, I just shook my head. "I'm not sure. The bakery still needs help, so I'll hang out there for a while, help Aunt Marie."

Sarah sat up again and reached for her bag. "I almost forgot," she said, unzipping a pocket on the exterior and reaching in. "Your passport. In case you need to flee the country."

She tossed it to me, and I grinned.

"Well, it's always good to have that option."

"The court mailed it back to the office along with all the paperwork exonerating your bond. You're now officially a free woman," she said, raising her bottle.

I raised mine, and we clinked them together.

"Thanks, Sarah," I said. "I appreciate all your help."

"Anytime," she said. "But I don't mean that you should go get in trouble again. Whatever you decide to do."

"What would you do in my situation?"

She thought about it for a moment then looked at me. "I'd probably use that passport, travel around, enjoy the fact that you're not tied to a job or a husband."

"Travel usually costs money, which I am plumb out of."

I didn't mention that the husband part of the equation was a sore subject with my recent run-in with Dylan.

"Doesn't have to cost a fortune," she said. "Plus, you've got credit cards."

Oddly enough, I still had excellent credit. I'd made really good money with Patterson Tinker and was responsible with my spending, so all my credit cards were gold and platinum cards with high limits. Apparently, the fact that I was fired from Patterson Tinker wasn't on the credit bureaus' radar, and since I hadn't run up any debt, the cards were all just sitting there with full credit lines at the ready.

"If you're not going to travel, at least go find a man—a *real* man—and go wild for a while," she said. Sarah had met Dylan when she and Burton interviewed him while they were investigating my case. She wasn't impressed.

"Hmm, like maybe Burton?" I mused and laughed when I saw the jealousy cross her face. In a flash it was gone, and she shook her head at my laughter.

"I'm not interested in Burton," she said. "Well, maybe his DNA. I mean, admit it, we would make incredibly beautiful children together."

This was true. Sarah's mother was Chinese and her father was French. She was a stunning mix of the best of her parents' genetics—green eyes with a slight almond shape, shiny black hair that hung straight as rain to the middle of her back, creamy skin that never required make-up. And she had a naturally willowy figure, despite her disdain for exercise. If she'd grown taller than 5-feet, 4-inches, she'd probably be a supermodel. I'd hate her if she weren't so damn nice.

"Maybe you'd have cute kids. Or maybe they'd get your height and Burton's bald head. You don't know how these things work."

She threw the sunscreen at me and laughed.

"Let's go get tacos for dinner," she said. "You need to put on a couple pounds."

I rolled my eyes. "Thanks, *Mom*. I work in a bakery. The pounds will find their way home soon enough."

We sat by the pool and talked about nothing important for a couple hours, finished off the beers, and then Sarah raided my closet for something to wear, and we got dressed to go out for dinner. As we walked to the restaurant on somewhat unsteady feet, it felt like a normal life, like any other 31-year-old woman would lead. It was the best day I'd had in a long time, and I reveled in it, ordering a margarita at the restaurant.

The taco plates arrived after my second margarita and Sarah's third.

"I'm sleeping on your couch tonight," Sarah said. I nodded and sipped at the tart cocktail, licking the salt off the rim.

The waitress set the steaming plates in front of us, and I inhaled the spicy roasted carnitas. I closed my eyes and let the savory fragrance wash over me.

Sarah laughed. "I don't think I've ever enjoyed something as much as you're enjoying those tacos. Not even sex."

I grinned and opened my eyes. It had been a long year and a half, but I felt at that moment finally fully relaxed. Life was good. Everything was going to be all right.

I rolled up the taco and took a bite, savoring the flavors.

Sarah did the same and then groaned. "Now I get it. These tacos are better than sex."

Looking over her shoulder, my gaze met that of a man sitting alone at the bar, a plate of food in front of him. He had a funny half-smile on his face, seeming amused by my encounter with the Mexican food. Sarah followed my gaze and turned to look at him.

She turned back and gave me a huge drunken smile. "Go for it, Miranda. He's hot."

My tequila-addled brain scrambled to keep up with the rush of hormones that the man had triggered. He was good looking— broad shoulders, wavy dark brown hair and intense dark eyes. He was still watching me, but now he was watching me study him. I gave him a smile and turned my attention back to my dinner.

I declined another margarita. It was only a three-block walk home, but any more alcohol and I'd probably head in the wrong direction. Sarah leaned back after polishing off her plate and one of my tacos. She ate like a linebacker. Damn her metabolism.

When the check came, Sarah grabbed it out of my hands and slapped a credit card down.

"My treat," she said, putting the folder in the waitress's hands. "We never got a chance to celebrate our win. Plus, I'll probably throw up later, and you'll end up holding my hair. So we'll be even."

I knew better than to fight with her, so I thanked her and glanced again toward the man at the bar. He was still there, lingering over a drink. He was watching me in the mirror behind the bar now, and I caught his eye again. This time, his expression was serious instead of flirty, and my brain woke from its boozy slumber and started sorting through memories trying to place him.

My smile faltered as the recognition clicked into place. His hair was shorter then, and he had been wearing a dark blue windbreaker with FBI emblazoned on the back. His strong hands grabbed mine, pulled them behind me, and snapped a pair of handcuffs on my wrists. Later, in a tiny room at the federal building downtown, he sat quietly taking notes while another man, the lead investigator, questioned me about the Sahara Fund.

"Miranda? Are you okay?"

I snapped back to see Sarah, leaning toward me, concerned. My throat closed, and the blood drained from my head.

I stood quickly, knocking the table with my leg. Sarah caught it and stood, too, grabbing her purse off the back of her chair.

"Let's go," I said.

Sarah waved toward the waitress and retrieved the check to sign the credit card receipt. I mumbled something about waiting outside and wobbled toward the door. Leaning against the stucco wall, I gulped down the still-warm evening air. My heart thundered and my hands shook.

"What's wrong? Is it the tequila?" Sarah said, joining me outside and putting her hand on my arm.

I looked at her, then past her as a shadow passed over the screen door and paused, the tall outline of the FBI agent silhouetted against the bright lights of the kitchen behind him.

"I'm fine. Let's go," I said, turning abruptly.

Well, it was nice being normal while it lasted.

CHAPTER FIVE

If Rob was the brains of the operation at his law firm, and Sarah the looks, then Burton Worthington was the muscle. He was at least 6-feet 3-inches tall and had improbably little body fat. When standing, he was the most intimidating man I'd ever met, and this was part of the reason why he was such a good investigator.

But he was also charming and easy to talk to, which made him a great investigator. People opened up to him. They trusted him. They told him things they really didn't want to share, things that they knew better than to tell him.

I kept that in mind as he held the door for me at the law firm.

"Welcome back, Miss Miranda," he said with a grin. He always called me that, though as far as I could tell, he didn't do that to anyone else—either coworker or client.

Burton's office was right inside the law firm's front door. He wasn't actually an employee of the firm, but he was hired on nearly every job Rob took, so the proximity worked for both of them. Theresa constantly reminded everyone that she worked for Rob, not Burton. But then she'd offer to type letters for the investigator, retrieve his messages, or even bring him coffee—which always annoyed Rob, since he couldn't seem to get that level of service from his secretary.

"How are you, Burton?" I asked, looking around the office.

Rob's door was shut, which meant he was probably on the phone. Theresa's desk was empty again, but Sarah was at her desk. She waved a hand and grimaced, motioning to the phone receiver in other hand.

"Are we going to have to find a desk for you?"

I grinned. "Sarah said I should take your office, since you're always out goofing off."

"Oh, she did, did she?" He nearly growled his response, and I saw a glint in his amber eyes.

She hadn't said any such thing, but I enjoyed teasing them both too much.

"I'll just wait for Rob in the library," I said, shifting the backpack on my shoulder.

Burton gave me a hug that nearly crushed the air from my lungs, the sudden show of affection surprising me.

"It's really good to see you, kid," he said.

I felt the sting behind my eyes and blinked quickly, not wanting to show exactly how much that meant.

"Yeah, thanks. You, too," I said.

I made my way to the large conference room, which doubled as the law library for the firm and set up the computer on the table to prepare for my meeting with Rob to discuss his new fraud case.

Rob's door flew open, and he rushed to the conference room and greeted me with a warm hug.

"I'm so glad you're doing this, Miranda. It will be nice to work with you on this. But first, I hear you have something else important to share."

I paused at his expectant expression. *How could he know?*

Then I remembered the box in my bag. I pulled out the pink cardboard container with the almond croissants inside. He grabbed the box and pulled a pastry from inside.

"Perfect. Tell Marie thanks for me. She knows the way to my heart, that woman," he said. His eyes sparkled as he bit into the flaky treat.

Sarah walked into the conference room and dropped a stack of paper napkins on the table next to Rob.

"Perfect timing. I've gotta go serve a bunch of subpoenas," she said, picking up a croissant and a napkin. "Sorry I can't stay to chat."

"You're taking Burton with you, right?" Rob asked.

She shook her head. "I can do it without him."

Rob frowned and glanced toward Burton's office. "If you're going into the south area, I'd prefer you and Burton go together."

Sarah sighed and then nodded. "Fine, I'll go with Burton."

"I'll drive," Burton said, appearing at the door as if summoned.

"Damn right you will," Sarah said, adding another croissant to her napkin. "I can't ride my bike and eat these at the same time."

"Oh no. Not in my car," Burton said, walking toward the office door with Sarah right behind him.

"Try and stop me, big guy. I had to skip lunch."

The front door closed, muffling the bickering duo's conversation and leaving Rob and me alone in the conference room. He gave me a smile and a wink. I wasn't the only one who saw the chemistry between them.

"Well, now that the important stuff is out of the way, I have a couple other items of news. First, Ralph and Tim were sentenced this morning. I attended the hearing."

My heart lurched. I knew the sentencing hearing was set for

this week, but it had been delayed so often, I didn't really expect it to go forward this time.

"What happened?"

Rob leaned back in his chair and frowned.

"They each got seventy months, a little less than six years," he said.

"What?" I was shocked. I had been looking at ten years if I'd been convicted. Federal fraud sentences are based, in good part, on the dollar amount, and thirty-seven million dollars stolen from more than 250 investors put the sentence at well past a decade. By their own testimony, Ralph and Tim were the masterminds of this scheme and profited by it, which added more years to the estimated sentence.

"Well, keep in mind that they pleaded guilty and agreed to cooperate and testify against you," Rob said.

"Yeah, but I was acquitted. Why do they get credit for lying on the stand?"

He shrugged. "The government felt they gave truthful testimony and recommended forty percent off their sentences," he said. "Remember, had they gone to trial and been convicted, they'd be looking at eighteen to twenty years. And they would have been convicted."

The numbers flew through my head. "But that would have been—"

Rob held up a hand. "The judge considered their age, lack of criminal history, and ability to pay restitution to the victims. They agreed to forfeit most of their assets, including art, real estate and cars, as well as bank accounts," he said. "But there's no way around it, they got a break. With good-time credit, they'll be out in just over five years. They also were each fined two hundred and fifty thousand dollars."

My face warmed as I thought about Ralph's mansion that overlooked a private lake on his estate. He could probably pay the fine with the money shaken from the many sofas in that huge mausoleum of a house. Tim, though not as wealthy as Ralph, lived in a ritzy neighborhood and collected art and baseball memorabilia. Both of them drove obscenely expensive cars and purchased similar models for their wives.

Most of it bought with stolen funds.

My head spun at the thought that I could have easily been right there with them, getting sentenced to that much time or even more since I wouldn't have gotten credit for pleading guilty and cooperating as a government witness. I tried to picture the impeccably dressed Ralph Tinker wearing orange jail garb, but it was hard to wrap my head around. He was in his 60s, and Tim was in his late 40s, and both had families and children. Ralph had a new grandson. I knew their families and felt sorry for them, for what they were going to lose when their loved ones went to prison.

But when I thought about Ralph and Tim testifying under oath that I was part of their scheme and had willingly helped them cheat clients out of their life savings, my heart chilled. I did not feel bad for the two men who would serve the sentences handed down this morning. Not at all.

Tim, especially, disgusted me. He had been an excellent boss and mentor, and I had been thrilled when I'd been promoted to work as his assistant. When I thought back to the four years I worked for him, I wondered how I could have missed the signs that he was a complete sociopath. I never had a clue that he was defrauding our clients, siphoning off their hard-earned money into his own pocket.

"What else did you want to tell me?" I asked Rob.

He leaned forward and paused, clasping his hands together. He raised his eyes to mine, and my heart stalled.

"You remember when we talked about the investors bringing a civil suit against Patterson Tinker?"

I nodded, not trusting myself to speak. Rob had explained that many of the investors had hired a lawyer to represent them in a civil suit, which would name Ralph, Tim and me personally, in addition to the investment house.

"Their lawyer called me this week. They're going forward with the suit."

"But I was cleared," I said. "They won't sue me, right?"

Rob bit his lip and my stomach dropped. "Well, see, you were cleared in the criminal case, but this will be a civil suit. The burden is less—only a preponderance of the evidence, instead of beyond a reasonable doubt."

I gave a bitter laugh. "Well, good luck getting anything from me. You know that saying about getting blood from a turnip? I have nothing. I make just over minimum wage."

Rob shook his head. "But you do have some interest in property."

I tilted my head, confused. "No, I sold the Tahoe cabin. And I never owned my condo. That was just a lease."

"Your aunt put your name on the bakery building and her house," he said gently. "It was years ago, a way to prevent you from having to pay inheritance taxes if anything happened to Marie."

I gasped. "No. They couldn't go after the bakery. Or Aunt Marie's home."

He nodded. "They could, if it gets that far," he said. "That's a long way off. Civil suits take a very long time to get through the courts, so please don't worry yourself too much right now."

Fat chance of that. My throat felt like it was closing around a softball-sized lump. I blinked back tears at the thought of Aunt Marie losing the Sugar Plum Bakery. She built that business herself and made it a thriving success. It hadn't been easy, either. Marie's business had only been open a year when her sister dumped me, a nearly feral three-year-old, at her doorstep and took off to follow yet another poor excuse for a man. But we'd managed. I played in the office, screened off from the kitchen with a baby-gate while she rolled out dough and filled pastries. When I grew older, I helped decorate cupcakes and cookies, and swept the floors. The employees at Sugar Plum Bakery stayed a long time, treated well by Aunt Marie who believed that everyone should benefit when a business makes a profit, and that everyone should earn a decent wage and have health insurance. They stayed so long, they became our family.

The tears spilled over as I remembered all the wonderful times I spent in the bakery with Aunt Marie. Rob leaned over and gripped my hand.

"Miranda, now don't you worry about this. Your aunt is going to be just fine. This is just another bump in the road. You have faced down worse than this," he said.

I was not reassured. This felt worse than going to prison. When I'd been charged with a crime, I was looking at a loss of my freedom. That would be hard on Aunt Marie, but she'd still have her life, her business, her home. Now that was all at risk, and it felt like a much worse sentence than a decade stuck behind bars.

"Why are they doing this?" I whispered.

He frowned. "They're trying to recover their lost savings, sweetheart. It's not personal."

But it was. It was so personal that I could hardly stand it.

"Is it that prosecutor, Donna Grayson? Is she trying to make me pay since I didn't get convicted?"

Rob scowled at the mention of the federal prosecutor. "I wouldn't put it past her, but no, the investors' lawyers have been looking at filing this suit for a long time."

My mind raced back a few nights to the Mexican restaurant.

"I just saw one of the agents who arrested me. The one

taking notes in the interview," I said. "Could he be following me?"

I knew it sounded paranoid, but panic was setting in.

"Jake Barnes, you mean? The FBI agent?"

"Yeah, I think so. Dark hair. Tall."

Rob nodded. "Yeah, he's a decent enough guy, for a fed, you know. He wasn't on your case long. Got moved from white collar to a different unit. It's probably just a coincidence, especially if you were dining near the downtown area."

I nodded. The restaurant was a popular place on the edge of the downtown office buildings. My mind was still not at ease. I hadn't seen Agent Barnes for months, and then he pops up just after my trial is over and the civil suit starts moving forward.

"The government can't come after you again. That would be double jeopardy. The criminal case against you is over and done. I can't imagine they'd have Barnes watching you," he said.

I breathed in, still not convinced but trying to calm myself.

Rob stood and walked to the sideboard and poured me a drink. He set the glass in front of me, and the scent of bourbon wafted up. I took a sip and felt the burn slide into my gut.

"Miranda, I won't let them take the bakery," he said. "I promised Marie that I wouldn't let them take you away. I kept that promise, didn't I?"

I looked up and saw the look in his eyes. It was a sheer determination that made my clenched heart relax a tiny bit. It was the look of a man who would do anything for the woman he loved.

I bit my lip and felt the tears burning again. Rob had been married once, Marie told me a long time ago. Marie had never married, and it was something that nagged at my conscience. She'd only been twenty-eight when I was dropped in her lap, and she had devoted herself to me. She'd dated some, but I couldn't remember anyone serious. Even after I moved out and went to college, she never mentioned any romantic interests.

"You love her."

He smiled and actually blushed a little.

"That's not your concern," he said, patting my shoulder.

He turned and poured himself a drink and when he turned back, he was more composed. At least more composed than I was.

"Why don't we talk about the new fraud case?" he said. "Maybe some securities fraud will take your mind off your troubles."

CHAPTER SIX

My eyes were dry and burning from hours of staring at a computer screen at my dimly lit kitchen table. I'd scanned thousands of pages of bank records looking for the transfers to some suspicious account, and my head was pounding.

Nothing made sense. Money flowed in from investors and then out to accounts where the investment guru was supposed to invest it in funds that would provide the best results for the clients. That's where the transfers should stop. But they weren't stopping there. The money might pause for a breath, but then it looked like it was skipping off to vacation in Switzerland, the Cayman Islands, Belize, and increasingly in Macau.

Patterson Tinker had offices overseas, including a thriving branch in Macau, where the economic boon was ripe for quick profits. But the clients who invested in the Sahara Fund were generally older, close to retirement or already retired, and wanted low-risk investments. Building high-rise condominiums or wind-generated power plants in Macau was not a low-risk investment. It was the opposite of that. The subsidiary in Macau was involved in casinos, housing and other businesses that could experience huge growth—or collapse and leave the investor with nothing.

Ralph often traveled there, and Tim had gone several times, too. Many people in my office had traveled there for meetings. On the one trip to the Asia office that I'd accompanied Tim on, I was stuck in a conference room for most of the week and didn't get much of a chance to venture out of the Patterson Tinker offices. I had a view of the city and the dozens of construction cranes and half-finished skyscrapers rising out of the urban landscape, over which a layer of dirty air lay. It felt miles away from the glamour and glitz of the casino scene, which Ralph and Tim raved about on the plane home.

There had been another trip planned, but I was arrested and fired about three weeks before I was supposed to leave. So reviewing records related to the Macau office was leaving me with a very bitter taste in my mouth.

I closed the laptop and left it on the kitchen table, and then got a beer out of the refrigerator. I took it with me to the bathroom and turned on the shower, downing the beer before I finished washing my hair. The warm water and the cold beer worked to relax me, and by the time I stepped out of the tiny enclosure, I was certain that I'd finally be able to sleep.

I dried off and wrapped myself in a towel and then stepped out of the bathroom to find some clothes. The nice thing about my tiny home was that everything was close at hand. The one-bedroom apartment was cozy. It was quirky. I'd fixed it up just as I liked it.

At least that's what I told myself.

My laundry basket was by the door, where I'd dumped it after coming back from using Aunt Marie's washer and dryer. I picked it up, rested the basket against my hip and was starting to return to my bedroom when I heard a loud knock on the door just feet from me.

"Jesus!" The sound came out of nowhere and startled the hell out of me. I glanced at the Mickey Mouse clock over the kitchen sink and saw that it was nearly ten o'clock. Who the hell would be knocking at my door this late?

I flipped on the outside light and peered through the lacy curtain covering the glass panes on the door.

My heart seized up at the sight of FBI Special Agent Jake Barnes.

"Fuck."

It was the only word that came to mind. My knees wobbled, and my mind raced back to the last time I'd had an unexpected encounter with the FBI—when they'd come into my office on a Friday afternoon and presented me with an arrest warrant.

"Ms. Vaughn?"

I was still staring at him, frozen in place. I dropped the laundry basket on the floor and opened the door the few inches the chain lock would allow.

"Yes?"

"I'd like to talk to you," he said. "Could I come in?"

He sounded polite, but I wasn't going to be fooled again.

"You got a warrant?"

He gave me a small smile. "No, it's not that kind of visit."

"Well, come back with a warrant, and I'll let my attorney know of your visit, Agent Barnes."

He looked surprised that I used his name, then uncomfortable.

"Please, Ms. Vaughn," he said. "I just need a few minutes of your time."

I shook my head, and my wet hair dripped onto my bare shoulders.

He paused, his lips tightened into a frown.

"I may be able to help you," he said.

My resolve slipped a fraction of an inch, but I was still rooted to the spot.

"Help me with what?"

He ran a hand through his hair and peered through the three-inch crack in the door at me.

"Can I come in? I'd rather not explain it standing out here, under this spotlight."

Moths dive-bombed his head as he stood beneath the security light outside the door. Still I waited, unsure of what to do. I seemed unable to make a decision.

"I promise not to arrest you," he said. "This is important."

I tasted blood and realized that I was biting my lip.

"It's about Patterson Tinker," he said.

"Wait here," I said, shutting the door. I picked up the laundry again, walked the twenty feet to my bedroom, and rummaged through the basket to find something to wear. Slipping on a pair of shorts and a tank top, I couldn't believe I was even considering letting a federal agent into my house. Rob had taught me better.

But he had information about Patterson Tinker, and that intrigued me.

I brushed my hair before it dried in a tangle and went back to the front door and unlocked it, opening it wider.

"It's late, Agent Barnes," I said.

He nodded. "I know. I apologize for coming by unannounced."

How polite. He made no move to come into the apartment, waiting on me to invite him.

Like a damn vampire.

I hesitated then opened the door fully. "Come on in," I said with a sigh.

He gave me a nod and entered my home, his eyes sweeping over the kitchen-dining-living room combo—what might be called a great room if that weren't so ridiculous in such a small space. I hurried to the kitchen table and swept up the paperwork and computer, stashing the documents on a bookshelf and putting the closed laptop on top of the pages.

"I hope I wasn't interrupting anything," he said.

I shook my head. "Just some work. Would you like to sit down?"

He glanced at the red couch that sat below the window overlooking the yard, and I quickly scanned the room for any bras or other embarrassing items lying around. The pitfall of living alone with few friends. He sat on one end of the loveseat, and I perched uneasily on the matching club chair across a low coffee table from him. The furniture had looked modern in my airy two-bedroom condo with a view of the city and the mountains in the background. Now the pieces looked like they were going slumming in my converted garage apartment.

"First, thank you for talking with me," he said. "This isn't about any investigation, doesn't have anything to do with your case."

"But if it did, you wouldn't have to tell me."

I knew the rules. If I lied to a federal agent, it was a felony. But he could lie to me with impunity.

"That's true, but I promise I'm not investigating you."

That promise meant nothing to me, so I just shrugged. "What is it you wanted to see me about?"

His lips tightened, and he appeared to struggle to figure out how to start.

"When you worked at Patterson, did you know Bill Macias?"

I nodded but kept my face neutral. I'd just spent a lot of my evening studying Bill Macias's email traffic and transfers to and from his office's general account.

"Are you investigating Mr. Macias?"

He shook his head. "No, I'm not. I'm not here investigating anyone," he said. "Did you work with Bill?"

"Not really. He was overseas, in London. Later he transferred to Asia," I said. This was information he'd easily be able to find out. Bill Macias was a vice president, and though Patterson was fond of giving out that title, Bill actually had responsibilities to go along with the nameplate.

"Yes, I know," he said.

"He headed up the energy group," I said. This, too, was easily accessed information. The company probably put out a press release on his promotion.

"What can you tell me about the energy group?"

I frowned. "That's a broad question, Agent Barnes."

"Call me Jake, please," he said. "Macias had been working with the energy group for a couple years, right?"

I nodded. "I believe so. I didn't have much interaction with him. Haven't seen him in years, since he was transferred overseas. We were on conference calls together. We emailed information to each other on occasion. That was the extent of my interaction with him."

"Did he have the authority to transfer funds?"

This was starting to feel familiar—a lot like when Jake Barnes's partner interrogated me about my job duties at Patterson Tinker. I crossed my arms and felt a chill even though the room was still balmy from the late summer heat. If I answered his questions, maybe he'd go away. But I'd thought that last time.

"I think I'd rather not answer any further questions, Agent Barnes."

He frowned and looked away briefly, his eyes taking in the spare furnishings before returning to me.

"I need to know about his job, who he would work with, answer to, that sort of thing," he said.

"Maybe you didn't hear me," I said, standing and walking toward the door. "I do not want to talk to you any longer."

I rested my hand on the doorknob, and he stood.

"This isn't about you, Ms. Vaughn," he said.

"I don't care."

"It's important."

"Please leave."

"You're being sued," he said.

The silence hung between us. I raised my eyes and looked at him.

"Yeah, so?"

I had done nothing wrong. I repeated that mantra to myself and kept my gaze steady on his face.

He stood and nearly filled the space. If he reached up, he could easily touch the low, sloped ceiling. His shoulders were broad and his arms bulged under the thin fabric of his t-shirt. I found my eyes on the muscles, my thoughts wandering to how they'd feel. I had a strong urge to poke one with my finger, to see if it was as hard as it looked. I resisted.

"I need your help," he said, his voice softer. His eyes were serious, and if he caught me ogling his biceps, he gave no clue. "Maybe we could help each other."

"The last time I saw you, you put me in handcuffs."

"Well, technically, the last time we saw each other you were making love to a plate of carnitas," he said, a flicker of a smile at the edge of his eyes.

Okay, maybe he had caught me staring. But I didn't want to flirt with Special Agent Barnes. Maybe if I'd never seen him before, didn't know what he did for a living. Maybe if he hadn't tried to get me thrown in prison for a decade. Then, maybe, I'd be open to a friendlier relationship. Oh, who was I kidding? I'd probably throw myself into those strong arms and against that wide, well-muscled chest.

I looked away quickly before I forgot who he was.

"If you change your mind—"

"I won't." I opened the door and held it for him.

He passed by me, and up close he was even larger than I'd remembered from our previous encounters or noticed while he was sitting on my couch. The scent of soap and something very male followed him. He paused, and I had to look up to look at his face. I was barely five-and-a-half feet tall and was trying to kick out a man who towered over me. And I was doing it while wearing next to nothing—just the shorts and tank top that I had picked out of the clean laundry.

Jake paused at the threshold and held out a hand. I hesitated then shook it. His firm grip made me feel small again, and I pulled back quickly. He took a card from his pocket and offered it to me.

"My cell phone is on the back. Call me if you change your mind."

I took the card, but shook my head. "I won't."

He smiled and nodded. "I understand."

I doubted that. He walked down the steps to the alley that doubled as my driveway, and a moment later I heard a motorcycle start up and then drive off into the dark night. The rumble faded into the sounds of the city, and I stayed on the landing, looking into the deep shadows of the yard and watched the strings of party lights from Aunt Marie's patio reflecting off the still water in the swimming pool.

Why was he asking about Bill Macias? The case was over, and Bill's name had never been mentioned. I remembered the vice president of energy in the Asia office—he was a charming man in his late 30s, ambitious, and a loyal Patterson Tinker employee. He had worked his way up from a fund manager to overseeing fund managers who studied the energy markets and invested money in companies and technologies that would pay the best returns.

I hadn't seen him since the short trip I'd taken to Macau with Tim and Ralph. Dylan had gone on that trip, too, and I gripped the railing tighter at the memory. I'd worked the entire time, but Dylan and Tim had found time to go out every night and party. When I'd complained to Dylan, he told me that it was part of his job—he had to spend time and Patterson Tinker's money entertaining clients. Then I had pouted and Dylan stormed out of the five-star hotel and didn't come back to the room until dawn. It had been a long, chilly flight back to the states.

I went back inside, turned off the porch light and locked the door. My plans to get a good night's sleep were blown out of the water. Taking the laptop with me, I went to bed to continue my research. This time, to focus on Bill Macias.

CHAPTER SEVEN

It would take Rob at least four weeks to get the evidence in his new fraud case, so I told Aunt Marie that I was thinking of doing a little traveling. She practically packed my suitcase for me. She had no idea about my plan but seemed happy that I had some goals and direction for a change. Of course, had she known my real plans, she would have probably locked me in the bakery's walk-in fridge.

I twisted the top off a bottle of water and checked out the view from the floor-to-ceiling hotel window. Macau was as amazing and impressive as it had been last time I'd been here, and looking out over the city gave me a little flutter in my stomach. The sky was white and overcast, and the air looked thick with the ever-present humidity. The haze at the edge of the horizon was tinged with a dusky brown smudge. That could be an effect from either the city's smog or an incoming storm front that would bring heavy rains, a risk of traveling to the southern coast of China in the summer months.

Checking into a hotel has always excited me. Maybe it's from a childhood where vacations were spent in a tent, but I've always loved exploring the little space, smelling the soaps, checking out the view. Unpacking my things and making this human-sized dollhouse my own for the duration of my stay.

It was more fun when it was an expensive five-star hotel paid for by Patterson Tinker. They'd always put their people up in the finest hotels, usually in suites. Having to pass my own credit card across the counter was more difficult, even for the smallest room at a slightly less prestigious hotel in Macau. I prayed that I could execute my plan quickly and get back to the states before I hit my credit card limits.

My room overlooked a series of bright blue swimming pools ringed by Greek columns and palm trees. The effect was more Vegas than world-class resort, but Macau itself seemed to be aiming at becoming Las Vegas on steroids, boasting more casinos than any other city on earth. One of the best parts of working for Patterson Tinker had been the travel I'd been able to do—Geneva, London, Paris, Stockholm and Frankfurt. It had been work, but I'd tried to fit in some sightseeing when I could.

The Mandarin Hotel was nice, but not as pricey as the one Patterson Tinker booked for me. It was close enough to my previous hotel that I'd be able to find my way around, so I paid more than I wanted to for that security. Plus, it was less likely that I'd run into visiting Patterson employees here. From the Mandarin, I could walk to the office building where my former employer, now called Patterson Investment Company, had its Asian headquarters. From my room I could see new buildings that had sprouted in the two years since I'd visited and recognized some landmarks in the historic center. It had been my first trip to Asia, and it made a huge impression on me. Dylan and I had even talked about spending our honeymoon exploring China.

Eager to shake thoughts of my former fiancé from my head, I opened my suitcase and dug around for the supplies I'd packed. Using an assumed name and a fabricated cover story, I'd made an appointment to meet with a personal wealth manager. It would get me in the office and past security so I could track down the man I needed to talk to.

And then? Well, I had a plan and it wasn't horrible. But it was risky. If Bill Macias called my bluff…

I forced myself to stop that train of thought. If I dwelled on that possibility, I'd lose my nerve. Instead, I unpacked my suitcase and hung up the clothes I'd wear the next day. I kicked off my shoes and made myself comfortable. My nerves were on edge. I'm not a fan of flying and can't sleep on planes. I was running on the very small amount of shallow sleep that I'd managed to get on the eighteen-hour flight from San Francisco. It was only 3 o'clock in the afternoon, but I was ready for bed. Unfortunately, if I did that, I would be awake at midnight with nothing to do until my afternoon appointment.

I still had plenty to do before then, so I ordered a room service snack and a pot of coffee. Nourished and caffeinated, I got to work, starting with the temporary auburn hair dye.

When I realized that all the money I was trying to track had gone through the general office account for the Macau energy-trading group, I knew I had to talk to Bill Macias. And before the FBI did, too. If they arrested him, I'd lose any chance to confront him.

As far as I could tell, he still worked for the Macau office as vice president of the energy-trading group. His office number still worked, though it went to his secretary's voicemail every time I tried to call. I never left a message, afraid that I'd tip my hand. Instead, I had dug into the documents that I'd swiped from my case files and found an internal company directory for the Macau office. Cross-referencing that with the trove of emails, I tracked down a wealth manager whose office was two floors below the energy-trading group and who was always complaining that he didn't have enough clients.

Martin Templeton was my entrée to the Patterson Investment Company.

I kept his emails in mind when I dressed the following afternoon. Martin was a chatty, social fellow. Born in East Anglia, England, the youngest of three brothers—and the least successful, at least according to the emails from his parents. His email traffic consisted of thirty percent work, thirty percent making social plans or chatting with friends in London, and forty percent forwarded photos of naked women. He also was a huge fan of all things Texan. Movies, music, travel. But he was especially interested in the Dallas Cowboy Cheerleaders.

When I left for the meeting, my hair was coiffed and teased into a brunette helmet that would make a beauty queen weep with envy. I was wearing more makeup than I'd ever worn at one time, including a hint of shiny blue eye shadow. My low-cut wrap dress emphasized my cleavage, which was supplemented to make it more impressive. The entire ensemble was based on a particular email chain that Martin had seemed fixated on, a half-dozen soft-porn photos of a Texas co-ed.

From the look on his face, I had hit the bulls-eye.

"Good morning, Mr. Templeton. I'm Lana Parker," I said in my best southern drawl. "I sure appreciate you taking the time to meet with me."

"Well, it's my pleasure, Miss Parker," he said. "Or is it Mrs. Parker?"

"Oh, Mrs. Parker is my mama," I said with a giggle. "You can just call me Lana."

Martin's face flushed pink, and he smiled widely. "Why don't we meet in my office?"

He led me past the reception area to a long, wide corridor lined with glass-enclosed conference rooms. The rooms looked out on the harbor. The conference rooms were empty, giving an unobstructed view of the city and the waterfront. Any fear that

I'd see a familiar face in the Patterson office was misplaced. Half the offices weren't occupied, and I wondered how well the company was really doing. When I'd visited two years ago, it had been bustling, taking up three floors in the high-rise and employing hundreds of workers.

Martin's office was a small suite with a sitting area by the windows. We sat in a pair of upholstered chairs, sipping tea and chatting before getting down to business.

"How can I help you, Lana?"

"Well, as I may have mentioned, my grandfather, may he rest in peace, left me a rather generous trust upon his passing. I just don't know the first thing about investing, and I really don't want to worry about that. My step-father suggested that the Patterson Company could be of assistance," I said. I was worried about laying the whole Texas thing a little too thick, but Martin seemed to be eating it up.

"And who is your step-father?"

"Lloyd Nash," I said, taking a sip of the tea and letting Martin make the connection. "He's an oil and gas man in Houston."

"Oh, Nash. Of course," Martin said, sitting a little straighter.

I'd done my homework. Lloyd Nash was a wealthy businessman with faint ties to the Asia markets, so his name would be known, but details of his family life probably wouldn't.

Martin offered condolences on my dead grandaddy and moved his chair closer and took my hand. "I can definitely help you, Lana."

I looked up at him through a thick fringe of fake eyelashes and blinked, as if tears were threatening to spill over. They were, but it was because of the damn glue on the false lashes. He offered a tissue, and I dabbed at my eyes and gave him a smile.

We agreed to meet the following day to review my current portfolio, and he was so eager at the prospect of his commission on such a large account that I almost felt guilty for my deception. By mid-afternoon tomorrow, I'd hopefully be on a flight back to California with the thirty-seven million dollars stolen from the Sahara Fund investors wired to a numbered account in the Caymans and an affidavit signed by Bill Macias attesting to my innocence.

Martin shook my hand vigorously near the elevators and seemed reluctant to let me leave, but the office was starting to close for the day.

"Are you relocating to Macau or here for a visit?"

"I'm afraid I'm only in Macau for a short time to spend time with my mama and Lloyd."

"Oh, is Mr. Nash in town?" Martin seemed eager to expand his portfolio of wealthy clients.

"He is in Macau. In fact, he said I should stop by and visit one of his friends while I'm here. I nearly forgot. Do you know Mr. Winthrop?"

Clint Winthrop was a senior analyst in the technology group, and if the information I had was correct, he worked on the twenty-second floor, one below the energy group.

Martin nodded eagerly. "Of course, of course. He's with the technology group upstairs. Would you like me to ring him up and let him know you're here?"

"Oh, if it's not too much bother." I batted my fake eyelashes and hoped that they would hold. Martin smiled and walked back to the receptionist, who placed a call upstairs while giving me a once-over. I knew she'd find nothing out of place—the expensive handbag, the pricey shoes, the classic designer dress. It was all genuine, remnants of my former life. The receptionist hung up the phone and gave Martin a nod, and he returned to me.

"He's in and would love to meet you. I'll escort you upstairs," Martin said.

"Oh, that's not necessary, Mr. Templeton," I said, taking his hand. "I'm sure you're very busy, and I can find my way up one floor."

I had to make sure Martin did not get into the elevator with me.

"Are you sure? It's really no trouble," he said, disappointed.

"I've already taken up so much of your time today," I said. "And I plan on monopolizing your day tomorrow, as well, so I would feel terrible keeping you any longer than necessary."

I flashed a smile and batted my eyes again. Those false lashes were getting a workout. He gave me a reluctant smile and walked me to a different elevator that ran between the three floors that Patterson Investment leased and took my hand in his.

"It's just up on the twenty-second floor, but you'll have to hurry. Sounds like he's running out the door."

Perfect.

"So lovely to meet you, Lana. I look forward to seeing you tomorrow. And then maybe I can convince you to go to dinner with me."

I squeezed his hand and smiled. "You charmer," I said. "I'd love to have dinner with you tomorrow night."

He beamed and held my hand as I stepped into the elevator and didn't let go until the door started to shut. Once the door closed, I hit the button for the twenty-third floor, letting out a deep breath and trying to calm my nerves.

The elevator passed the twenty-second floor, where Mr. Winthrop was waiting for Lana Parker to come introduce herself. He was going to be disappointed. The doors opened, and I stepped out into the lobby of the twenty-third floor, prepared to bluff my way to the suite belonging to the vice president of energy. The lobby area was silent, and the reception desk was empty. I walked toward it, my high-heels clicking on the marble floor.

When I reached the middle of the lobby, the sound of my

footsteps echoed off the walls. I passed the receptionist's desk with the mute phones, and stepped onto a plush carpet that led down a wide hallway. It was the same layout as the twenty-first floor, where I'd met with Martin Templeton. The sitting area past the reception desk featured low modern couches and glass tables on which several financial periodicals were arrayed. The floor-to-ceiling windows featured the same view as on the main floor—a panorama of the city and the harbor.

I peered down the long hallway, expecting to have to produce my cover story—that I must have hit the wrong button in the elevator—but no one walked out of the offices that lined the corridor.

The hair on the back of my neck stood on end. There was something eerie about the deathly quiet space. It was close to 5 p.m., and the offices two floors down were packing up for the day. But this floor had the feeling of a space that had long ago shut down.

I moved down the hall, looking at the nameplates on the doors. The names were familiar because I had studied the employee roster for the energy section. The office doors were closed, and I reached out and tried a door knob, but it was locked. I grew bolder as I made my way toward the end of the hall, trying the doors and peeking into the offices that were unlocked.

They were all empty.

The plaque on the door of the corner office said it belonged to Vice President Bill Macias, and my fingers trembled a little as I turned the knob. Like the rest of the floor, it was empty. But unlike the other offices I had poked my head into, there were papers strewn everywhere. One wall was bookcases with long filing drawers beneath them. Several of the drawers had been pulled out and left open, the contents stacked on the floor haphazardly.

I approached Bill Macias's desk, a sense of foreboding flooding my body. His desk sat near the wall of windows. It was a massive wooden desk, an old-fashioned style that matched the built-in bookshelves and coordinated well with the Persian rug. The whole room had the feel of an antique library, not an investment analyst's office. The room was in such disarray that I expected to find a body on the other side of the desk, but there was nothing there but a large leather chair, resting on its back. I pulled it away from the desk and poked through the desk drawers. I had no idea what I was looking for—a forwarding address, maybe?

With a sigh, I looked around the empty room. This was not what I expected to find. What was going on? There was no indication downstairs that the energy group had moved or closed. But the twenty-first floor where Martin and other "front office" wealth managers worked had seemed rather sparsely populated, too. This floor, though, was sinister in its silence and in the manner the office had been closed—as if a fire alarm had been pulled and no one on the twenty-third floor returned after the drill.

A soft ding sounded and my heart stopped. I froze and listened to the sound of footsteps on the marble floor. Crap. It was probably security, wondering what happened to the visitor who was expected in Mr. Winthrop's office. I clutched my purse to my chest as the footsteps ceased. That could mean that the person walked the opposite direction from where I was. Or that he was heading down the carpeted hallway toward me.

I stepped out of my shoes and crouched behind the desk, crawling into the knee hole. I exhaled slowly and tried to control my pounding heart. I couldn't see if anyone came into the room, so I listened for any sound that might tell me when it would be safe to emerge from my wood-paneled cave. I hoped that whoever it was would glance around the room and not see me, and then leave.

In the silent room, the only sound I could hear was my heartbeat, which sounded like it was echoing through the empty halls. Then I heard it, a slight creak and then the sound of footsteps, the whisper of shoes against the carpet. I held my breath and stayed as still as possible.

The footsteps were closer, and I peeked down at the two inches of clearance under the desk. I couldn't see a damn thing. Not even a shadow. I'd have to lay flat on the floor to see anything, and I didn't dare move. Then the toe of a man's shoe appeared, and I heard the sound of items on the desk being moved just over my head. I pulled my knees closer to me and took slow and shallow breaths. I closed my eyes. How was I going to get myself out of this mess?

The sounds stopped, and the shoe moved out of my line of sight, and I heard the sound of drawers opening. Not in the desk, though. The other person in the room must be looking through the drawers in the built-in bookcases.

Wait. Why would a security guard be rifling through filing cabinets?

Before I could dwell on that, I heard the footsteps near me again. I held my breath and looked skyward, as if God would help me in my predicament. As I did, I saw something on the underside of the desk, way back from the opening I'd crawled through. I reached up and touched it and traced the packing tape that secured a flash drive to the wood. My fingernail found the edge of the tape, and I slowly tugged, but the crinkling of the cellophane tape was louder than I expected. I froze, and then slowly drew my hand back, closed my eyes, and prayed that the man in the room hadn't heard me.

No luck.

A strong hand gripped my upper arm and yanked me out

from my hiding place. I smacked my head on the underside of the desk before emerging into the brightly lit office. I fought back, struggling against the man who ripped me from my hiding place, but he pinned my arms against my sides and pushed me against the wall of bookshelves.

"I don't believe this."

At the sound of the man's voice, I looked up.

And into the eyes of a very angry FBI agent.

CHAPTER EIGHT

Jake Barnes's fingers dug into my upper arms, and he had me immobilized against the bookcase.

"What the hell are you doing here?" His voice was low, almost a whisper. An angry whisper.

I gasped, trying to catch my breath. "Me? What are you doing here?"

My own whisper was more a furious squeak, like a cartoon mouse. He growled and let go of my arms, but didn't answer.

"Stay quiet," he said.

"Why?" I hissed.

"We're not alone."

The thought that there was someone else on the floor hadn't occurred to me. I had seen no signs of life since I entered the floor. But as soon as he said it, I listened and heard it. A faint sound, shoes on carpet perhaps. It was coming toward Bill Macias's office, from the opposite direction of the lobby.

Jake pushed me toward the desk. "Hide."

I crawled back into the knee hole of the desk. Again, I could see the faint outline of the flash drive taped under the desk, and I wanted to grab it, but I didn't want to rustle more than necessary. Instead, I held my breath, waiting to hear the inevitable sounds of Jake Barnes being confronted by the building security officer.

Countless minutes passed, and I finally heard Jake's whisper.

"It's clear." His hands reached down, and he helped me out, more slowly this time. "We've got to get out of here."

I scrambled for my shoes under the desk, and as I did, I reached up and yanked at the piece of tape, my fingers closing around the plastic case and keeping it hidden in my palm. I planned to stash it in my purse, but as I emerged from the desk, I saw Jake holding my bright blue clutch. I turned away, resting my closed fist on the desk to steady myself as I slid my feet into the shoes. Still holding my purse, Jake walked to the office door and peered down the hall. While his head was turned, I shoved the device into my bra.

He looked back at me and nodded toward the hall. "Let's go."

I shook my head. "No. I'm not going anywhere with you."

He stared at me like I was out of my mind. "Look here, Ms. Vaughn. You're trespassing in a closed office. In a foreign country. You really want to try and explain that to the local authorities? Or the security personnel working for your former employer?"

He had some good points, but I wasn't convinced that it was a better idea to go off with an FBI agent who had already arrested me once.

"What are you doing here?"

He shook his head, his lips compressed in a line. "Let's catch up later."

The soft ding of the elevator announced that we weren't going to be alone for long. I moved toward the door. I'd take my chances with the U.S. authorities on the trespassing charge. The devil you know, and all that.

We hurried down the hall in the opposite direction from the

lobby, and I followed Jake blindly, hoping he knew where he was going. I knew there was a staircase that linked the three floors, but it was near the internal elevator that had brought me to this floor. Jake turned down a hall that appeared to end, and I nearly stopped, but he reached back and grabbed my hand, pulling me into a darkened room. It had been a break room, and there was still the scent of stale coffee in the air. I heard a soft click as Jake locked the door.

He looked around the dimly lit space, pulled me to the corner and opened a door marked "supplies." We barely fit into the tiny space, and I was petrified that we would knock something off the shelves or kick a mop bucket. He closed the door and moved us so he was between me and the door.

I heard the sound of the break room door rattling, then the jingle of keys and the door opening. Jake's arm tightened around me, and I could feel his breath on the top of my head. The footsteps on the tile floor drew closer. I closed my eyes waiting for the door to the closet to be yanked open, but nothing happened. I opened an eye and saw a brief flash of light at the edge of the door, probably a flashlight being waved around the room. Then the door closed firmly, and the footsteps faded away. In the distance, I could hear indistinct voices.

"Wait," Jake whispered in the dark.

He still had his arm around my shoulder, and I found myself nearly wrapped around his body. Not like there was anywhere else to go in the small closet. But that didn't quite explain how my leg came to be wrapped around a very solid thigh. In any other circumstances, I'd be completely embarrassed by the full-body contact. At the moment, though, I had too many other concerns competing for room in my head—were we going to be dragged out and tossed onto the street? Arrested? Shot? Why was the FBI here? Were they following me? And if so, why?

Jake slowly and quietly turned the knob and opened the

door, letting in the weak light from the break room. The room was empty and quiet, and I loosened my grip on him. He stepped out of the closet, and I followed. He turned and pointed at my feet.

"Take off your shoes," he whispered.

I didn't ask questions, just did what he said. We made our way across the room, the smooth floor cool under my bare feet. At the door, he put a finger to his lips, and I nodded. He again paused, then quietly cracked the door and listened.

In the distance, a door slammed, and he looked back at me.

"How did you get up here?" he asked, his voice barely above a whisper.

"The elevator from the twenty-first floor," I answered, keeping my voice low.

With a nod, he opened the door wider and taking my hand, pulled me into the hall. He closed the door quietly and keeping a grip on me, led us back toward the reception area. I pulled back, afraid to head toward the noise we'd just heard.

He shook his head. "Come on."

The lobby was silent, and we crept past the empty reception desk, toward the elevator that had brought me to this eerie office. Then Jake pulled me past the elevators and the door to the staircase that led to the two other Patterson floors, and then down another hall. I barely breathed as we moved quickly toward a door that appeared to be the emergency exit.

Jake put a hand on the doorknob, looked down at me and gave a quick nod toward the door. He pushed it open, and I cringed, waiting for a shrieking alarm. Nothing happened. He ushered me into the narrow staircase and closed the door quietly behind him. I barely heard the click as the metal door met the frame.

Quickly, we started down the stairs to the twenty-second floor, then to the twenty-first floor. I paused, but he yanked my hand again, and we continued down. By the fifteenth floor, I was regretting my lax cardio regimen. Jake, though, seemed to handle the quick descent without any heavy breathing.

At the tenth floor, I stopped and doubled over. "Wait," I gasped.

"No."

He reached for me, and before I could catch my breath, he swung me up and over his shoulder, and he continued down the steps.

"Jesus! That's not what I meant," I said, as my head bounced off his rock-hard back.

"I know," he said.

"Just put me down!" This was more embarrassment than one person could take in an afternoon.

"No, this is faster."

Then he sped up, and we bounced the rest of the way down the steps to a set of double doors, where he finally put me on the ground. He opened the door and looked out and motioned for me. I was putting my shoes on and trying to regain my breath. Also, I was a bit dizzy from all the blood that rushed from my head.

"Are you trying to get arrested?" he asked, yanking me out of the building and into an alley.

I gasped and immediately regretted it. The alley smelled of exhaust and garbage that had been stored too long in the steamy, late-afternoon heat. Once outdoors, Jake headed away from the street, dragging me along with him. We ducked into another alley, rounded a corner, and he finally dropped my hand and turned to look at me. I took a deep breath and started to talk. I had a lot of telling-off to do.

He held up a hand. "Stay here. Do not go anywhere."

I shut my mouth, my brain still struggling to form words and thoughts after its recent jarring. He turned and ran down another alley, and I lost sight of him.

"Well, that's just great."

I had no idea what to do. Wait for Jake Barnes, who was almost certainly going to arrest me? Or take my chances with Patterson's security guards?

As I hesitated, I heard a familiar sound. I turned to look behind me and barely caught the helmet Jake Barnes threw my way as he pulled up on a gleaming black motorcycle.

"Put it on, and get on," he said, sitting astride the bike.

I shook my head and took a step back, but he grabbed my arm and looked into my eyes. His anger was evident, but he tamped it down when he saw my fear.

"The people chasing us are going to take the elevator when they figure out we're no longer there. We need to leave now."

"Who—?" I still struggled to form complete sentences, but he seemed to understand me.

"Bad guys."

I took a deep breath, handed Jake my purse. He unzipped his jacket and slid the clutch inside, securing it against his chest. I exhaled and put the helmet on. Then I turned to the bike and paused. I was wearing a knit wrap dress and three-inch heels. There was no way to mount this machine without getting indecent about it.

He must have sensed my horror, because he looked away while I threw a leg over the leather seat. I wasn't even seated when he reached back and grabbed my thigh, pulling me snug against him, and gunned the engine. I clutched at his back and closed my eyes.

"I hate this. I hate this. I hate this," I chanted. This would be a good time to pray, but God and I were not on speaking terms presently, so I settled for voicing my discontent.

"Just hang on," Jake said, and the bike surged forward and shot out of the alley like it was fired from a cannon.

He didn't have to tell me twice. I wrapped my arms around him and opened my eyes to see where we were going. The last thing I saw was the front door of the office building opening and a half-dozen blue-shirted security guards running out before I squeezed my eyes shut.

The bike weaved in and out of the stalled traffic, and the warm air brushed across my bare legs. I opened one eye and saw the blur of cars we were passing. I quickly shut my eye again and tried not to think about the fact that my last few minutes on earth were apparently going to be spent in abject terror.

Jake leaned into a curve and, as I was glued to him, I did, too. Sarah was never going to believe me when I told her I rode on a motorcycle. She'd been trying to get me to ride with her since we met. But I was sure the two-wheel contraptions would result in certain death.

I was more convinced than ever of that.

The bike leaned the other direction, and the driver and I moved like one. I tried to go to a happy place, but perhaps it had been too long. I tried to recall the warm kitchen at the Sugar Plum Bakery, Aunt Marie's family room with the plush loveseat under a bay window where I used to curl up with a book when I was a kid. Anything. Any place other than where I was.

"Where are you staying?"

Between the helmet and the fact that my head was pressed tight against his back, I could barely hear Jake's question.

"What?"

"Your hotel. Which one are you staying at?" he yelled back.

"The Mandarin, by the harbor."

The bike turned, and we were on a frontage road that looked over a stretch of water. The air was cooler and cleaner here, with a breeze coming off the harbor. I realized that I had opened my eyes at some point and was enjoying the view. Except the part where the bike zipped in and out of traffic. That part was making me pretty nauseated.

"Keep an eye out for anyone following us."

The bike leapt forward, and I turned my head to look behind us, unsure of what I was supposed to look for. There was heavy traffic, but nothing that looked like a car full of private security officers hired by an investment bank.

If there was a threat out there, I didn't see it. Unless it was the one I was snuggled up against on a bike racing through Macau.

CHAPTER NINE

Jake parked the bike in an alley at a casino parking garage a couple blocks from the Mandarin Hotel. I climbed off and tried to compose myself, pulling off the helmet and reaching up to feel the damage to my hair. My carefully coiffed hair was now suffering the effects of helmet head—smashed flat and matted. I peered into the side-view mirror of the bike and let out a yelp of horror.

"It's not that bad," Jake said, his voice amused.

"I have to walk back through that lobby like this. How is this not bad?"

"A little vain, are we?" He cocked an eyebrow.

I glared at him. "Trying not to attract too much attention."

There was no way the desk clerk wasn't going to remember me now. I'd tried to keep a low profile, but this just wasn't part of the plan. Not that I had a *great* plan, but I did have a rudimentary scheme that I was determined to follow. Of course, that plan had relied on meeting with Bill Macias. I needed to recalibrate my next move, and I needed to do it alone.

I fluffed my hair back up as big as I could make it and wiped the smudged mascara from under my eyes then started toward the hotel. Jake Barnes was at my side, and I wondered how I could ditch him. He seemed to read my mind, handing me my purse and putting an arm around my shoulder as we entered the hotel's opulent lobby.

I smiled at the concierge as we passed the desk on the way to the elevator. He didn't give me a second glance, so I must not look as disheveled as I felt. We took the elevator up to the ninth floor in silence, alone in the mirrored box, a piano concerto playing softly in the background.

As we walked to my hotel room door, I tried to remember how I had left it. But unlike last time Jake Barnes had barged into my life, this time I wasn't worried as much about stray undergarments. Had I left my computer out? The papers I'd compiled? The hard drives?

My heart was in my throat as I unlocked the door. Jake opened the door, keeping me from entering the room until he'd scanned it, then pulled me in and locked it behind me. I also looked around the room and then exhaled a sigh of relief when I saw that my computer and other items were safely out of view.

"So, what's with the get-up?" he asked, looking me over.

"What are you talking about?" I tried to sound offended. "And what are you doing here? Isn't this a little out of your jurisdiction?"

God, I hoped it was out of his jurisdiction, but I honestly had no idea how far the FBI could travel to investigate a crime.

Jake strode across the room to look out the window and ignored my question. "Nice place. Have you stayed here before?"

"No."

I watched him, unsure of what to do. Was he here to investigate me? Arrest me? Did he know what I was doing here? If so, he would surely cuff me, and not in a fun way. But how could he know my plans? He turned and studied me and I shifted in my high heels, uncomfortable in the scrutiny. Then I took a deep breath and moved toward the closet to get a change of clothes from my suitcase.

Pulling some comfortable clothes from my bag, I thought about the flash drive in my bra. My laptop was in the locked safe below my suitcase, but I couldn't very well open it in front of the FBI agent. Not without raising a lot of questions I didn't want to get into.

"I'm going to go change my clothes," I said. "Try not to violate my Fourth Amendment rights while I'm gone."

I saw a hint of a smile on his face before I raced to the bathroom and slammed the door. I quickly discarded the designer wrap dress, now a wrinkled mess, for a pair of jeans and a red and white striped t-shirt. I slid the flash drive into my pants pocket, and then washed my face and removed the stupid false eyelashes. When I was done, I looked in the mirror and saw my familiar face—not the Texas beauty queen I had been just a couple hours earlier. The brown hair was still a shock every time I passed a mirror. It made my blue eyes stand out, and I hoped was enough of a change that any Patterson employee who'd briefly met the blonde Miranda Vaughn two years ago wouldn't recognize me when I met with Martin Templeton.

When I emerged, Jake was sitting on the edge of the king-sized bed.

"We need to talk," he said.

"Fine. You first," I said, closing the closet door, as if that would keep him from seeing what was in the safe. "Why are you in Macau?"

He didn't respond right away, keeping his gaze on the window. The sun was setting and the slanted light beginning to fade. I didn't move to turn on any lights.

"I'm looking into a missing person."

"Bill Macias?"

He looked back at me with narrowed eyes and nodded.

"Why is the FBI interested in him? How long has he been missing?"

Jake gave me a tight smile and then shook his head. "No. That's not how this is going to work. You tell me why you're here."

I frowned and tried to come up with something that I could tell him that wasn't technically a lie. My mind drew a blank.

"Are you going to arrest me?" I blurted out.

He studied me again. "Should I?"

"No! I mean, what are you investigating? Is it Bill Macias? Or his disappearance? Why is the FBI so far from home?"

A long pause and I shifted, my toes digging into the plush carpet. Jake stared at me, his eyes hard.

"I'm not here on official business," he said.

"Then why are you here?"

"If I tell you, you have to come clean with me."

I nodded, reluctantly. There was no way in hell I'd tell him everything, but I could dole out some truthful information to placate him.

"Bill Macias has been missing for several weeks. The local officials aren't taking it seriously," he said.

I sat on the settee across from the bed and met his very direct gaze, then reached for a pair of socks to put on. "So, the U.S. government is investigating?"

He paused, his lips tightening. "Bill used to be married to my sister."

That wasn't what I was expecting to hear.

"Is that why you were taken off my case so early? Because your brother-in-law worked for Patterson Tinker?"

"I was only brought in for support that day. The lead agent knew I had a tenuous connection, and I was barely involved in the investigation," he said.

"So you flew halfway around the world to investigate? Are

you sure this isn't an official investigation?" I slipped a pair of running shoes on. What they lacked in style, they more than made up for in comfort. And I had done enough walking in high heels for one day.

"I wouldn't be here if it were at anyone else's request, but my sister asked me to find out what trouble Bill's in. And if this were an official investigation, I'd be here with a partner," Jake said, crossing his arms across his chest. "Now you. What are you doing here? And why were you in Bill's office?"

I bit my lip and tried to think of a good reason for any of that. There wasn't one. So I went with the simplest explanation.

"Someone set me up."

The phone on the desk next to me rang, and I nearly jumped out of my skin. My hand trembled as I picked up the receiver, the adrenaline coursing through my veins.

"Miss Vaughn?"

The caller ID on the phone showed the call was coming from the concierge, not the front desk. The caller's voice was distinct and low.

"Yes," I said.

"Your guests are on their way up."

"What guests—?" Before I could finish my question, Jake's hand cut off the call.

"We're checking out," he said.

I stuffed the clutch purse into a leather messenger bag and followed Jake toward the door, wondering if I'd be able to return to the hotel room.

"Wait!"

I dove into the bottom of the closet, fumbled with the combination on the safe and then withdrew my laptop and the hard drives and slid them into the bag. A folder of papers and a notebook full of my handwritten notes went on top. Then Jake

Barnes yanked me up off the floor and out the door, and we were running down the hall toward the stairs.

We rounded the corner at the end of the hall, and Jake grabbed me and pulled me against him, both of us up against the wall. He peered around the corner, just as we heard the ding of the elevator. He pulled his head back and cursed under his breath. I reached into my bag, fumbled with my clutch and pulled out a compact and handed it to him.

Jake took it, but gave me an uncertain look. I took it back, opened it and tapped the mirror with my fingernail. He nodded and used the mirror to watch down the hall outside my room. From my position, I couldn't see anything in the reflection except the gold baroque wallpaper.

The sound of a hard knock on a door startled me. A moment later, I heard the sound of a door opening, followed by muted voices and a door closing. Jake closed the compact, slipped it into my purse and nodded toward the end of the hall, where there was an exit sign over a metal door.

Great, more stairs.

"They're going to know we saw them go into the room," he said quietly, nodding toward the corner of the ceiling at the black glass bubbles that concealed the security cameras. They'd also know we were taking the stairs. I was just happy that it was a mere nine flights this time. But at the end of the staircase, where would I go?

I stayed close on Jake's heels in the stairwell—an easier task with sneakers on than in the expensive heels I'd just abandoned in my hotel room. The messenger bag banging at my hip now contained everything I was going to have until I could get back into the room, which was probably being tossed by the Macau police.

At the bottom of the last flight, Jake pushed the door open, peered in both directions, and then pulled me into the hallway.

Hand in hand, we walked briskly toward the main entrance, down the wide corridor flanked by doors that opened into business conference centers and well-appointed sitting areas for travelers.

The tall, slim figure of the concierge rounded the corner and made eye contact with me. He hesitated and his face briefly registered shock, then he gave me a quick shake of the head and continued into the first open door. I yanked on Jake's arm, and ducked into a sitting alcove.

"What?"

"We can't go that way."

The alcove was empty, but didn't have any door except the wide entrance to the hall, making us trapped and exposed. I peered around the corner and down the hall in time to see a half-dozen men crossing the hall and walking briskly toward the elevators. I jerked my head back and bit my lip.

"Who did you see?"

"Six men, heading to the elevator."

"Uniforms?"

I shook my head.

"Could they be guests?"

I paused and thought about what I'd seen. Something about them had a law enforcement vibe. Was it the nondescript suits? The short haircuts? The walk—fast, as if they were trying to hurry but not draw attention to themselves by running. The way they walked in pairs, almost like military formation.

"Pretty sure they're cops."

"Chinese?"

"No, they were white."

"Probably Patterson's security," he said, moving me so he could look out in the hall. "It's clear. Is there another exit?"

I had walked down to check out the pool this morning. It

was hard to believe that was just a matter of hours earlier. It seemed a lifetime ago.

"The pool area has a fence, pretty high. I don't remember an exit. We'd have to cross the lobby to get to the pool anyway," I said. "What about the kitchen? There must be a service entrance."

He nodded. "Which way?"

"This way," a soft voice said behind me. I jumped and suppressed a scream, finding the concierge standing three feet from me.

He nodded to a door that blended into wall, and after a brief hesitation, we followed him. He shut the panel behind us, and I realized that it wasn't a secret entrance, just a way for the hotel to expand a meeting room to accommodate a larger group. The other side of the door was another alcove, but it opened to both the hallway and another conference room.

"Stay behind me," the man said.

Jake gave me a questioning look, and I shrugged. I had no idea whether to trust him or why he was helping us.

"Miss Vaughn, you have very little time," the concierge said.

"Why are you helping me?"

"We take care of our guests."

He gave me a pointed look, and after a few seconds I nodded. Maybe this wasn't the first time the Mandarin's hotel staff had to help a guest evade police. He turned and headed into the dark and empty conference room, staying along one wall. At the corner, he unlocked a door and let us into a hallway.

Then he stopped.

"Go through the double doors, turn right. Follow that hall to the end and you'll find the door to the service alley." He reached into his pocket and withdrew my passport, which I had given the clerk when I checked in.

"Won't the police be watching the back entrances?" Jake asked.

The concierge gave us a puzzled look. "Those men are not police."

I swallowed hard at his tone, took my passport and stammered out a thank you. Jake grabbed my hand and pulled me away.

We ran down the empty hallway, following the directions to the exit. We were in a service hall, and the only people we passed were a few housekeeping staff and servers, but they didn't pay much attention to us. Jake pushed the exit door open and looked outside, and then pulled me out into the alley. The concierge was right—the men looking for us were not covering the back entrance. We hurried down the alley toward a street behind the hotel.

Jake led us on a convoluted path away from the Mandarin, and I had to jog to keep up with his long strides. The oppressive heat didn't help. No offshore breeze penetrated the maze of city buildings where we were and the air was thick with humidity.

"Where are we going?"

"To my hotel," he said as we passed a bus stop.

"The bike?" I asked, my breath coming in gasps.

"A rental. It's fine where I left it."

As we left the casino and modern buildings behind us, the architecture changed from modern to Macau's own blend that reflected Asian influences and those of the region's Portuguese settlers. My feet slid and stumbled over the cobblestone streets that snaked between squat and cramped buildings. The exotic scent of incense from an open market mingled with the heavy exhaust fumes from Macau's impressive traffic. It would have been a lovely walking tour, if we weren't being chased. And if we weren't nearly running.

Jake looked up at a storefront, paused and then yanked my hand and pulled me into the front door of a convenience shop.

He went over to a display of tourist staples—hats, sunglasses, t-shirts, postcards. He grabbed a large black t-shirt and two baseball caps and paid with cash. Taking the plastic bag, he led me back out the door, his hand gripping my elbow as if I'd flee. He didn't have to worry. I had no idea where I was. I didn't speak the language, and I had no clue who was chasing me. I may not trust him, but at that moment, Jake Barnes was my lifeline.

At a corner, where the alley ended at a boulevard, Jake pulled out one of the baseball caps and put it on. He handed me the t-shirt.

"What am I supposed to do with this?" I asked, holding it up and reading the slogan for an American beer company.

"Put it on. In that shirt, you look like the main character in *Where's Waldo*?" he said.

I looked down at my shirt with its wide horizontal red and white stripes. "Isn't that good? No one can find Waldo."

He frowned, and I sighed, putting the t-shirt on over my shirt. He handed me a cap, and I put that on, too. He shook his head, took the cap off my head, and handed it to me.

"Tuck your hair up, best you can," he said.

I did as he instructed, trying to coax my hair into staying beneath the cap. With an impatient sigh, he took the cap and handed it to me, then pulled my hair up in a sloppy pile and held it with one hand. He took the cap from me and fit it over the mess, tucking a few stray strands up, his fingers brushing my face.

"Good enough," he said.

"Way to make a girl feel special," I muttered, as he started off in a new direction. I had to nearly run to keep up with him.

As the sun set, the sky turned a dingy shade of orange, then a deeper grey-orange shade from the light pollution. We wove through a couple more alleys, turning corners that seemed to lead deeper into dark corners of Macau. Gone were the shining buildings of the financial center and the glittering five-star hotels. The doors we passed now were unmarked, or covered with peeling signs for cigarettes. Occasionally, we'd pass an open door and the tantalizing scent of spicy Cantonese cooking wafted out, making my stomach rumble in protest.

Even in running shoes, my feet were tired and achy when we finally walked across a pedestrian overpass, and Jake pointed to a low squat building.

"We'll stay here tonight," he said.

It was a far cry from the Mandarin, but I didn't care. I wanted to take a hot shower, wash the dye out of my hair, and put my feet up. Maybe get something to eat. Definitely sleep for a long time.

There was no concierge in the lobby of the motel, and the front desk was occupied by an older woman watching a soap opera on a table-top TV. She didn't even look up from the screen as we passed and walked up one flight of stairs. Jake opened the motel room door and after scanning the room, held the door for me.

The room smelled of disinfectant and stale air-conditioned air. I stood in the middle of the room, unsure of what to do next. It was a typical Ramada/Best Western style room—just with a few Asian touches, like the bamboo plant near the window, and the sign on the outside wall in Cantonese characters.

"Have a seat," Jake said.

I sat in the small, upholstered chair next to the desk by the window, clutching my messenger bag to my body. Jake sat on the edge of the bed, facing me. We were only a few feet apart.

"Now," he said, his voice low. "Tell me what the hell you're doing here. And don't lie to me this time."

CHAPTER TEN

I stood in the narrow shower and let the hot water pour over me. After the third time shampooing my hair, the suds were no longer muddy with the temporary dye. Which meant I no longer had an excuse to stay in the steamy privacy of the tiny hotel bathroom and avoid Jake's questions.

I'd begged off answering his interrogation until I was able to shower, convincing him that the people chasing us wouldn't be looking for a blonde, and I should wash the dye out before we had to run again. But I couldn't hide in the shower forever.

With a reluctant sigh, I turned off the water and stepped out of the tiled stall. A knock on the door caught me off guard, and I clutched the thin towel around my body.

"You decent?"

"Not remotely."

"I have some clothes for you," Jake said.

Intrigued, I went to the door and opened it a crack. Sure enough, he was holding a department store bag, which he held up.

I reached through the door, but he pulled away.

"Let's make a deal," he said with a smile.

"No, let's allow me to get dressed." I was not in the mood to play games. I glanced around the bathroom for the clothes I had been wearing and realized that they were missing.

"I took them," he said. "Don't worry, they're safe."

I looked back at him through the several inches I'd cracked the door. "Where? Why?"

"Didn't want you to leave while I was out," he said.

I turned again and looked at the empty counter, not believing my eyes. "You just came in here? When I was in the shower?"

"Yep."

I saw the strap to my messenger bag under the counter and nearly exhaled in relief that he hadn't grabbed that.

"Can I please have my clothes? Any clothes?"

He gave me a half smile and leaned against the wall.

"Why are you here in Macau?"

I slammed the door shut and stood there, fuming. Running my fingers through my wet hair, I looked around the steamy room. There was nothing I could wear here. There was another towel and two washcloths. No bathrobe. Maybe I could use the shower curtain, if I got creative.

Damn it.

I opened the door and he was still there, waiting. Smiling.

"I told you. Someone set me up. I came to Macau to find out who," I said through gritted teeth.

He frowned and then shook his head.

"I don't think that's the whole story," he said. He reached into the bag and pulled something out and handed it to me. "But you have these."

"Socks?"

"Don't worry, I'll give you a chance to earn more clothes."

My head started to pound with suppressed rage. I took a

deep breath, counted to ten, and set the socks on the bathroom counter.

"Now, why were you in Bill's office?"

Thoughts of what I would do to Jake Barnes when I was fully clothed marched through my head. Most were impractical—where was I going to find a cattle prod in Macau at this hour? But no matter how creative, they all were satisfying my lust for revenge.

"Bill Macias was in charge of the energy group. Some of the money from the Sahara Fund investors went through his office's general account."

He gave me another piece of clothing—a navy blue t-shirt. Great, now I had a shirt and socks. And nothing else but a soggy towel.

"You're saying Bill set you up?"

I could hear the disbelief in his voice.

"Yes."

"How do you know this?"

"You owe me another piece of clothing. You asked if I was saying Bill set me up, and I answered," I said.

He rolled his eyes, reached into the bag and pulled out a pair of pink lace underwear, dangling the delicate fabric from his finger. I grabbed it and added it to my meager pile.

"I found the evidence in the discovery from my case. If your coworkers had followed the money, they would have seen that the money was siphoned off from the Sahara Fund trust account to the ones set up in my name—by *other* people," I said, stressing that last part. "But then it was transferred to accounts under other Patterson Tinker offices, mostly Macau's energy group."

Jake looked thoughtful as he pulled out a pair of khaki pants and handed them to me.

"So, are you saying that the fraud scheme included more than just Tinker, Norquist, and you?"

"*I* was not involved," I said, my voice rising.

"What exactly were you going to tell Bill?"

I put the pants on the counter and tried to gather my thoughts. If I told him my actual plan, he'd probably arrest me. But he still had something in the bag, and I hoped it was a bra. And maybe a comb.

"I wanted to show him the trail of the money transfers and see what he knew about it."

He narrowed his eyes and stared at me, and suddenly, the damp towel and the door I was standing behind didn't seem like much protection. Then he shook his head.

"That one is a lie," he said.

"Why do you say that?" I really wanted to ask how he knew I was lying. Did I have a tell? Or was he really that good at reading people?

"Because you believe Bill set you up. You're not here to ask questions." He tilted his head and gave me a long stare. "And because I know Bill. He's a good poker player. He'd never give you the answers you want."

"Can I please have another piece of clothing?"

"Tell me your plan."

Damn it.

"I was going to convince Bill to transfer the thirty-seven million stolen from the Sahara Fund investors to an account so the victims could get their money back," I said.

Deliberately, he opened the bag and looked in, then slowly drew out a bra that matched the panties he'd already handed me. The man had pretty good taste in lingerie.

I took it and slammed the door again. I ripped off tags and dressed quickly, marveling at how everything fit fairly well. The khaki capris were good quality, as was the t-shirt. I turned sideways and looked in the mirror. He was a little optimistic on the bra, but it would do. I dug into the side pocket of the messenger bag and found the flash drive from Bill's desk and tucked it into my pants pocket. I hadn't been able to look at it yet, but I knew it was important. Bill Macias wouldn't have hidden it there if it were inconsequential.

Taking a deep breath, I opened the door and started to walk out but ran smack into Jake's chest.

"You're still here?"

"If you would have answered another question, you could have had the rest," he said, handing me the shopping bag. I peeked in and saw a smaller bag from a drug store. Inside were a toothbrush, a comb, and shampoo and conditioner. I looked up and felt a wave of emotion that threatened tears.

"Thank you," I said, setting the items on the counter. I didn't know why such a small gesture was making me teary. It was just more thoughtful than I was expecting. Especially after he held my clothes hostage. I decided to blame jet lag and exhaustion, since I'd just walked all over half of Macau.

"It's just toothpaste and stuff," he said, seeming uncomfortable with the fact that he'd just disarmed me with some drugstore toiletries.

I started trying to comb my hair, which was even more tangled after the temporary dye and thorough washing with cheap hotel shampoo. Jake stood in the doorway of the bathroom.

"You'd never convince Bill to willingly send thirty-seven million on your command. You know that, right?"

I smoothed some conditioner through my hair and ignored his question.

"I mean, the man doesn't even pay his alimony on time," Jake said, watching me fight the snarls in my hair with the cheap comb.

"Well, this isn't his money. It's the right thing to do."

"Let me see if I understand this. Your big plan was to fly to Macau, blackmail a former coworker by promising not to tell the authorities about his involvement in the scheme, and get the money back to the victims?"

This time, I didn't answer. When he said it, it sounded ridiculous. In my head, it had seemed like a semi-solid plan with at least fifty-fifty odds of success. He looked incredulous.

"That is a terrible plan. I mean, I've heard you're smart, graduated at the top of your class, worked your way up to a responsible position. You know this would never work, don't you?"

"Why won't it work? My plan clears my name and makes the victims whole again. I'm not trying to save the world, just the life savings of a few hundred people."

"It won't work because it's illegal. You're going to blackmail someone," he said.

"No, I am going to convince someone to return something he stole. It's not blackmail, it's doing the right thing."

"How were you going to get the money to the victims?"

"I'm not sure yet. Maybe through their lawyers," I said, finally freeing the plastic comb and moving to another section of knots. "As you pointed out, they are about to sue me."

He crossed his arms and leaned on the doorframe.

"You could talk to the U.S. Attorney's office. They'd be interested in getting the victims reimbursed."

"They think I stole it in the first place," I said.

"You didn't?"

I shot him a furious glare and finished combing out my hair.

"Can you show me what you found about Bill's involvement in the money transfers?"

On one hand, I could do that, very easily. I had tracked the money to Bill's doorstep, and beyond. And the beyond part was the problem. I could show him why his brother-in-law was involved with a thirty-seven million dollar fraud scheme. But Bill was involved in so much more, and that was my only leverage.

"I can show you the transfers," I said, reaching for my bag. I'd just have to be careful and hope Jake didn't ask too many questions.

We moved from the damp bathroom, and I set my messenger bag on the desk by the window. Jake pulled the curtains shut on the dark sky outside. He sat on the foot of the bed again and watched as I pulled out my laptop and the paperwork I'd compiled.

I tossed him a packet of about twenty pages, stapled along the side into a makeshift booklet. It was a report I'd compiled, similar to the ones I'd put together in my days working in finance. But this one was different in that it was the story of the Sahara Fund fraud, told in charts and graphs. And names. I named everyone.

He started to read, then looked up at me. "You wrote this?"

I nodded, and he flipped through the pages quickly, taking it in. Then he stood and went to the other end of the bed and sat with his back against the headboard, his legs stretched out on the bed, and started reading at the beginning. When he finished, he lifted his gaze to mine, his eyes serious.

"What is Bill up to?"

Biting my lip, I paused, unsure of what to tell him.

"Look, I'm no fan of the guy. He left my sister with two kids under the age of five. But he's Henry and Lily's dad. He was a lousy husband, but he was a good father. He wouldn't willingly abandon his children. And now he's missing. He hasn't been in touch with my sister in three weeks. His office—hell, his entire department—is MIA. There's something going on. If you know something, please tell me."

Oh, great, guilt with a side of absentee father—my kryptonite.

"I don't know anything about Bill or where he might be," I said. "How long have you been here looking for him?"

He ran a hand through his hair and leaned forward. "Just a few days. I've gotten nowhere."

The silence hung between us.

"Why do you think the guys following us are bad guys?"

"Because I saw them at Bill's apartment two days ago."

He swung his legs over the side of the bed and rested his forearms on his knees, staring intently at the carpet.

"They'd trashed the place. It looked like his office. And now they know you're poking around. What name did you use to get into Patterson Investments today?"

I hesitated only a second before answering. "Lana Parker."

"Who is Lana Parker?"

"She's the stepdaughter of a Houston oil man who came into a large trust and needs assistance managing her wealth."

He gave me a hard stare. "That worked?"

He couldn't have been more surprised than I was. "To an Englishman, I can sound Texan."

"Did you use your real name at all?"

"Of course, for my flight and the hotel," I said.

He nodded.

"They're looking for Lana Parker now, so ditch anything you have with that name on it. And they obviously figured out your real name."

"But how?"

"If I were heading their security team, I'd have asked the front desk clerk to identify you from a still from a surveillance video. That's not important right now. What matters is staying off their radar," Jake said. He tossed my report on the bedspread. "Why did you put together your case against Bill in a report like this? Seems like a lot of work to accuse someone of a crime."

"Well, that's your area of expertise, not mine," I snapped. "I researched a series of financial transactions and summarized my findings in a report. That's what I used to do at Patterson Tinker."

It was a familiar task, and somehow compiling the evidence as if it were a year-end report on one of Patterson's investment funds distanced me from the true object of the report—the fact that someone used my name to funnel a ton of money off Patterson's books and into their own pockets.

"I don't know what you did or didn't do at that company," Jake said, standing. "But I'll help you."

I sat still in my uncomfortable chair, immediately suspicious. "Why would you help me?"

And did I even want his help?

"Well, the U.S. Attorney tried to convict you without success. Do you know what the odds are of that?"

I did know—something like ninety-six percent of cases indicted in federal courts end in conviction. Of the very small fraction of cases that didn't, only a handful were acquittals after a jury trial. Rob had made sure I understood that I was nearly guaranteeing my conviction by going to trial.

"And I don't know if you're delusional. Maybe you're trying to recover the missing money for yourself. But I need to find Bill. And you're the only lead I have at this point."

He walked to the scarred white door leading to the closet and opened it, and pulled out a plastic bag and dumped an assortment of snack foods onto the bedspread.

My stomach growled at the sight of the food, and I realized that it had been a long time since my light breakfast at the Mandarin. Jake tossed me a bag of chips, which I ripped into without concern about the flavor indicated by the Chinese characters on the label. Turned out that salty potato chips are the same the world over, at least if you're hungry enough. The contents of the bag were gone in minutes. While I inhaled the chips, Jake paced and re-read the report I'd given him.

Finally, he paused and ran a hand through his hair and then rubbed his face. His expression was grave and exhausted. With a sigh, he sat on the edge of the bed and stared at me.

"It sounds like we both need to find Bill," he said. "It will be easier for both of us if we work together."

"I don't know how to find Bill," I said. "I only know where he works. I didn't have his home address, I don't know where he hangs out."

"I think you know more than you realize," he said, nodding toward the two external drives that were resting inside the gaping opening of my messenger bag.

The massive volume of information on those drives included a large number of Bill Macias's emails, expense reports for several years, and his daily calendars. With enough time, I could probably learn a lot about the man. But I didn't have a lot of time. I figured I had no more than three weeks to travel before my credit cards either maxed out or the bills came due—and I wasn't sure I'd be able to cover the minimum payments yet.

Palling around with an FBI agent wasn't part of my plan. There was no way I could tell him everything I knew about his brother-in-law and the bigger scheme, which I was only beginning to understand. And he certainly wasn't going to let me blackmail his family member.

"If I let you search the hard-drives, will you help me get the money back to the Sahara Fund investors?" I asked.

He tilted his head and then nodded. "I won't let you blackmail Bill. Or anyone else."

Of course not. But what he didn't know...

"Fine, let's look at the drives," I said.

He stood up and walked toward the bathroom. "You get started," he said. "I'm going to grab a shower."

The bathroom door clicked shut, and I turned on my laptop and was happy to find an open Wi-Fi signal. I quickly opened my email program, and at the top was an email from Sarah, just hours earlier.

Hope you're having a good vacation. Hate to be a bummer, but call me when you can. Got some news.

She didn't say it was good news, just news. That meant it was bad news. I looked at the closed bathroom door and heard the shower running. Then I took a deep breath and reached for my cell phone.

CHAPTER ELEVEN

"Hey, *chica*! How's the vacation going?

It was so nice to hear Sarah's voice over the phone that I almost wept with homesickness. It had only been a few days since I left California, but it felt like a lifetime ago. The Mandarin had all the comforts of home, and then some, so it didn't feel foreign. But this sparse motel room Jake Barnes was staying in felt a million miles away.

"It's great, really nice to get away, you know," I said, trying to keep my tone casual despite the panic that I could feel within arm's reach. "What's up?"

Over the phone, I could hear her take a deep breath before answering, and I steeled myself for the news.

"I really hate to interrupt your holiday, but I thought you should know what's going on here," she said.

"Lay it on me," I said, closing my eyes and running a hand through my damp hair.

"Well, the lawsuit was filed yesterday."

Okay, I knew that was coming. Rob had warned me that could happen at any time.

"Is that it?"

"No," she said. I could tell she was reluctant to tell me the rest. "They're also trying to get a court order to freeze all of your assets, so you can't dispose of anything you own before the lawsuit is resolved. Since you don't really have any assets in your own name that means it was served on Marie, since you and she are joint owners of the house and the bakery building. Rob accepted service on your behalf."

My eye started to twitch. Rob had warned of this, too. Didn't make it any easier to think of Aunt Marie getting served legal papers because of me.

"Is there anything Rob can do about that?" I asked.

"He's fighting it," she said. "There's something else, too."

"Is Aunt Marie all right?"

"Oh, yes, she's fine," Sarah said quickly. "Rob isn't going to let anything happen to your aunt."

Again I had that feeling that Rob's interest in my aunt was growing more than friendly. Or maybe it had always been that intimate, and I was just oblivious to the attraction before. Or maybe I just wanted there to be someone like Rob keeping an eye on Aunt Marie's well-being.

"No, this is about Ralph Tinker," Sarah said.

"What about Ralph?"

"He died. Yesterday. In prison."

"What?"

I sat up in the chair, and my hand flew to my mouth. During the long months leading up to the trial, my feelings toward Ralph Tinker had swung dramatically—from disbelief that he could have defrauded his clients, to shock and disgust when I learned he pleaded guilty to doing just that. Then when he testified against me, I hated him. I knew he was lying. His prison sentence would depend on how well he cooperated with the prosecutor, which would be measured by whether I was convicted.

But after Rob told me that Ralph had been sentenced to prison and I tried to think of the older, white-haired man in orange prison garb, my feelings softened to something closer to pity. I hadn't forgiven him—not remotely. I hadn't really thought of him much since he was sentenced to prison. But when I did, it was as a sad old man whose family was paying for his greed.

And now he was dead. A small chill ran down my spine.

"How did he die?" I asked, conscious of the sudden lack of sound from the bathroom. I hoped that Jake hadn't heard my question.

"He, uh, killed himself," Sarah said.

The breath escaped my lungs, and I didn't know what to say. "Oh."

"Yeah, it was kind of a shock to everyone," she said. "He had only been at the federal camp for a couple days and wasn't on suicide watch."

"I just—Damn."

"I know." She took a deep breath. "I'm really sorry to be such a bummer while you're trying to escape reality. Rob thought you should know what was going on."

"Of course," I said. "Don't worry about it."

"Well, at least tell me something good, Miranda," Sarah said with a forced laugh. "Tell me you're on a beach somewhere, drinking girly cocktails. Tell me you've met some handsome stranger and are having acrobatic, *but safe*, sex all over some exotic country."

The bathroom door opened, and Jake Barnes emerged wearing nothing but a towel wrapped around his lower half. His wet hair was tousled, and drops of water dotted his nicely muscled chest. It should be illegal for a man built like that to walk around in a towel. No telling what riots he'd cause. He raised an eyebrow at the sight of me using a cell phone but then continued to the open duffel bag in the closet. I swallowed hard as he turned and leaned over the bag to get his clothes, the damp towel leaving little to my quickly overheating imagination.

"Hello, Miranda?" Sarah said. "Did I lose you?"

I turned away quickly and stared at the closed drapes, focusing on the faded yellow fabric. "No, nothing like that," I said. "I should go. This is probably costing a fortune. I'll call you in a couple days, okay?"

We said goodbye, and I disconnected the call. Jake had stepped back into the bathroom, and I was alone again. I closed my eyes and leaned back, trying to make sense of the news from home.

"Who died?"

His quiet question jolted me out of my thoughts.

"Ralph Tinker," I said, opening my eyes. He was wearing clothes, thank God, but his hair was still damp and sticking up at odd angles. I could imagine how the short wet strands would feel between my fingers. I tried to stop that train of thought.

"Were you close to him?" Jake looked puzzled now.

"No, not at all."

He nodded and sat in the other chair.

"Who was on the phone?"

"My friend Sarah."

"Does she know where you are?"

I shook my head.

"Feel like going out?"

"Out where?" I asked, wary of another walk. The last one was a little too long and dangerous for my tastes.

"I want to go back to Bill's apartment. I went before, but it had been tossed, and I didn't have much time there. Maybe with your help, I can find something that will help us."

"What are you looking for?"

He frowned. "I'm not sure. An address book, something that would indicate who he trusts. He and my sister, Molly, have been divorced for a year. Maybe he's dating someone who knows where he's hiding out."

I bit my lip. Jake's words triggered a faint memory. I'd been studying Bill's email traffic, but it was mostly work-related. Anything social was related to Patterson's clients. But there was something that tickled the back of my brain.

"No one uses address books anymore. But I think I might be able to help you," I said. "And we won't even have to put on shoes."

I reached for my laptop and plugged in one of the hard-drives, looking for the emails.

"Bill's phone synced with his email program. His contacts will be here," I said. "But that's not going to help you unless you know who you're looking for. He's got thousands of contacts."

"Doesn't sound particularly helpful."

It wasn't the contacts I was searching for. There had been a certain tone in some of Bill's emails to a coworker—a female coworker. I quickly scrolled through the dates until I found what I was looking for.

"Here it is," I said, taking the laptop with me to sit on the edge of the bed, so Jake could see the screen. "His emails with Cecily Ho seem friendlier than with others in his office. I think he's been involved with her for a while."

As I said it, I wondered how long Bill had been separated from Jake's sister. I knew several of Patterson Tinker's executives who transferred overseas didn't bring their families, at least not right away. And as you'd expect, this often led to marital problems.

"That wouldn't surprise me. Molly said Bill had started dating as soon as they'd separated, but I think she suspected maybe he started sooner."

He scooted near me and leaned in to peer at the laptop, and my stomach flipped at the nearness. The memory of him wearing only that towel flashed through my mind, and I felt myself blushing. Quickly, I scrolled through the list of emails that I'd sorted.

"See, here, he asks a casual question about whether she's around to assist him on the weekend, and she replies that she is," I said, trying to focus on the research.

"Why does that mean they're sleeping together?"

"It might not. But his assistant is Philip who works on weekends all the time for Bill."

"Seems a little thin," he said.

"There are more emails like this. Many more. She was always available to work on weekends, but there's never ever mention of what they're working on or emails to other people about what they did," I said.

Jake nodded and read the emails. "Can you find out where Cecily Ho lives?"

I nodded. "There's an employee directory, but it's a couple years old. I might be able to track it down."

"How long will it take to find it?"

I shrugged. "There's a lot of stuff on these drives, but I've got it pretty well organized. Maybe an hour or so."

He sat on the edge of the bed and put his shoes on. "I'm going out to get us something to eat. Something that's not junk food," he said, watching me carefully. "Are you okay staying here alone?"

"Yeah, sure."

"I'm not going far."

"I'll be fine."

He stood and walked to the door, then turned back. "You'll be here when I return?"

"Where would I go?" I asked, frustrated.

He didn't answer, just opened the door and left.

I turned my attention back to the computer. As I expected, it took me ten minutes to find Cecily Ho's personnel information. Provided she hadn't moved I had her home address and phone number. I jotted the information down on a hotel notepad and then listened for any sound outside the door. Hearing nothing, I pulled the flash drive from my pocket and slipped it into the port. It was time to find out what Bill Macias was hiding under his desk.

The 32-gigabyte drive was nearly full, and contained a backup of a laptop and multiple folders, each one holding hundreds of files. I tried to find some logic to the organization, sorting everything by date and started with the newest dates. Most of the files were encrypted, but the most recent ones were spreadsheets that I was able to open without passwords.

The names scrolled by while I looked at the account numbers and the figures representing money flowing in and out of those accounts. Some of the accounts were numbered, and some were in the name of various corporations that all had suspiciously vague names. As I reached the bottom of the list, names started popping up associated with accounts. I had some experience with the various types of bank accounts. The numbered account could be used by anyone who could present that number and a passcode, usually more numbers. The passcodes were all listed, cross-referenced in the complex spreadsheets.

The named accounts, though, could be accessed by the person on the account or others given permission by the account owner or through electronic access with the correct passcodes. I had no idea who else had access to this information, but there must have been a reason Bill had it hidden under his desk.

I studied the dollar amounts and the dates, flipping between spreadsheets, trying to trace the transactions. I understood what I was looking at, but it didn't make sense. Funds were being transferred between accounts, ledgers kept showing incoming money and the percentage being skimmed off to "overhead"—presumably Patterson's bottom line—and then funneled into other accounts.

Why would a respected multinational financial institution like Patterson be engaging in large-scale money laundering? Why would the bank risk its reputation and criminal prosecution?

On the other hand, a small division of rogue employees could operate this scheme and bury it in the many millions of transactions and various accounts. It could go unnoticed for years. For about ten years, if these spreadsheets were correct.

The rattle of the doorknob sent my heart into overdrive, and I quickly ejected the flash drive while Jake set the bags of food and water down on the dresser.

"I hope noodles are acceptable," he said, taking a couple containers out of the bag.

"Sure. I'm not a picky eater," I said.

We ate spicy noodles and vegetables out of Styrofoam containers, the unfamiliar heat of the peppers barely cut by the sweet coconut milk. I wasn't sure if I'd worked up an appetite or if it was the best meal I'd ever eaten. By the time we'd reached the bottom of the to-go boxes, I had shown Jake what I found about Cecily Ho.

She was local to Macau and worked as an interpreter and executive assistant—or at least she had when the government seized the corporation's computer files almost two years ago. Cecily was twenty-nine, fluent in Cantonese, Mandarin, French, Portuguese, and English and started working for Patterson about six years earlier. Her emails weren't among those seized from the corporate computers, so I didn't know much about her besides her resume and home address.

"We should go visit her tomorrow," Jake said, standing and

clearing the empty food containers. "In the meantime, we should get some sleep."

I nodded, and my gaze fell on the bed. I looked up at Jake, and he grinned. "Hope you don't snore."

I frowned at the thought of sharing a bed with him, at least under these circumstances. He tossed me a t-shirt from a black duffel bag and then left to take the trash out.

Great. A slumber party with the FBI. I put the laptop away and then went to the bathroom to change into the too-large t-shirt and brush my teeth. When I returned, Jake was still gone, so I turned off the light and climbed into bed, taking the side by the window. I left the lamp on his nightstand on, but the room was dim and quiet, and the pillow soft. Within a few minutes, I could feel my body relaxing and my thoughts drifting off.

The bed shifting under Jake's weight woke me, and I bolted upright.

"Sorry," Jake whispered. "I was trying not to wake you."

The room was dark now, lit only by the moonlight coming through the window and a slim wedge of light coming from the half-open door of the bathroom. The bed creaked as he settled under the thin blanket.

"What time is it?" I asked, still disoriented.

He looked at his watch. "It's about nine. I got a call when I stepped out. I didn't mean to be gone that long."

I had only been asleep a half hour at most. I lay back down and tried to calm my heart rate. My mind was racing nearly as fast as my pulse. I turned and looked at Jake, who was on his side now, watching me. His hair was still mussed and his expression concerned.

"You okay?"

"Yeah, yeah, fine," I said, tugging the blanket up to my shoulders.

"I need to ask you something," he said, his voice low.

"Sure."

"What did your friend tell you about Ralph's suicide?"

I shivered in the warm room and pulled at the blanket again. The thought of Ralph's death chilled me.

"Just that he killed himself in prison. He had only been there for a few days and wasn't on suicide watch," I said.

"That's not what happened," he said softly.

"What happened?" From the tone in his voice, I had a pretty good idea what he was going to tell me. I closed my eyes and exhaled slowly.

"His death is under investigation. It wasn't a suicide."

"So it was murder?"

"Yes."

"Who?"

He paused. "I don't know."

"Another inmate?"

"That's pretty unlikely at the camp where he was. He should have been safe there. It's all nonviolent offenders, fraud defendants, like he was."

"So, who then? A guard?"

Another long pause followed my question. "I don't have any information about that."

The hair on the back of my neck stood on end. Who would kill Ralph? I thought back to the list of accounts and the large sums of money being laundered by Patterson. A decade worth of money laundering. There could be a large number of powerful people who would want to ensure Ralph's silence.

"Is Tim at risk?"

"He's been moved to a protected unit," Jake said, rubbing his eyes. "How did you get involved with these people?"

I thought about it for a long minute before answering.

"I didn't," I said, trying to find the right words that would finally convince him. "I trusted the Patterson Tinker name. The investment house has been around for twenty-five years. It has a good reputation. Well, it used to. Billions of dollars are entrusted to Patterson each year. Probably tens of billions, maybe more. And yes, it looks like there are some criminals doing some shady things, but a large portion of its business is legitimate, just as most of the employees there aren't knowingly breaking the law."

Jake rested his elbow and studied my face.

"You had no idea what was going on?"

I shook my head.

"I would never have gone along with it," I said. "I know you don't believe me. Fine. But I know that I did nothing wrong."

That was going to be cold comfort when these credit card bills came due, unless I could find a way to clear my name. If the government would admit I was innocent, not merely not guilty, I could get a job, rebuild my savings.

"You beat the case. Why isn't that enough?"

"Because I don't want to spend the rest of my life working at the bakery, serving coffee to people whose paychecks I used to approve."

"No luck finding a new job?"

"Well, when your public image is being led out of your last job in handcuffs…" I gave him a long stare, and he had the decency to look away. He should, since he had been the one leading me out of the building in cuffs. "Apparently, I'm radioactive in the financial services industry."

"Where have you been working?"

"For my aunt at her bakery," I said, hugging my arms around me. Lying in the dark talking to Jake seemed natural. But I wasn't sure if it was wise. "It wasn't supposed to be like this. I'm the first person in my family to graduate from college. Now everyone thinks I'm no better than my parents. Just another criminal."

He continued to study me, his head tilted.

"Your parents were criminals?"

I shrugged. I hadn't meant to go there, but since I was unburdening my soul, might as well get free therapy out of this little chat.

"Petty stuff, some drug possession, theft to support drug habits. They were seventeen when I was born, so I was raised by my Aunt Marie since I was three years old. My dad split shortly after I was born. My mom floated in and out of my life once in a while, but she died in a car accident when I was ten."

"And your dad, where is he now?"

"He died when I was twenty. Overdose. I never knew him."

"Any siblings? Other family besides your aunt?"

"No, it's just the two of us," I said, staring back at him, wondering what he was thinking. "That's why I have to do this. She sacrificed everything for me growing up and then again when I got arrested. She doesn't deserve this. To have the bakery taken from her. To lose her home."

The tears spilled over, and my breath hitched.

"I can't do that to her."

The strong hand that took mine offered comfort, strength. And a dose of reality. I couldn't trust Jake. And I couldn't trust myself around Jake. I needed to get a grip.

I pulled my hand away and wiped my face.

"I'm sorry," I said. "I'm just jet-lagged."

"No, you're upset. It's okay." His voice was low and deep and lulled me into looking at him. Big mistake. The moonlight highlighted the rugged planes of his face. His eyes watching me. Staring into his dark eyes was like falling into a warm, comforting embrace.

"You should get some sleep," I said.

"I will," he said.

But he still lay there, and I realized that I was gripping his hand now. His thumb stroked the skin on the top of my hand.

Each touch left a tingling trail, and my heart quickened. He leaned in and smoothed my hair away from my face.

"Get some sleep, Miranda."

I pulled my hand away to break the contact, but the tremors in my stomach remained.

CHAPTER TWELVE

The afternoon sun was low and slanting over the city the next day as Jake and I left the motel to hail a cab to take us to a residential neighborhood away from the city center.

I had spent some time surreptitiously studying Bill Macias's flash drive while waiting until the afternoon, when we planned to go visit Cecily Ho after she got home from work. By mid-day, I was pretty sure I knew why Bill had gone underground. He was in trouble—deep trouble. It wasn't about Sahara Fund investors losing thirty-seven million, either. That looked like chump change compared to the figures I saw on his spreadsheets. Unfortunately, my few hours of studying Bill's secret flash drive wasn't enough to figure out exactly what was going on. And there were so many more encrypted files that I couldn't read.

Jake whistled, and a cab pulled to the curb. He handed the driver a note with the address written on it and said a few words in Cantonese, and the man opened the door for us to get in the backseat, an apparent agreement that he would get us to our destination. Once settled in the backseat, I studied Jake with growing suspicion.

"You speak Cantonese?"

"Only a little."

There was so much I didn't know about Jake Barnes. It made me uneasy, being tied to him now. But I was stuck with him for a while. I wasn't comfortable returning to the Mandarin, and if there was a chance that Bill Macias was still in Macau, I needed to stay here.

I fought off a yawn as the sun streamed into the warm and muggy cab. Though I was exhausted last night, every movement in the bed caused me to jolt wide-awake. I wasn't used to sleeping next to someone, especially someone who was essentially a stranger. When I finally drifted off, I dreamed about being chased by through Macau by the men at the Mandarin Hotel. I awoke feeling like I'd just run a marathon.

As the cab crept through Macau's late afternoon traffic, I mulled over what I'd seen in Bill's secret files. Money was being transferred willy-nilly from various banks in a dozen different countries, then to other accounts—some not belonging to Patterson Investments. Some had no names associated with them, just strings of numbers. Some had generic-sounding names that meant nothing to me—Christopher A. Jenkins, Robert S. Stafford, Jr., Jerome Knight, Marie de Jesus Santiago. I dug deeper into the account list and found a trove of boring corporate names—ABC Holdings, Corp.; Seabreeze Island, Inc.; Millennium, LLC. They had some of the most preposterous fake addresses I could imagine—unless there really was a 123 Main Street, Anytown, New York. I'd bet my last dollar they were shell corporations used to hide assets.

Then I saw my name.

Miranda Marie Vaughn.

And not just on one account, but on a half-dozen. Two in Switzerland, two in Belize, two in Macau. I knew I hadn't opened accounts there.

The last entry on the spreadsheet was just over three weeks

earlier, right around the time that Bill disappeared. I had quickly added up the incoming and outgoing sums in "my" accounts and was disappointed to learn that I wasn't rich beyond my wildest dreams. The accounts were simply pass-throughs on the funds' way to numbered accounts in other counties.

"Are you okay?"

Jake's concerned voice startled me.

"Yes, fine. Why do you ask?"

"You looked a million miles away," he said. "Did you sleep much last night?"

I shook my head. "Not really."

I had been able to get a nap this afternoon. Jake thought it was too dangerous for us to be out wandering in Macau, so we stayed in the cramped motel room until late afternoon.

The cab swerved down a tree-lined street and turned onto a smaller lane that wound past a row of small apartment buildings. He pulled to the curb and pointed at a white building that sat in the shade of several large trees.

Jake paid the driver, and we got out of the cab.

"This way," Jake said, taking my arm and leading me down a path between two buildings. The doors were sheltered from the street and opened onto the courtyard between buildings. A cluster of flowering trees shaded us from a bright but overcast sky. The branches barely moved in the thick, moist air. Each entrance was private with gated patio and shrubs. We walked to the end of the building, and Jake peered over the last gate. "This is it."

He pressed a buzzer on the gate, and a moment later, a young Asian woman answered the door.

"Cecily Ho?" Jake asked.

"Yes. Who are you?" she asked.

"Bill Macias's brother-in-law," he said.

Her eyes widened, and her face paled. "I don't know Bill Macias."

I rolled my eyes. "Yes, you do. You worked with him at Patterson Investments."

She looked at me with a confused expression. "Yes, you're right. But I don't know him well."

I looked to Jake, then back at her. "You've been seeing Bill outside of work for quite some time," I said.

She frowned, looked around and stepped out on to the patio and motioned for us to come through the gate. She closed the door to the apartment behind her and crossed her arms in front of her. She was very pretty, with sleek black hair cut in a chic chin-length style. She was wearing a suit skirt and blouse, as if she'd just come home from work.

"I don't know where Bill is. I haven't seen him since he was fired about three weeks ago." Her voice was low, and I had to lean in to hear her.

"Are you still working at Patterson?" I asked.

Again she shook her head. "No, the energy division was disbanded. A few people transferred to other departments. Most of the local staff, like me, we were laid off."

She composed herself and looked Jake in the eye. I saw the flash of diamond earrings through her thick dark hair. "I can't help you, I'm afraid. I haven't spoken to anyone at Patterson since I left. I got a good recommendation and started a new job almost immediately."

I got it. Cecily Ho had probably accepted a fat severance package and signed a nondisclosure agreement in return for a good recommendation.

Jake sighed and ran a hand through his hair.

"Can you tell me where he might be? Any friends of his who might know. His family is worried," Jake said.

"Family? He said he was divorced." Her voice rose slightly, and her body stiffened.

"He is divorced. But he has two children with his ex-wife." He pulled out his cell phone and turned it on, then handed it to Cecily. "That's Henry and Lily. They're three and five years old."

She tilted her head, and her eyes softened as she looked at the images on the phone. "They look so much like their father," she whispered.

"If he's in trouble, we're his best bet at helping him," I said, lowering my voice.

Cecily bit her lip, and after a minute, she nodded. "He's just trying to get out."

Her voice was barely a whisper.

"Get out of what?" Jake asked, lowering his voice, too.

"It would be better if he explained it to you," she said.

"Where is he?" I asked.

"Stay here," she said, turning to the front door. "I'll be right back."

She entered the apartment, and Jake and I stood awkwardly on her patio. Was she going to get Bill? Calling Patterson's security department? The police? A few minutes later, she returned and handed Jake a piece of paper, folded in half.

"He'll meet you there in an hour," she said. "Now, please go. I don't want to be involved."

She backed into the house and shut the door, and Jake held the gate for me to leave. We walked back to the street and then to the corner, where traffic was heavier.

"Do you believe her?"

"Not entirely," he said. "You?"

"I think she cares for him."

"Why?"

"Because she's trying to protect him."

"From what, though?"

I stayed silent while Jake punched the address Cecily gave him into his phone's GPS map. "We're not too far."

"Do you think he was inside the apartment?" I asked.

"Yes, probably," Jake said, frowning.

We walked along the residential streets as the sunlight faded. The street ended at a busy boulevard, and we headed toward the harbor that we could see in the distance. By the time we reached the vast parking lot for a defunct ferry service, the sky was inky black, and the streetlights had come on. Jake's gaze swept the acres of empty asphalt continually as we approached the boarded up building.

"Why would he choose this place?" I asked, dreading the answer.

Jake didn't say anything, just looked at his phone again.

"We're a little early. Let's look over there," he said, pulling me around the building.

The alley between the main building and what looked like a machine shop was completely darkened, untouched by the lights in the parking lot. Though it was still warm, a shiver ran down my spine at the thought of venturing into that alley. Jake, though, seemed to have no fear of what might lie ahead. He pulled me a few feet into the alley and then leaned against the wall, keeping me behind him. I peered around him to watch the parking lot, or at least what we could see from our hiding place. My heart thumped in my chest, and I struggled to keep my breathing normal. But all I could think of was whether Bill Macias was setting us up. Why else would we be meeting in an abandoned ferry yard?

The high-pitched whine of a motorcycle engine cut through the silence, and my heart nearly stopped. Jake reached back and pressed me against the wall behind him.

"Stay here," he whispered. He turned to look at me, but all I could see was his silhouette against the yellow light of the parking lot. I nodded. "I mean it. No matter what happens, you need to stay hidden."

"I understand."

It was like he didn't trust me or something.

Jake stayed still, and I leaned forward to peer around his back. The motorcycle came into view and stopped near the stairs that led up to the old ferry terminal's main building. A man stepped off and looked around, shifting nervously. He walked up the steps, turning back to look over his shoulder at the empty lot. As he hurried behind a wide column, he took off his helmet and faced away from where Jake and I were standing just about twenty-five feet behind him. He peeked around the post from time to time to scan the parking lot.

Finally, Jake stirred, squeezing my hand and then putting his hands on my shoulders in a silent command to stay in the darkened alley. I nodded but wasn't sure if he would see my response in the pitch-black space. Then he stepped out of the shadows.

"Hello, Bill."

The man by the post jumped nearly a foot straight up. The helmet he was holding crashed to the ground and rolled a few feet away.

"Jesus, Jake! You scared the hell out of me," he said, his hand at his throat. "Cecily said it was you, but I didn't know what to believe."

"It's me," Jake said, moving out under the light.

"Is anyone with you?" Bill asked, looking into the alley. It felt like he was staring right at me, but I knew he couldn't see me. "Cecily said there was a girl with you."

Jake nodded. "There was."

"Who was it?"

"I think you know who it was."

"What are you doing here, Jake?" Even in the dim light from the security lamp, I could see Bill's face was shiny with sweat.

"You fell off the grid three weeks ago. No one has heard from you. Molly was getting worried."

Bill ran a hand over his head and paced a few feet away, then back toward Jake.

"Are they okay? Molly and the kids, they're safe, right?"

"Safe from what?" Jake asked, his voice more angry now.

"Just—It's complicated, all right? Just make sure that they're safe," he said.

"You're not making any sense, Bill. Just calm down and tell me what is going on."

Bill continued to pace, his nervousness nearly palpable in the silence.

"Aren't you worried about your girlfriend?" Jake asked.

"Cecily is fine. She's not involved in this. She doesn't know anything. And no one knows about her, anyway."

Bill had conveniently ignored that Jake had tracked Cecily down and made the connection.

"Look, I'm only here because I need to get something I lost. Then I'm outta here. I'm starting over. A whole new life. Molly won't have to worry about money for the kids or anything," Bill said.

Jake grabbed his brother-in-law by the shoulders. "Tell me what's going on."

"Jake, I can't tell you. Not just because you're FBI, but it's not safe." Bill looked around nervously again and stepped away from Jake. "Look, you shouldn't have come here. You're messing with things you know nothing about."

"So tell me."

Jake's quiet, calm voice seemed to steady Bill, and he walked back toward him.

"You don't want to know," he said quietly, shaking his head.

"I can help you."

"Not unless you can break into my old office," Bill said.

"What happened at Patterson? Why is the third floor empty?"

"You went there?"

Jake nodded. Bill grabbed his arm. "Did you find it?"

"Find what?"

Bill released Jake's arm and backed away.

"Nothing. Just forget it."

"Jesus, Bill, just tell me what sort of trouble you're in. I can help you."

Bill stood still and looked at Jake. The orange light of the security lamp left his eyes in shadows, but I could still see the fear on his face from where I remained hidden.

"I uncovered something. I'm pretty sure it's illegal," he said, his voice lowered, as if he feared being overheard. "I think someone at Patterson Tinker was laundering money. I think it might be that woman who was arrested in California, Miranda Vaughn."

My stomach clenched at the mention of my name and at the accusation. I started to push myself off the wall, but remembered my orders. Taking a deep breath, I watched Jake's reaction.

"That's such bullshit, Bill," he said. "What's going on?"

There was a long pause as Bill paced in front of Jake. Finally, he stopped, running a hand through his hair.

"Patterson is into some bad shit," Bill said. "With some bad people. I went along with it, but I'm not taking the fall for everyone. And I'm not going to lose my head over it, either."

Jake crossed his arms. "What bad people?"

"Patterson Investment moves money—big money—for bad people. It's become the banker for the world's arms traffickers, narco-terrorists, actual terrorists. Anyone who needs to launder illegal funds."

The words hung in the warm night air, confirming my suspicions about what I saw on the flash drive. In the dark alley, I hugged my arms around me, suddenly chilled in the warm tropic evening.

"Who else is involved with this?" Jake asked.

"At Patterson? There are a couple guys who know, real higher-ups. But something must have happened because they shut down the energy division on an hour's notice. I need to get back in the building. I left something behind, and if I get it, I can probably save myself," he said, his voice starting to reach peak whine.

"What do you mean they closed the division? How can they do that?"

Bill continued pacing. "The energy division was a front. There were a couple guys who researched that sector, but mostly it was used for money laundering."

"What did you leave at the office?"

"A small computer drive," Bill said.

In the low light, I saw Jake's jaw clench. "The drive, what's on it?"

"Accounts. Passcodes. Names of account holders," Bill said.

"Where is it?"

Bill stopped and looked around, as if he expected someone to overhear. "In my office, twenty-third floor. West wing of the building, corner office. Under the desk, way in the back, I taped a flash drive in the corner. You'll have to crawl all the way under to see it, but it's there." He wiped his face with both hands. "God, I hope it's there."

Jake nodded. "I'll see what I can find. Then what?"

"Bring it to me. I'll finish the transactions that are pending, and then I'm done. I'm out of there. I'm not built for this."

"I can't do that, Bill. I can't help you commit a crime."

Bill grabbed Jake's arm, and I could see the panic on his face. "You don't understand who you're dealing with," he gasped. "They'll kill me, Jake. But just to make their point, they'll come after everyone I love. They'll go after the kids, after Molly."

He wasn't faking it. No one was that good an actor. Bill Macias was scared to death.

Jake pulled his arm away and put a hand on Bill's shoulder. "Calm down. I'm not going to let anything happen to Molly and the kids. Or to you. We'll get you into protective custody."

Bill shook his head. "I don't know, Jake. I don't think you'll be able to protect me. I've thought about this a long time. How to get out. What I need to do."

"Bill, don't do anything stupid. I'll get the drive. We'll figure out what to do then. I'll make some calls."

This made Bill look even more uneasy. "No. No, don't call anyone. Not yet. These people, they have allies everywhere."

Jake shook his head. "I have someone I trust, who can help you."

"I don't know," Bill said. "God, I can't believe I envy Ralph and Tim right now. They're spending some time in Club Fed, but when they get out, they'll be rewarded for keeping their traps shut. Stupid, greedy bastards had to have their own side game going on."

"Ralph is dead."

Even in the eerie yellow light, I could see the blood drain from Bill's face at the news. "He's dead? How?"

"Suicide."

Bill looked around the empty lot again and swallowed hard.

"I gotta get out of Macau," he said, almost as if he was talking to himself. "They're cleaning up all the loose ends. I'm a fucking loose end, Jake."

He started to back away. "Take care of Lily and Henry, Jake. You gotta promise me that you'll make sure nothing happens to them or Molly, okay? Promise me you'll keep them all safe. And tell them I love them so much."

He kept backing away, and Jake followed.

"Bill, don't leave," Jake said.

"I gotta think this through," he said, picking up the helmet from the ground. "You don't know who these people are. I need that drive."

"Then you've got to work with me, Bill. You've got to trust me. Let me talk to some people."

"No!"

"If we have the drive, we'd have the leverage."

Bill paused and ran a hand over his face.

"I'm out of here tonight. I'm leaving Macau before they figure out I lost the backup drive," he said.

"Where are you going?" Jake asked, edging closer to Bill's motorcycle.

"I've got it all set up. A new life. This is the only way Molly and the kids will be safe," he said. "I just have to make one stop, and I need you to help me. If you do this one thing for me, I'll give you everything. Every name. Everything the FBI needs to make this bust. It will be the biggest case of your career."

"I really don't care about that, Bill. I just want to make sure you're safe." Jake held up his hands, and Bill nodded.

"It's the biggest money laundering scheme ever. And I'll tell you every detail," Bill said, as if Jake never spoke. "But I want protection."

Jake nodded. "I can do that. What do you want?"

"Meet me in Belize," he said, coming back toward Jake and pulling a card from his pocket. "This is Cecily's number. She'll know how to reach me."

He turned and climbed on the bike, starting it up.

"Fine," Jake said. "I'll be there."

"Not alone," Bill said. "Bring Miranda Vaughn with you."

The bike roared off, and Jake watched it go. I stayed in the shadows until the bike crossed the empty parking lot and turned onto the frontage road, the lights disappearing as it joined traffic on the busy street.

I stepped out of the alley as Jake turned toward me. Even in the low light, I could see the set of his jaw, the tension in his shoulders.

"What the hell are you involved in?"

"I am not involved in any of that," I said.

"Where's the flash drive?"

I paused. If I shared it, I lost the leverage I had over Bill. But why did Bill want me to go with Jake to Central America?

"I know you have it," Jake said.

I briefly thought about whom I'd rather have on my side— the steely eyed FBI agent who pulled me out of the Patterson office? Or the man who was laundering money for the mob and every other bad guy in the world? I nodded at Jake. There was no going back now.

"Yes, I have it."

And with that, I kissed off the thirty-seven million dollars I traveled around the world to recover.

There was a long pause and a deadly look in Jake Barnes' eyes.

"It's time for you to start talking," he said.

CHAPTER THIRTEEN

Twenty-eight hours after boarding a plane in Macau, I walked out of the airport in Belize City. My stomach churned from too little sleep and too much adrenaline. It was a long, long series of flights to travel halfway around the globe—made even longer by the fact that the FBI agent at my side was snappish the entire time.

I could understand, from his point of view, why he was angry with me. Sure, I hadn't shared the fact that I found Bill's flash drive. Or that I had reviewed the files he saved. Or that I had mostly figured out the money-laundering scheme Bill was involved in.

It's not like I had asked for a partner on this investigation. All I wanted was to get *someone* to transfer thirty-seven million dollars back to the U.S. so I could clear my name and start over. And maybe he could be a little sympathetic about my distrust of government agents, given my recent past.

Throughout the flight, Jake had quietly grilled me on what I knew. When we were able to, I had taken out the laptop and shown him the files on the drive and tried to explain the significance of the long strings of numbers.

Whoever masterminded the scheme was brilliant. The money came in from various banks around the world, concentrated into a stream of millions of dollars that then flowed through various accounts. Fake invoices to and from the shell corporations were issued to provide the thinnest cover for the illegal transactions, and then somewhere in the labyrinth, clean untraceable funds emerged. Then the funds disappeared, back to the parties who set the transfers in motion. Patterson would take a commission for its trouble. Even a small percentage would result in huge profits, if the numbers in the spreadsheet were correct.

Who were they? I had no idea. I showed Jake the encrypted files and the backup copy of a computer. I suspected those would provide clues to who was laundering the money, but that would take more technical skills than I possessed.

After I ran through my theories, Jake was mostly silent the rest of the trip, barely even making a sound as he herded me past the baggage carousel to the taxi stand. A cab pulled up to the curb and Jake threw his duffel bag into the trunk then opened the back door for me. As the car pulled away, he gave the driver an address and conversed in easy Spanish.

"You speak Spanish?" I asked.

"You're a California native, and you don't?" he countered.

"Languages have never been my strong suit," I said, defensive. "I'm better with numbers."

I had tried numerous times to learn Spanish, starting in high school. My accent was atrocious, and I could never get past present-tense conversations about libraries. But give me a string of numbers and I could add them up in my head, find the median and the mean, or just memorize them. Numbers were constant and were something I grasped intuitively.

Jake leaned back in the seat and rubbed his face. "When we get to the hotel, I'm calling for backup," he said quietly.

I gave him a sidelong look. "What's that mean?"

"We can't do this alone," he said.

"Maybe we should talk later," I suggested, as the driver caught my eye in the rear view mirror.

Jake nodded and closed his eyes. I thought he might be asleep and studied his face—the way his thick eyelashes rested against his skin contrasted with the dark scruff from two days without shaving, which gave him a dangerous edge. His dark hair was tousled and his clothes wrinkled from traveling. Even scruffy, he had a magnetism that I had to work hard to resist. If only, I thought. If only he weren't a law enforcement officer and if only he didn't think I was a criminal. If only...

As the car slowed to pull into the drive in front of the hotel, his eyes opened, and I quickly looked away, embarrassed to be caught staring at him. He helped me out and grabbed his bag. I had only my messenger bag that I grabbed when we left the Mandarin two days earlier. I had abandoned my trendy clutch purse for a fabric pouch with a long strap I could wear across my body. My few pieces of clothing were in his duffel bag. My world, though, was on the computer and the drives that I clutched close to me through the various airports on our route.

As I turned to look at the hotel, the ground shifted beneath me, and my vision dimmed around the edges until I was looking through a dark tunnel. A strong arm caught me before I toppled over, and I leaned into Jake's chest. Whether it was the exhaustion or something else, I nearly didn't pull away from his embrace. Jake righted me and took my messenger bag from me.

"We'll get something to eat after we check in," he said.

I blinked and nodded, steadying myself and following him into the lobby of the mid-level hotel. He set me and the bags on a padded bench in the lobby and went to check us in.

He had booked us two rooms with an adjoining door. Dumping my bag on the queen-sized bed, I went to the window to let in some fresh air. The room was bright and cheery, over-looking a small park two floors below. Our rooms shared a balcony, and I stepped out to take in the view.

The colors below were vivid in the bright sunlight. Lush green grass, brightly colored flowers. Even the sky was an almost surreal shade of blue with fluffy bright white clouds drifting by, pushed by a soft breeze that made the tropic heat bearable.

"I'd prefer it if you would stay indoors," Jake said from behind me.

"Why?"

"It's safer."

Trying not to think of what the threat would be, I walked back through the sliding glass door to my room, and Jake followed me from the balcony.

"I'll run out and get us something to eat," he said. "I won't be long. Stay in the room."

I bristled at his command, but was too tired to argue. "Yeah, sure. You don't have to steal my clothes this time."

"Don't open the door for anyone but me."

I shrugged. It wasn't like I was expecting company. Jake handed me a stack of my clothing that had been in his bag, along with the few toiletries, closed the adjoining door between the hotel rooms, and I was alone. Jake's absence made me nervous. I was in a new country, on an idiotic mission, and I was running on few hours of sleep and two bags of peanuts. It was hard to believe it had only been a few days since Jake Barnes had pulled me from underneath that desk. It seemed like a lifetime.

After a long, hot shower, I stretched out on the bed in my *Where's Waldo* shirt and closed my eyes.

I'll get up and do more research, I thought. *I should see if any of the account numbers on Bill's drive match up with the accounts in the case discovery.*

Then I let the exhaustion overtake me like a wave, pinning me to the mattress, and fell into a sweet, black abyss of sleep.

The pounding on the hotel room door jerked me awake in a disorienting rush of adrenaline. I ran to the door and peered through the peephole and saw Jake on the other side. I opened the door and remembered I wasn't wearing pants.

"Nice look," he said, brushing by me with a fragrant bag of food.

"Is that tacos?" I asked, my mouth watering and my half-naked state momentarily forgotten. I grabbed the folded pair of khakis from the bed and slipped them on. According to the bedside clock, I had been asleep for less than an hour.

Jake set the bag on the small table by the window, and I followed like a cartoon dog following a scent trail. My stomach rumbled at the thought of food that hadn't been packaged by an airline. He slid a stack of napkins toward me and then ripped open the bag to reveal tamales, still steaming in the husks.

"Oooooh," I murmured, my eyes on the food. I looked up to see him smiling, the first time I'd seen that expression since he learned about Bill's flash drive.

With a shake of his head, he pushed the food toward me. "I remembered that you had an unnatural affection for Mexican food. Hope these will do."

I nodded and bit into the tamale, the sweet corn dough mingling with the spicy pork filling.

"Hmmm, this is so good," I managed to get out.

Jake watched me eat for another few seconds, raised an eyebrow, and then reached for the tamales. Maybe he'd never seen a woman actually eat in front of him before. I knew girls who did that. I was never that kind of girl.

After we had wiped out the pile of tamales, Jake leaned back and rested his feet on the bed. He looked as tired as I felt, his eyes shadowed and his face a little pale. I knew he hadn't slept much more than I had in the past few days.

"I called the States. Talked to a friend of mine at home."

I put my feet up, too, and leaned back in the chair, waiting to hear the news.

"We have a new plan," he said.

"We had an old plan?" I asked. "Because I was just kind of winging it at this point."

"Yeah, I gathered that," he said. "We're going to meet with Bill tomorrow morning and find out what he knows and why he wants to meet here."

"Do you trust him?"

He paused and looked thoughtful. "Bill? No, I don't. Why do you think he insisted on meeting here?"

I was pretty sure I knew what Bill wanted. Several of the accounts were in Belize, including two in my name. If he didn't have the drive with the account numbers and pass codes, he couldn't transfer money out of the accounts. According to the spreadsheets, the balances in the Belize accounts in my name totaled a little more than $10,000. But that information was three weeks old. There could have been transactions after the last update, and if the previous sums were any indication, there could be more money in those accounts.

"He needs the flash drive to access the accounts," I said.

The drive was the only leverage I had against Bill Macias at this point. If Bill found out that I gave it to the FBI, he'd have no incentive to do what I needed him to do. I was counting on Bill's greed to help me out—I'd offer him the drive in return for the funds being transferred. What he did with it after that wasn't going to be my concern.

Jake's expression told me he didn't believe me, or at least thought I was withholding information. He was a perceptive guy.

"Okay, fine," he said after a pause.

"Who did you call in the States? The person helping us?" I asked, a feeling of dread seeping into my stomach.

Jake glanced up and looked almost apologetic. "Matt Reese."

I exhaled as an image of the young prosecutor crossed my mind. The dark haired, reed-thin man in his early thirties, his black-frame glasses giving him a Buddy Holly vibe. I could even hear his voice in my head, calling me a thief and a liar during his closing arguments.

"That guy hates me. Why is he helping me?"

Jake shook his head. "He doesn't hate you."

"He called me a thief."

"He was doing his job."

"He tried to send me to prison for a decade."

Jake bit his lip, and his brow furrowed. "I told him what's going on, tried to the best of my ability to explain it. I've worked with Matt for several years, and I trust him. And I told him he can trust you."

And I was sure that Matt Reese would put aside the nearly two years he spent prosecuting me, Ralph, and Tim, and embrace me and my investigation of a worldwide money-laundering operation. I reached up and rubbed my forehead and tried to erase the throbbing pain in my temples.

"How do I know I can trust *him*?"

There was a long silence following my question, and I looked up to find Jake staring at me.

"Do you trust me?"

That was a tough question.

"Mostly."

He leaned back in the chair and grinned. Something about his relaxed posture and warm smile broke the tension, and a fraction of the tension in my shoulders gave a little.

"We'll meet with Bill in the morning, hear him out. But I can't let him transfer the funds to some drug cartel."

"How do you stop him? If we give him the account information, that's what he's going to do. He's too scared of them not to follow his orders."

Jake frowned. "Yeah, it's a problem."

I didn't want to leave without getting what I came for. The money in the Patterson accounts might not be the same dollars stolen from the Sahara Fund account, but damn it, those investors deserved to get their money back. And I deserved something, too. Not money. That wasn't what I wanted. Just the ability to get a job. To see my former coworkers on the street and not feel uncomfortable, wondering what they thought of me. Was that too much to ask?

"He doesn't know we have the drive, right?" I asked.

"Right," Jake said, giving me a sidelong glance that was full of suspicion.

"Then we tell him that you couldn't get the drive from Patterson's office. I'll be there with you, though, and if he's smart, he'll realize that I have access to at least some of the accounts—the ones under my name."

Jake didn't say anything, just leaned back and studied me.

"I can go to the bank and access the accounts in my name. If there are funds there, I can move them, withdraw them, whatever I want," I said, the idea forming quickly in my brain.

He nodded slowly, but his brow furrowed. "Bill wants to move the money back to the criminal enterprise to save his ass."

"Yes, but I can move it anywhere," I said. Like to the account I opened in the Cayman Islands, anticipating Bill's willingness to transfer the money back to the Sahara Fund investors once I showed him that I knew what he was really up to. Well, what I had thought he was up to. Now I had even more leverage—if I could talk to him alone.

Jake reached into his shirt pocket and pulled out a folded paper. "If you can get Bill to cooperate with you, that is. We've got an account set up to receive the funds for the Sahara Fund investors."

He slid the paper across the small table to me, and I unfolded it and saw the long string of digits.

"Why do you have this?"

"Because that's what you needed, right?"

I nodded, dumbfounded. "You said you wouldn't let me blackmail anyone, though."

He sighed. "I won't let you blackmail anyone. But I talked to Matt about it. We think that if you were to convince Patterson executives to part with the funds for the investors, that wouldn't amount to blackmail. As long as you weren't threatening to turn them in to authorities, or otherwise cause them harm."

That had been my plan, but I could adapt it.

"Sure, I can do that," I said, studying the twenty-two digits. I read it several times committing it to memory, and handed him the paper.

"Keep it," he said, pushing it back. "You need that to transfer the funds."

"I'll remember it."

"The account was set up by the U.S. government, and anything that gets moved there will be passed on to the Sahara Fund's investors, even if it's not the full amount they're owed," he said, then he paused. "And what do you mean you'll remember it?"

"I memorized it."

"That's impossible."

"Try me."

He took the paper back and looked at it as I recited the digits back to him.

"How did you do that?"

"I told you. I'm good with numbers. Like, *Rain Man* good."

He still looked suspicious, one eyebrow raised slightly. "Really? Can you count cards, too?"

"That's a limited universe of options—each deck has fifty-two cards, four suites, thirteen numbers or face cards. Even if you have multiple decks, it's not hard to figure the probability of what's going to come up next," I said. "But no, I don't cheat at cards."

He stared at me a little longer, his head tilted slightly. "Okay, back to the plan. You're going to transfer the money, close the two accounts, and get out of the bank."

"That's it?"

"Well, you're also going to turn over evidence you developed to me so I can give it to the Department of Justice, including the flash drive you took from Bill's office," he said. "And any cooperation you can provide in deciphering the bank records would be greatly appreciated."

"How appreciated?" I asked.

"What do you want?"

I want my old life back.

It was my first thought, but I didn't say it out loud. I wasn't even sure if it was true, anyway. Did I want my old life back? I'd be married to Dylan by now, still working at Patterson Tinker and going to Holland family functions at the country club on special occasions. It sounded so drab and shallow. Dylan had turned out to be a weasel, and I had never warmed to his family anyway. They certainly weren't all that welcoming to me, either. Patterson Tinker was a corrupt institution, and the thought of working for the criminal underworld's bankers, even unknowingly, was nauseating.

So what did I want?

"A public apology from the U.S. government, acknowledgement that I wasn't involved in the Sahara Fund scheme, recognition for everything I've done to get the money returned to the victims of Ralph and Tim. And if the government could repay my Aunt Marie for my legal expenses, that would be great."

He looked down at the floor, his lips tight, and my hopes sank.

"I'll see what I can do," he said, looking back up at me. "I can't make any promises."

"Right. The Department of Justice doesn't like to admit mistakes. If they apologize to me, it makes it look like they were lazy and believed two lying, convicted felons rather than doing the legwork to uncover what really happened at Patterson Tinker."

His jaw tensed. "Something like that."

"When do we meet with Bill?"

"Tomorrow morning," he said. "Tonight, just try and get some sleep, okay?"

He stood up and moved toward the door to his room.

"It's only six o'clock," I said.

"Well, I'm exhausted," he said. "You can do whatever you want. Just don't leave the hotel room."

"That leaves me tons of options," I muttered as he pulled the door between our rooms nearly closed, leaving it open just a few inches.

I heard the shower run in Jake's room and lay down on the bed to get some sleep. But my mind was off and running. It felt like I was missing something. I tossed and turned and finally heard the bed springs in Jake's room groan. After a little while, I could hear his rhythmic breathing. I pictured him in the bed on the other side of the wall from me, wondering what he slept in. Boxers? Or less?

Jesus. I sat up and shook my head. Lusting after Jake Barnes was exactly the wrong thing to do. What did I even know about him? He was at least semi-fluent in Spanish and had some conversational Cantonese skills. He had a sister, and he thought I was a criminal. I wasn't even sure that we liked each other. We certainly didn't trust each other. It simply wasn't going to happen.

No matter what my hormones wanted.

CHAPTER FOURTEEN

The resort where Bill wanted to meet was a beachside affair that was lightly populated with tourists brave enough to travel during hurricane season. The rush of holiday travelers wouldn't hit for another month, when the rain and humidity let up. As I followed Jake along the pebbled path that led to a covered patio, I could feel my cotton shirt absorbing the ambient humidity. The morning air was warm, and clouds were already forming overhead.

Bill was at a table at the edge of the patio that overlooked a stretch of gentle surf, alone with a drink that featured a spear full of fruit. I hadn't seen a girlier drink since my last stint as a bridesmaid.

Giddy relief flooded his face when he saw us approach. He stood and greeted Jake with a warm handshake.

"You made it," he said. "Great, great."

He sat down and stood again quickly. "You guys want a drink?"

He waved at the waiter then sat perched on the edge of the chair—a bundle of frayed nerves in a loud Hawaiian print shirt.

"No, we're good," Jake said, taking the seat that let him scan the patio. The restaurant wasn't open yet, but the bartender took a break from wiping down glasses to make another daiquiri for Bill.

Bill sucked down the last of his drink and started on the next immediately. Between sips, he kept his gaze on me, as if he was studying my features.

"So, you didn't have any trouble leaving Macau?" Bill asked. The air was cool with the promise of a hot day in the near future, but Bill's forehead was already dotted with sweat.

Jake eyed him and then shook his head. "Why would we?"

"No reason," Bill said with a shrug. "Just you know, international travel."

"Why are we here, Bill?"

Jake was apparently done with small talk.

Bill's glance flickered over me again, and I was growing increasingly uncomfortable, as if I was the bargaining chip the two men were fighting over.

Bill slurped down the last of the drink and fidgeted with the skewered fruit. "Did you get it? The drive?"

Jake shook his head. "No."

He was a consummate liar. No elaboration, no unnecessarily complicated explanation. I made a mental note.

The faint hope in Bill's expression drained away at the single word. "I'm going underground."

I looked at Jake, who was still watching his brother-in-law. "You're abandoning Henry and Lily?"

Bill put his hand to this temple and rubbed his forehead, genuine grief on his face.

"It's better this way," he said softly. "I can't go back to the States. Not now."

"Where are you going?"

Bill looked at Jake and shook his head. "I can't say. But I need a favor."

We'd just traveled around the globe at his request, and I wasn't in the mood to grant Bill any further favors. Neither, it appeared, was Jake, who raised an eyebrow at the request.

"What sort of favor?"

Bill looked away, concentrating on the pineapple chunks in front of him.

"I, uh, need to get something. It's, uh, complicated. But uh, well—"

"Spit it out, Bill," Jake said, bringing his hand down hard on the table and leaning forward. "We're not here for a vacation."

"I need you to go to a bank," Bill said. Only he wasn't talking to Jake any longer, he was looking at me.

They were both looking at me.

"What? Why?" I sat up straighter in my chair.

"Because there are a couple accounts in your name," he said. "I wouldn't need you if I had the flash drive with the account information, but now I can't transfer the money unless it's in person."

I felt my face flush. *Damn it.* I hated being right about Bill's stupid plan.

"You want me to go into a bank and do what?"

Bill swallowed hard. "I've set up an account. All you have to do is transfer the money to it. Then that's it. Just walk out. Simple."

I doubted it would be as simple as Bill said.

"Why are the accounts in my name?"

Bill looked around again, and Jake and I did also. It was still just the three of us on the patio. Even the bartender had gone. Bill's nervousness was contagious, and I found myself on the edge of the metal chair, ready to flee.

"That wasn't my idea. We just, uh, needed someone whose information was already available to us, and you were on some of Patterson's legitimate accounts," Bill said. "But here's the thing. We have to hurry. We need to do this today. Tomorrow at the latest."

"What's the rush?" Jake asked, his eyes narrowing as he leaned toward Bill again.

"The money was supposed to be transferred, and if it's not done soon, heads are going to roll. And I mean that literally. I need to get in there and move the money," Bill said. "If not, well, I'm a dead man."

"And you're just going to disappear using what? Your retirement account? You're taking the money for yourself, aren't you?"

Bill started to shake his head but then laughed and looked down, his lips pursed. "You know, Jake, you're a pretty good investigator. Yeah, I'm taking a small percentage for myself. Not enough to put a target on my back. Just enough to let me start over. They won't even miss it."

"Who is involved in this?" Jake asked.

Bill shook his head. "If you do this, I'll give you all the information I've got on this scheme. Everything. You'll take down the entire Patterson empire with this information."

Jake leaned back. "Start talking."

Bill shook his head. "No, I need you to do this first."

"That's not going to happen."

Jake's voice had taken on an edge I hadn't heard before, and I got the impression that his feelings toward his brother-in-law had been suppressed over many Thanksgiving dinners in the past.

Bill pushed away from the table and stood, Jake following him. I started to stand as well, when Bill leapt in my direction, grabbed me and spun me around. The cold metal of a gun barrel against my neck made me go still, not even daring to swallow.

"No, Jake. We do it my way."

Jake backed up half a step and put his hands up. "This is not necessary, Bill."

Bill pressed the gun barrel into my neck and I could feel my pulse pound against the metal. Jake caught my eye and my breath quickened. The panic rose in my gut and I fought to keep myself calm and not set off the nervous man with the gun to my neck.

"I won't hurt her. I promise. I just need her to do this. Then I'll let her go," Bill said.

And then the target would be on me. It would look like I stole the money being held for the big bad guys that Bill was afraid of. And he'd be off living under an assumed name. *Nice.*

"Just stay calm," Jake said, meeting my eyes.

I tried to nod, but the gun bit into my jawbone. Bill's grip tightened around my body as he pulled me backward with him, away from the patio and toward the path Jake and I had just used.

At the parking lot, he kept me at his side, the gun now jammed into my ribs. He opened the driver's side door of a small rental car and pushed me in, forcing me across the center console to the passenger seat. As he climbed in behind me, I grabbed the door handle, but felt the gun push into my side again.

"Oh, no, you don't," Bill said. "You're staying with me."

I sat back in the vinyl seat and tried to follow Jake's advice—taking deep breaths as the car fishtailed out of the parking lot, Bill's attention divided between me and the road. I turned and saw Jake racing toward a motorcycle, then we rounded a corner, and I lost sight of him.

My heart sank. I was alone with a highly unstable and armed idiot who put all the pertinent information about his complex criminal scheme on a flash drive and didn't even bother to encrypt it.

Bill looked behind us, his face pale and sweaty. He wiped his hands on the fabric of his shorts and then gripped the wheel.

"God, I can't believe this," he muttered, probably to himself.

"Look, just keep calm. We'll get out of this," I said, figuring that it was better to have a calm kidnapper than a fidgety one.

He took a deep breath and turned the car onto a wide boulevard, merging with a steady flow of traffic.

"I'm sure you didn't think it was going to come to this," I said, trying to engage him in conversation. If he would talk, I could get more information about what was going on.

"Of course not," he said, turning to me. "I'm not a bad guy. Really. I just need your help. There's no other way."

"What happened at Patterson?" I asked, lowering my voice and trying to stay calm.

He shook his head, and I thought he wasn't going to answer me. Then he inhaled deeply. "It just exploded. I don't know what happened, but whatever it was, it went down quick. There wasn't time to do anything."

I nodded sympathetically. "What does that mean for the clients?"

That didn't seem like the right term, but I didn't know what else to call them. The criminals?

"There was no way to tell them to stop transferring funds, but without the laptop or the backup, I can't get in and complete the transactions," he said. I didn't have a clue as to what he was talking about, but nodded again.

"If there's a chance we can get some of the money moved, that will pacify them. Buy me some time," he said, looking past me at the traffic alongside the car. "Buy me some time to fix things."

He wasn't holding me hostage to fix things. He was going to take the money and run like hell. And I didn't blame him.

"What happens if you can't—if I can't move the money," I asked.

He frowned and wiped his hands on his shorts again. "Bad things, so make sure it goes well."

"Who are the clients?"

He gave me an incredulous look. "Don't be stupid, you know who they are."

I shook my head, and he laughed. "Fine, act dumb. Let's just say you'll be on the wrong side of the worst people if you don't go into that bank and do exactly what I tell you to do."

I swallowed and nodded. "Are you going in with me?"

He shrugged, and we drove in silence for about ten more minutes, weaving in and out of traffic and making random turns onto small side streets. I looked behind us whenever I could but never saw anyone who looked like Jake on a motorcycle. When I thought about not having Jake at my side in a foreign country, my heart started racing again. How had I become so dependent on him so quickly?

"Okay, here's what we're going to do," Bill said, speaking quickly and drumming his fingers on the steering wheel in a manic pattern. "We're going to the bank. You're going to go in and transfer the money to my account. Then when we walk out the door, you go one way, and I'll go the other. Got that?"

I closed my eyes and took a deep breath. "How much is in the account?"

"I'm not sure exactly, just transfer everything, okay?"

He had the gun in his lap, and with his right hand he reached over and gripped my purse strap. He fumbled with the clasp until it opened and then rooted around in it. He withdrew my passport and wallet and tossed them to me.

"Good, you have your ID. That's all you need," he said.

"This is never going to work," I said, stuffing my passport and wallet back into the bag.

"It better work," he said, picking the gun up again.

He steered the car into a parking lot and parked in the very back, near an alley. I looked around but didn't see the bank.

"Don't even think of running off," he said, keeping the gun pointed at me as he got out of the car. I nodded and got out of the car. He didn't seem experienced with a gun. If I ran, he was as likely to shoot me on accident as on purpose. I didn't want to get shot either way, so I decided to wait for an opening to get away. If that didn't work, I had an idea to thwart his plan once we got in the bank.

Taking my arm, Bill forced me down the alley behind the parking lot. We turned left down a narrow path between two tall buildings. It wasn't so much an alley as a grimy, dark walkway that was probably home to large angry rats. I stepped over a broken bottle and around a pile of cloth that I didn't examine too closely.

At the end of the hundred-foot building, the path opened up, widening to about ten feet wide. Bill's hand gripped my elbow painfully as we passed a wide opening, a metal grated door open halfway.

"Keep going," Bill hissed, as I peered inside, hoping to see someone.

The room, a bare storage area, was dark and empty. We passed the door and continued toward the other end of the dark path, where I could see cars zip past on a busy boulevard.

Where was Jake? Was he able to follow Bill's car?

I stumbled over a stray piece of wood, nearly falling as Bill yanked me along with him.

"Hurry up!" he snapped.

I looked up, annoyed, and saw a man behind Bill, whose attention was focused on me. At the sight of the familiar face, I gasped and stopped in my tracks.

"Hello, Miranda."

I still didn't believe my eyes, but he still stood there even after I blinked several times. Bill whirled to see who I was looking at, raising the gun as he turned.

My throat constricted, and my mouth went dry. A million questions raced through my brain, but I could barely get out one word.

"Dylan."

He gave me that grin that used to melt me, but the expression didn't reach his eyes.

Bill gripped my arm hard and started pulling me back down the alley, toward where we had come from and away from Dylan.

"You son of a bitch," Bill said, his voice shaky. "God damn you. You have it, don't you?"

"Have what?" Dylan asked, walking toward us as Bill backed down the alley forcing me with him.

"The flash drive, the backup," Bill said.

Dylan shook his head, that grin still on his face. Bill stumbled, nearly knocking me over, as Dylan slowly stalked us. I could feel the fear coming off Bill's body in waves. Even considering our past, I would normally run to Dylan. I had trusted him once. But Bill's fear was primal and contagious, and there was something about Dylan's expression that made me uneasy.

"I don't have it," Dylan said.

"Then, why are you here?"

"I have another key," he said with a smile.

"There is no other key, you moron," Bill spat out. His hand gripped my forearm so hard I thought he might break it. I twisted to get away from him, but his grip was strong.

"Sure there is," Dylan said. His stride lengthened, and his pace picked up.

Bill shook his head, his eyes focused on Dylan. "No, there

can't be. I had the only copy of the accounts and the pass codes. And I have Miranda."

"And so do I." Dylan's smile chilled me. I realized that he was looking beyond Bill and me. I turned.

And saw Katrina Lore, looking more like me than I did at that moment. Her blond hair fell straight to her shoulders. She wore a simple white sleeveless blouse and a pair of light pink capri pants, and she looked like a well-heeled tourist—except for the silver handgun in her right hand.

Well, crap.

CHAPTER FIFTEEN

"Miranda, sweetheart, I need you to cooperate with me."

Dylan's voice and the condescending tone set my nerves on edge. The fact that his fiancée was holding a gun on me didn't help, either.

"I am not your sweetheart," I said.

He smiled and reached behind him, pulling a handgun from his waistband. "That may be. But I need you to work with me."

"Go to hell."

For so many reasons.

"You'll cooperate with me, Miranda. If you don't, I'll make sure that every cartel member in Latin America has Marie's address."

A chill ran up my spine at the threat.

"He's bluffing," Bill said. "Dylan doesn't deal with people like this. He doesn't get his hands dirty."

"You're an idiot," Dylan said. "Who do you think brought the Latin American clients in? Tim and I did that. Tim's locked up safe now, but I need that money moved, or we're all dead. You got it, Bill?"

Bill stayed silent, and I watched my former fiancé with a new horror.

"You did this," I said, as the reality of my situation hit me full on. Dylan and Bill were desperate. They were dealing with bad people. Very bad people.

"Yeah, well, I didn't start it," Dylan said. "I just expanded the program to new regions. Now get over here."

"We don't need her, Dylan," Katrina said from behind me. "I can do this."

I refused to turn back and look at her, just kept staring straight ahead at Dylan. The pieces fell into place. I thought about how Katrina had changed since I'd seen her last—the hair color, the clothes. Dylan had been grooming her for this. Literally grooming her. I felt sick.

"No, this is better, Kat," Dylan said. "This is much better."

"But I have a passport."

God, she was whiney.

"A fake one. This is the real deal. The real Miranda Vaughn. She'll be the one who moved the money. And took it for herself."

Katrina was close behind me, and I heard her exhale in frustration.

"You did this," I said again, watching Dylan's face. "You set me up."

He gave a slight shrug, his expression unchanged.

"Didn't mean to cause you any trouble, Miranda. You were merely convenient."

I swallowed hard at the betrayal. Of course it was Dylan He'd known everything about me—he had access to my entire life. We worked together. We practically lived together. He knew I had signing authority on other Patterson accounts. How hard would it have been to use that information on illicit accounts?

How had I not seen it? How had I loved him?

A sudden sharp pain in my side brought me back from my

self-pity as Bill grabbed me around the neck and jammed the barrel of his handgun into my ribs.

"I swear to God, I will shoot her."

"Bill, I have a back-up," Dylan said, nodding toward Katrina. "If you shoot Miranda, Kat's going to walk into that bank a block away and transfer the money."

Dylan kept his gaze on me as Bill dragged me in front of him, keeping me between himself and Dylan. If Dylan was concerned for my well-being, he was sure good at hiding it.

"Yeah, but you said it yourself. It's better to have Miranda do it. Less risk of getting caught, right?" Bill said. His voice portrayed his panic, as did the increasing grip on my upper arm.

"So what do you want, Bill? You want a cut? Is that it?"

Bill gave a derisive snort and pushed me another few feet ahead. "A cut? Fuck you, Dylan. I'm not risking my life to take a few crumbs."

I stumbled and nearly fell, but Bill pulled me up and pinned me to his body, using me as a shield. If either Dylan or Katrina shot at Bill, the bullet was very likely to hit me.

How had this happened? How did I end up here, where everyone had a gun except me?

Bill's body tensed, and he went still. I twisted and saw Katrina behind him, her gun against the back of his head.

"Let Miranda go," Dylan said softly. He focused on Bill with a cold intensity. "Let her go, and you can walk away. You won't have any money, but I won't say anything about you being here. You can start your life over. Just not in the same style to which you've become accustomed."

Bill shook his head and whimpered, the gun in my ribs shaking. I closed my eyes and took a deep breath. How would Aunt Marie be notified of my death? Would Jake identify my body? Take my remains back to California?

The pressure in my side let up, and I opened my eyes. Bill

held the gun up and pointed it away from me.

"Fine, okay, take her," he said, pushing me forward and away from him. I stumbled a few feet at the sudden release and rested my hand against a large metal trash bin against the side of the building. "You're of limited value, sweetheart. Once he's done with you—"

"Throw down the gun," Dylan said, pointing his firearm at Bill. "Do it now."

I felt exposed, between Bill and Dylan, both armed. I took a couple steps toward Dylan, keeping an eye on his right hand, which held the black handgun, as I edged toward the corner of the trash bin. When I reached the corner, Dylan reached out and grabbed at me, but I dodged him, slipping past his arm and into the corner where the trash bin met the concrete wall.

Bill's words echoed in my head. I knew he was right. Dylan's plan to have me walk into the bank and transfer the funds didn't end with me walking off into the sunset. Once he was done with me, I would be a liability. He could go back to California with Katrina, continue his career at Patterson. But for that to happen, I couldn't exist.

As soon as there was an opening, I would run for the end of the alley. I only hoped that Katrina wouldn't risk firing at me if Dylan was in the alley, too.

"Where did you put the account information?" Dylan asked, motioning at Bill with the gun.

"It's in my office," Bill said.

I crouched down lower, leaning against the metal bin. This made Dylan have to split his attention between me and Bill.

"What the fuck, Bill? You didn't take it with you?"

"It's not my fault!" Bill's voice was agitated and high-pitched. "You think I got a chance to pack up my office before the operation was shut down? I was escorted out of the conference room. I didn't even get to go back to my office."

"God damn it," Dylan hissed. He ran his left hand through his hair. "Okay, okay. We just have to get back there and get the information. It's got it all, right?"

"Yes, yes," Bill said. "It's all there."

"Where's the laptop?"

"In the bottom of the harbor," Bill said. "I told you, it wasn't safe to keep it. I kept a backup."

Dylan glared. "Is there a code? Did you encrypt it?"

"What? When would I have had time to do that? This was a last minute decision. I couldn't reach you."

This explained so much. Patterson must have either uncovered the in-house scheme and shut it down to avoid criminal prosecution, or gotten wind that the bank's illegal profit-making scheme was going to be busted. Either way, it sounded like a sudden decision.

"Okay, fine. Katrina and I will go to Macau and get it. Where is the backup?"

"I told you, it's in my office."

"Where in your office?" Dylan's voice rose.

"No, forget it. If I tell you, then you don't need me anymore."

"You already told me it's in your office. I'm not the only one looking for it, you moron. Just tell me where it is, so we can undo this mess."

The money was stuck, I realized. Once he was kicked out of Patterson's office, Bill couldn't access the account information, which meant he couldn't transfer the funds back to the original owners.

"You got her now," Bill said. "You can move some of it."

"Not enough," Dylan said. "We have a lot of business to take care of. A lot of clients depending on us."

My blood ran cold with his words. I knew what I'd seen on that drive, and the numbers I saw were huge—hundreds of millions of dollars flowing in and out of the accounts. How many illicit clients were Bill and Dylan serving?

And how screwed would they be when they found out the FBI had already seen the files on the flash drive they were fighting over?

"Dylan, we have to get out of here," Katrina said. "Let's just go to the bank now."

Her voice sounded less confident.

"Sure, sweetheart," Dylan said. "Bill, give Katrina your gun."

"No way!"

"Just do it!" Dylan's face grew pink at Bill's refusal to comply.

"So you can shoot me? Forget it!"

They were so involved with each other, I wondered if they forgot I was there, cowering behind the Dumpster. I stayed still as Dylan moved toward Bill, stepping just beyond the corner of the bin.

"Give me the gun, Bill," he said.

I looked to the side and saw his attention was focused on Bill, and gauged the distance to the end of the alley. About a hundred feet. Could I make it? Did I have a choice?

I pushed off the Dumpster and ran for the busy boulevard, ignoring the shouts from Katrina and Dylan behind me.

The sharp crack of a handgun echoed off the concrete walls, but I kept running. The thin soles of my sneakers slapped against the uneven pavement, and I heard the next shot hit metal, probably the trash bin, but I wasn't about to turn and look. Shouts echoed down the alley, following me, and I focused on the corner where the sidewalk met the pockmarked pavement of the alley, beyond which I might be safe.

Another shot and a scream, a higher pitched voice. I pushed ahead, the alley ending in just a few more steps, and heard the heavy steps behind me.

No! I reached the corner and grabbed at the building,

propelling myself around the side, stumbling with the momentum of my sprint, and out of reach of any stray bullets. The sidewalk was nearly empty, and I wondered if anyone even heard the gunshots. I continued to run, still trying to outpace the footsteps behind me.

I ran blindly, panicked, unsure where I was going. Ahead, I saw the red traffic light and the speeding cars in my path and turned right at the intersection, hoping against hope that no one tried to sneak past the red light. At the other side of the street, I ran flat out for another two city blocks before daring to look behind me.

No one was following, and I let my pace slow slightly, looking back every few feet for any sight of Dylan or Bill. This was a busier area, and I tried to blend in with the growing crowd, but as far as I could tell, I was the only blonde on the street.

Now if only I could remember where my hotel was, maybe I could find Jake and just go home.

What was I thinking trying to force an international bank to do anything, let alone transfer a large sum of money? I was an idiot to think I could pull this off. Now how was I going to get out of this mess? All I had was my passport and four high-limit credit cards that would be cut off in a few weeks when I wasn't able to make the minimum payments.

And where was Jake, anyway? If he was looking for me, how would he even know where to find me? If I could get back to the hotel, I could wait there until he returned. It was the best plan I could come up with, so it was going to have to work.

I stopped at the curb and waved toward a taxi then remembered that I had no cash on me. I stepped back, unsure of what to do and heard someone call my name. I turned toward the voice and saw Dylan—a tall, blond figure striding toward me, a half a head taller than everyone else on the street.

Without thinking, I ran in the opposite direction, right into traffic. The squeal of the taxi's brakes filled my head, and I jumped, expecting the next sensation I felt to be the car's grill taking out my legs. I squeezed my eyes shut and waited for the impact, but it never came.

Instead, there was the sound of shouting and in the middle of that, I again heard my name.

"Miranda!"

Dylan's shout followed me as I bolted again, away from him and toward the other side of the street.

Ignoring the stares of other drivers and the irate yelling by the taxi driver, I wove through the stopped cars until I reached the curb and ran toward the corner. I had no idea where I was going. I just knew that I needed to get away from Dylan.

I turned down random streets and up alleys until I was fairly certain I'd shaken him, and slowed slightly to a jog. My heart was racing, both from fear and exertion, and I had a killer stitch in my side. If I survived this, I promised myself, I would take better care of myself. Go jogging, at least once in a while.

Turning another corner, I found myself on the edge of an open-air market. Crowds filled the spaces between the tables and tents. It would be a great place to blend in, but I was the only blonde, and I stood out like a beacon. I looked down at my *Where's Waldo* shirt and cursed under my breath. Once again, I was dressed like a damn target.

I took a couple deep breaths and tried to calm myself. *Think, Miranda. What would Jake Barnes do?*

I reached for my purse, strapped across my body, and pulled out my wallet. I had a few American coins, some *pataca* from Macau, but no Belizean dollars. There were various cosmetics, pens, and a small perfume sample that I had swiped from my room at the Mandarin Hotel.

Looking around the tables and booths, my gaze fell on a

young woman selling hats and scarves and I made my way toward her. The table in front of the woman, who was probably still more of a girl, held an assortment of multicolored clothing, too. I picked up several items, searching for something that would fit my needs.

"*Hola*," the girl said with a shy smile.

"*Hola*," I replied, nearly exhausting my Spanish-language skills.

I lifted a straw hat and a linen tunic.

"Uh, *que*, uh, no. *Cuando?* No, that's not right," I stammered, trying to dredge up something from high school Spanish class.

"Twenty dollars," she said in heavily accented English.

"Oh, thank you," I said, my breath rushing out in relief. "Uh, I don't know if I have that."

"Fifteen dollars."

Opening my purse, I dumped the contents on the table between us. There wasn't much there and I sorted the items I couldn't lose—my passport, the flash drive, my favorite lipstick—and tucked them back in my purse.

"I don't have any cash," I said quietly and watched her face.

She raised an eyebrow and looked at the items remaining on the table.

"*Es perfume?*" she asked, pointing at the small glass bottle of perfume from the Mandarin Hotel. It was a promotional item, but a high-end one—a tiny replica of the real designer perfume bottle.

I nodded and she picked it up and sniffed it. After a quick glance around, she slipped the bottle into her pocket. She gave me a smile and a quick nod and I scooped the rest of the debris into my purse.

Then I looked around. "Is there a place I can change?"

She gave me a smile and a shrug, and I tugged the dark blue linen blouse over my striped shirt, hoping it gave me enough cover for now. With the hat also in place, I started to walk away, then returned and fumbled in my purse again. I found a piece of paper and pen and wrote the name of my hotel on it.

"Directions?"

She glanced at the paper and then scanned the crowd and waved to someone. A young man walked up with a smile, and she handed the paper to him and said something in rapid-fire Spanish.

He nodded and began speaking, also in Spanish. The girl giggled.

"*No, en Ingles.*"

The handsome young man grinned, his eyes sparkled, and I patted myself on the back for finding a teenager in love when the only currency I had was a quarter-ounce of cologne.

The young man took my pen and paper and drew a map. He pointed to the other end of the market and then tapped the map. I nodded, following his motions and thanked him, gave the girl a wink, and left the two lovebirds alone at the booth.

Looking back, I scanned the crowd and saw Dylan, just entering the market, his hand raised to shade his eyes, searching the crowd.

Damn it, I couldn't keep running from him. He'd just follow me back to the hotel.

Keeping my head down, I backtracked to the same booth where the teens were still exchanging flirty glances and giggles.

"Ayudame."

It was the one word that Señorita Perlmann had insisted we learn on day one—*help me*. "It might get you out of a jam one day," she had said. I silently sent her my gratitude as the girl's face turned serious, and she nodded. I hunched over, trying to be invisible to Dylan.

"El Americano over there—" I nodded toward the tall fair-haired man slowly proceeding through the crowd. "Es muy—"

I had to really dig for the word. "Peligroso."

The word was on every warning sign at every beach in Southern California, so I hoped it meant "dangerous" and not "high tide."

The girl grabbed my arm, yanked me around the display of hats and shawls, and forced me to the ground. I rolled under the folding table and curled up, as the light around me dimmed. My new friend had unfurled a wide length of fabric and was draping it around the edge like a tablecloth.

From my hiding spot, all I could see now was the young man's worn leather boots near the front of the table, his stance solid and protective. He'd be no match against Dylan and his gun, though. All I could hear was my heart pounding, louder than the sounds of the market.

"Hola."

The sound of Dylan's voice chilled me, and I became hyper aware of the thin piece of fluttering fabric that separated us.

"Busco a una mujer rubia."

"No, lo siento."

The sound of Dylan's footsteps faded, and I waited for a cue from my guardian angels. After what felt like a long time, the young woman lifted the fabric and helped me out. She pointed to the entrance of the market where I had entered and from where Dylan had come, too. She mimed walking with her fingers, and I got the point—Dylan had gone back in that direction.

I thanked her, tucked my hair up under the hat again and headed in the opposite direction, following the rudimentary map that might get me back to my hotel.

And with some luck, to Jake Barnes.

CHAPTER SIXTEEN

As I walked, I tried to formulate a plan. Option one—go straight to the airport, buy a ticket to California and forget this horrible misadventure ever happened. I'd be several thousand dollars deeper in debt, with nothing to show for my trouble, no way to get a job, and with a reputation in tatters. And I'd be facing a lawsuit from the Sahara Fund investors, which if they won, would mean that Aunt Marie and I could be homeless, as well.

For all its downsides, that plan did have a low probability that I would end up shot dead by Dylan, Bill, Katrina, or some angry Russian arms trafficker looking for someone to blame when he learned Patterson had lost his money. But running home now wouldn't guarantee my safety. I knew too much now, and that was a threat to Dylan and to whomever he was working with and for.

That meant I needed to see this through. The key to that was in my purse, rattling around with the lipstick and hotel pens. I could go back to the bank, transfer the money myself and then turn the flash drive over to Jake or some other American official. But that option pretty much drew a target on my back. Somehow I doubted a drug cartel was going to write off the loss of millions of dollars, even if it was used to reimburse some American retirees who got fleeced.

The smell of roasting peppers wafted out of a door open to the street, and I peeked in to see a small diner, empty except for the man behind the counter and someone working in the back. My mouth watered, and I realized that I was starving and thirsty. I'd been walking for about forty-five minutes in the growing heat. Young Romeo's directions seemed to be pretty good, but they weren't to scale. I wasn't sure how much longer it would be until I got to the hotel. And once there, I had no idea whether Jake would be waiting for me.

The man waved me in, but I shook my head and raised a hand. "*No dinero.*"

He smiled and tapped a faded logo taped to the counter. "Visa."

Bless you. I was at the counter in a fraction of a second, ordering a plate of tacos and the largest bottle of water in the restaurant. As the man ran my credit card, it occurred to me that it might be risky to keep using my own credit here. Could Dylan or someone else use that to track me?

A steaming plate of food distracted me from that thought, and I took my meal to a table with a view of the street through the dusty window. I dug into the tacos and kept an eye on the passersby, watching for Dylan. The cold water and spicy food refreshed me, and I headed back onto the street with a renewed optimism.

I was going to do the right thing and end this scheme. Maybe I could negotiate some sort of protection from the government for my cooperation. My mind, and hormones, went immediately to the thought of Jake Barnes providing that protection, and I had to shake my head to clear that image. He might not even be looking for me right now.

No, that was wrong. He was a good guy, a professional white-hat wearing, Dudley Do-Right type. He'd just seen me taken at gunpoint by an unstable criminal—he was probably looking for me. Unless he went to the embassy to get assistance. In which case, he wouldn't be looking for me. Maybe I was more trouble than I was worth, and he decided to put my fate in his colleagues' hands. Given what I'd put him through in the past three days, I wouldn't blame him for that.

The street I was on was starting to look familiar, and I consulted my map. Unfortunately, my map was focused on the main streets, which were all wide boulevards with lots of traffic. This made me nervous, so I tried to stay close to that route, but on smaller side streets. Glancing around a corner, I saw the wide sweeping driveway of my hotel and exhaled in relief. I waited and watched the street and the people going in and out of the hotel.

I didn't see Jake, but I also didn't see Dylan. I'd been walking long enough that I wondered if Dylan gave up and resorted to a new plan himself. I waited for several minutes, and decided it was as safe as it was going to get. Keeping my head down, I scurried up the drive, staying close to a curving hedge.

I kept my hat on and the brim low as I entered the lobby and peered around the room but didn't see any familiar faces—either friend or foe. The hall outside my room was empty, and I let myself in and shut the door behind me quickly.

"Jake?" I called out quietly, but the room was silent in response.

I cracked the adjoining door to his room and peered in. It was empty and it looked like he hadn't been back since we left this morning. Exhaling in frustration, I turned away and slumped on the edge of the bed.

Unsure what to do while I waited for Jake to return, I went through my luggage—that is, my purse and my messenger bag —and pared down my belongings, figuring that we'd be running again soon. And I hoped that wouldn't be literally running because my legs and feet were killing me. I picked up the flash drive and looked at it. A couple inches of plastic that could destroy so many people. Instead of putting it back in the purse, I slipped it into my pants pocket—wanting to keep it as close as possible to me. If I lost this, I'd lose everything.

I went to the bathroom and washed my face, trying to compose myself. I'd only been back in the room for about twenty minutes, but the silence and the absence of Jake was making me twitchy. Where was he?

As I dried my face with the hand towel, I heard something outside the door and sighed in relief.

Finally. I put the damp towel on the counter and was turning to leave the bathroom when the front door exploded into the room.

"Fuck!" I dove to the floor and slid to the wall, trying to reach the bathroom door to close it. A second shot hit the door, and I saw more wooden shards fly past the opening.

It was too late to try and hide in the bathroom. Dylan stood in the doorway, gun in hand.

"Get up," he said.

My ears were ringing from the gunshots, but I could hear the cold hatred in his voice just fine. When I didn't move, he grabbed my arm in a vise-like grip and hauled me to my feet. He yanked me into the room and pushed me toward the bed.

"Get your passport."

Shaking, I picked up my purse and slipped the strap over my head and across my body. Dylan looked around nervously, and his gaze settled on the messenger bag.

"What's in there?"

Without waiting for my answer, he opened the flap and shook out my computer and the two hard drives.

"I knew it. That coward didn't destroy the laptop," he said

with a tight smile. He put the drives back in the bag with the computer and carried it to the door, keeping the gun trained on me. "Let's go."

"Where?"

My voice sounded like it was in a tunnel, and my heart was racing from the adrenaline.

"You're going to go transfer some money," he said. "Then we're going to go for a boat ride."

"I'm not doing anything for you," I said. "Let Katrina do it."

"Katrina's dead."

He said it without any trace of emotion. My mouth went dry at his casual announcement. "Oh my God," I whispered.

I didn't like her, not a bit. But she certainly didn't deserve to die in that grimy alley. For the first time, I noticed the blood on his shirt cuffs.

"What about Bill?" I managed to croak as my throat tightened.

"Let's just say he won't be bothering you any longer."

I closed my eyes and gulped down air, trying to stay calm. In the distance, a siren grew louder. Dylan looped the strap for the messenger bag over his shoulder and grabbed me by the arm. He pushed me toward the open door, the frame jagged from his bullets. He pulled me toward the end of the hallway and then down the stairs. He kept a tight grip on my arm and my skin crawled at the contact with him. My mind scrambled to come up with a way out of this mess.

Outside, he hurried me toward a car parked at the corner. He tucked the gun into his waistband and then unlocked the door. He forced me into the car, withdrew the gun and rested it under my jaw as I leaned back in the seat, trying to get away. The barrel sank into the soft flesh under my chin, and he chuckled.

"If you behave yourself, you just might get out of this alive. If you don't, I'll shoot you. And then I'll make sure your darling

Aunt Marie suffers, too." He pressed the gun harder. "Understand?"

I tried to nod.

"Is that a yes?"

"Yes," I whispered.

He pulled the gun away, slammed the passenger side door and walked around to the driver's seat. He tossed my messenger bag into my lap and got into the car.

"Keep that safe for me, babe. I'm going to need it later," he said.

He was awfully jovial for someone who just lost his fiancée in a gun battle. How would the sociopath react when he realized that this wasn't Bill's computer? On one hand, I didn't want to be around to see his rage when that happened. On the other hand, if he thought he had all the account information, he no longer needed me.

We drove through downtown Belize City, passing a police car speeding in the direction of the hotel we had just left. Instead of heading toward the downtown district where Bill had taken me. Dylan turned north, and we traveled along the waterfront. Just out of town, he turned right into a marina, and my heart dropped. Dylan's words came back to me.

You're going to transfer some money. Then we're going to go for a boat ride.

He thought he didn't need me to transfer the money now so he was skipping that part and going directly to the end—the part where he shoots me and dumps my body in the ocean, I guessed.

"It's not Bill's computer. It's mine."

Dylan slammed on the brakes, the car skidding to a stop on the gravel road.

"What?"

The fury in his voice would probably haunt me for years. I

swallowed and gripped the messenger bag tight, my fingers finding the edges of the laptop under the canvas.

"I said it's my computer. Not Bill's."

He hit me so quickly I didn't have time to duck, my head jerking to the left and smacking the headrest of my seat. Pain radiated from my jaw to my temple, and I could taste blood from my lip.

"You're lying."

I opened my mouth to make sure my jaw wasn't broken. "It's mine."

He gripped the steering wheel with both hands and stared straight ahead, and I saw an opening. I shoved the messenger bag at Dylan's head as hard as I could. I heard a satisfying thunk as the computer hit him in the face, then I opened the car door and ran.

CHAPTER SEVENTEEN

I scrambled over the loose gravel as I heard the car door slam behind me, followed by Dylan's outraged shout. My feet hit the grass along the side of the road, and I gained some traction, flying over the park-like median toward the marina, a safe-haven in the distance.

A truck was pulling out of the parking lot, and I waved frantically toward it. The driver started to slow, concern on his face, and then I heard the crack of a gunshot. The driver yanked the wheel to the side and dove into the seat. I turned to see Dylan running toward me, gun in his hand and gaining ground.

I jumped over a low rope fence that separated the grassy area from the parking lot. If I could get across the parking lot without a bullet in my back, I could find a place to hide or someone who could help me by calling the police. The shouts behind me grew louder, and I dared to turn and look.

Dylan ran across the grass, only fifty yards behind me. Behind him the driver of the truck was getting out of his cab, waving and shouting.

And behind him, crossing the field at a dead run, was Jake. He lowered his shoulder like a football player and launched himself at Dylan, taking him down. Both men rolled several yards, and the gun flew out of Dylan's hand.

Without thinking, I turned and ran toward the struggling figures, worry for Jake overwhelming me. He landed a good punch, stunning Dylan, but only for a few seconds. Dylan recovered with an elbow to Jake's head, and I saw the blood flow from his nose. It was enough of a blow that Jake reeled back, and Dylan took advantage of the respite from the attack. He scrambled to his feet, picked up the gun, and turned to Jake.

"No!" I screamed.

Dylan turned and saw me, and I froze.

"Miranda, run!"

At Jake's shout, I turned and bolted toward the marina again.

Another shot, and I cringed, expecting to feel the impact of the bullet. Nothing.

I turned and saw Jake lying face down on the grass, arms out. My knees buckled, and my head spun. The tears in my eyes nearly blinded me, but I was still able to see Dylan, still coming, now focused on me.

With a ragged breath, I turned away and ran. The marina was nearly empty, the boats tied off at the dock put away for the rainy season, and I looked around, desperate for someone to help me, but the business office and the store were locked and empty. The docks were quiet, with only the sound of seagulls and the creaking of the swaying docks. I turned back as I approached the end of the sidewalk and saw Dylan was still there.

I had the choice to go left or right at the end of the path and turned to the right where there were more boats moored and tied up against the labyrinth of docks. There must be someone there who could call for help. My feet hit the floating dock, and I could feel the soft swell as the gentle waves rocked it, but I kept running, turning down docks that looked like they either had boat owners or a place to hide. When Dylan hit the dock, I felt the impact under my feet.

"Miranda, there's no place to go," Dylan called. "Stop running. I won't hurt you."

Liar.

I turned a corner to a short pier and looked in both directions. On my right was a sailboat, a forty-eight-foot sloop with a wide sweeping deck. I could see a padlock on the door. To my left, a smaller fishing boat with an open wheelhouse. It had several large storage boxes on the deck, one covered with a tarp, and would provide me with more cover.

I jumped onto the boat and crept behind the small square room that hid me from Dylan's line of sight. I knelt and peered up the dock and saw Dylan walking slowly now, looking up and down each branch off the dock and at each boat that was tied off.

Looking past him, I could see the empty marina. The truck driver who Dylan had nearly shot stood at the top of the path to the parking lot, hands on his hips.

Please call the police, I prayed silently.

Then he pointed in the direction of the dock, and I saw Jake limping past the driver, scanning the marina until his gaze locked on Dylan. The breath left me, and relief flooded through me. He was still alive. He was going to call for help. Bring in the police or the Belize army or someone.

Right?

I lost sight of Jake and focused on Dylan's slow and methodical search, getting closer and closer.

Looking around, as much as I hated to admit it, Dylan was right. There was nowhere to go from here. I'd run out of places to run. I could jump in the water but then what? I wasn't going to out-swim a bullet.

Dylan seemed oblivious to Jake's presence as he stalked me,

like I was his prey. The midday sun beat down on me, and it felt like I was under a spotlight. I shifted and felt the hard plastic case in my pocket, reminding me that I couldn't jump in the water. I reached in and found the drive, grasping it tightly in my hand. It held the key to my future—clearing me, putting things right for the victims. And if I could get it to the right people, they could shut down Patterson's illegal scheme.

"Miranda, come on now," Dylan said, his voice closer. "I'm going to find you eventually. Let's not drag this out. I'm on a deadline here, sweetheart."

I slid down, my back against the wooden structure, sweat trickling between my shoulder blades. Inching up just enough to look through the glass window above my head, I saw Dylan's head swivel as he noticed Jake at the end of the dock.

"Look, this is personal man," Dylan called out to Jake. He held the gun behind his back. "You don't need to get involved."

I took advantage of the distraction to move positions, scurrying to a wooden box and crouching behind it. If I had to, I could leap into the water from here, and it wasn't as exposed if Dylan made it to the short pier this boat was tied to. I crawled forward and looked around the edge of the wooden container. Dylan had his back to me, and I couldn't see Jake from this position.

"Looks to me like the young lady could use a hand," Jake said.

"Just a lovers' spat," Dylan said. "You need to leave."

"I don't think so."

I saw Dylan's grip on the gun change, his finger sliding to the trigger. Without a thought, I leapt up.

"No!"

Dylan whirled around. Jake lunged toward him. He grabbed the gun, and it waved around madly as the two men grappled. Then I heard Jake yell out and saw Dylan emerge with a silver handgun in his left hand—the pistol Katrina had been holding. He leveled the gun at Jake's chest, and my heart stopped.

"Dylan, no! Don't hurt him!"

I jumped from the boat to the dock and ran forward. The black gun was sitting on the dock, between Jake and Dylan. Slowly, Dylan leaned down, watching Jake the entire time. He picked up the gun and turning sideways, pointed it at me and still keeping the silver handgun aimed square at Jake's heart.

I gave a quick glance behind me. I was at the end of the pier. Beyond that was a bright blue open bay. I was out of options for escape.

"Just come down here, Miranda," Dylan said. "Then your hero can go."

"If I do, you'll let him go?"

"I promise."

I rolled my eyes at that, but reached into my purse and fumbled until I felt the plastic case I was looking for. I held the black plastic case between my finger and thumb.

"You want this?"

"What is it?" He looked at me with suspicion, squinting in the bright sun, trying to discern the small object in my hand.

"It's Bill's back-up drive."

Dylan smiled and took a step toward me, but I shook my head and backed up two steps, gripping the plastic case tight in my fist. I was just feet from the edge of the dock.

"Don't come any closer," I said.

"Or what?"

"Or I'll throw it in the water."

He stopped, glanced back at Jake then turned to me.

"You let him go," I said, nodding toward Jake. "Or I swear to God, Dylan, I will throw this into the water. Do you know what salt water does to computer components? Kills them dead. Even if you let it dry out, the salt is too corrosive. All the information on this drive will be gone. Forever."

Dylan froze, his face a mask of pure hatred. "Bitch," he spat out. "Fine, you want your hero to walk away. That's fine. He can go."

"No."

Jake said it quietly, but the word carried across the water.

"Jake, just go. He's already killed his fiancée. That's what happened isn't it, Dylan? Bill didn't shoot her. He was in front of her. He would have been aiming at you. You shot at Bill but killed Katrina, didn't you?"

Dylan gave me a tight smile. "You were always so smart."

He waved the gun at me.

"Put the drive on the ground, and I'll let him go," he said.

Jake's stance stiffened, and I heard the sound of a boat behind me. A big one, coming in fast.

Dylan must have seen it, too, because he paled, and his eyes grew wide. I turned and saw the vessel—a sleek, fast racing boat bearing down on the marina at breakneck speed.

"Hurry, Miranda, throw it to me," Dylan said, the panic evident in his voice. He edged closer to me. "Do it now!"

My fist tightened around the plastic case, and I looked behind me again. The boat showed no sign of stopping.

The gun in Dylan's hand shook, and he looked between me and the boat, seeming to have forgotten Jake was behind him.

"Miranda, get down!" Jake yelled, just as rapid bursts of gunfire erupted from behind me.

I dove onto the short pier between the sloop and the fishing boat, shielded from the gunshots. Covering my head with my arms, I could hear the bullets chewing up the wood side of the boat. Looking up, I saw Dylan on the dock, lying flat on a short pier about thirty feet closer to the marina. His face was pale, and

I saw both guns were in the middle of the main pier, abandoned in Dylan's haste to get to safety.

The pier bounced from the boat's wake, and water sloshed over the edge. The ropes tying the boats to the dock groaned at the strain of the swells. I couldn't see Jake, and my heart started racing. *No, no, no.* I thought he was dead once today, and I couldn't bear the thought. Staying below the side of the sailboat, I crept toward the main pier and saw that Jake was on deck of the fishing boat I had taken refuge in just minutes before. I exhaled and tried to calm my heart rate. I'd hate to survive the gun battle only to die of a heart attack.

The roar of the boat increased, and it sounded like it was about to make another pass. My heart pounded, and I could only think of getting to the marina, but if I ran down the pier, I'd be exposed.

"Stay down!" Jake yelled. He pushed himself to his feet and staying low, crept to the edge of the boat and dropped onto the pier and rolled over to me.

"Are you hurt?" he asked.

I shook my head. "Are you?"

"I'll be fine," he said, and I saw the dark stain on his jeans, just above his knee.

"You were shot," I said, my panic rising.

"No, Miranda, look at me."

He took my face in his hands, and I looked into his eyes. He didn't break eye contact for the longest time, and the more I looked deep into his eyes, the more calm I felt.

"I am fine. We're going to get out of here."

I nodded.

"Miranda, throw me the drive," Dylan yelled.

I turned to Dylan, not believing his nerve. He was holding the silver gun again and was kneeling in the shelter of a boat in the slip. I felt Jake take my hand, squeeze it hard.

I looked at Jake, and his eyes flicked toward the end of the pier. The boat was getting closer, and I expected another blast of gunfire any second.

"Now," Jake said.

He pushed himself up and pulled me with him toward the end of the short pier, just as the bullets started flying again. This time I heard them hitting the dock, the boats, wood splinters flying around us as we ran to the end of the dock.

"No!"

Dylan's voice behind me was nearly drowned by the gunfire, but I could hear his anguish as Jake and I dove off the end of the dock into the bay. One hand was still gripped in Jake's, the other wrapped tightly around the hard plastic case.

CHAPTER EIGHTEEN

My lungs were bursting when I finally surfaced, my hands, now empty, grasping at the slick side of the *Maria Belen*, the fishing boat I'd hidden on earlier. My nose was filled with oily water, and I gagged at the smell of shallow, fetid saltwater with a hint of diesel. My hand found a rail and gripped it. I gasped and wiped the water from my face. Gulping air, I looked around for Jake and found him a few feet from me, holding on to the opposite corner of the fishing boat.

For the second time that day, I heard the sound of approaching sirens. The marina was again silent, except for the faint sound of shouting coming from the parking lot. Jake pulled himself up and onto the back of the *Maria Belen*, then reached down and took my hand, lifting me out of the water. Once I was on the boat, I could see people running from the parking lot, at least six people hurrying down the slope toward the docks.

And one running away—Dylan.

I squeezed the water from my tunic and felt for my purse. It was still attached at my hip, my passport soggy, but secured inside.

"We're going to have to answer some questions from the local police," Jake said, his voice low.

I looked up and saw his face was pale, but concerned about me. Then I looked to where I'd seen the stain on his leg. It was hard to see the blood stain since his pants were soaked through, but there was a ribbon of blood threaded through the water pooling at his feet.

"Oh my God, we have to get you to a hospital," I said, feeling a little faint at the thought of his injury.

He shook his head. "No, the little prick had a knife in his pocket and cut me. He punched me there when we were wrestling on the dock," he said. "It's just a minor cut. Nothing life-threatening."

He leaned closer to me, putting both hands on my shoulders and examining my face. He traced a finger along my jaw, to my lips. "He hit you?"

My hand flew up to my mouth. "Oh, yeah. When I told him the laptop wasn't Bill's."

Jake swore under his breath and gently traced my bottom lip, which had started to swell. His touch left a trail of fire in its wake. If he continued to touch me like that, look at me so intensely, my clothes would be dry in minutes. I found myself self-consciously licking my lip as I met his intense gaze. My stomach fluttered at the closeness and the tenderness.

He leaned in and touched his lips to mine, and I closed my eyes and sank into him. My body arched as if possessed. My fingers gripped his hard-muscled bicep, and I pulled myself closer, desperate for more. With a groan, Jake pulled away, and I swayed at the absence of his touch, his kiss, then exhaled a long breath.

"Oh, my," I whispered, my heart pounding in my veins.

"We should get out of here," Jake said. He took my hand, led me to the side of the boat, and jumped onto the dock.

"Wait!"

I leaned down near the supply box where I had hidden and dug my fingers into the tarp covering the supply box until I found what I was looking for.

Jake held his hand up to help me off the *Maria Belen*. "What's that?"

"The drive." I held up the small, black plastic case.

He shook his head. "What was in your hand?"

I sighed. "My favorite lipstick. Went to a watery grave, I'm afraid."

He grinned. "May it rest in peace."

Dripping, we walked up the dock toward the marina. "If we get questioned by the officials, just follow my lead."

Two police officers jogged down the pier toward us, and Jake held up a hand and greeted them in English, giving the officers our names.

"What are you doing here?" one of the officers asked, his eyes narrowing as he looked us over.

"We were looking for a friend on his boat when the men started shooting."

I nodded as Jake spoke, grateful that he wasn't sharing the full story, or we'd be here all day. Or for twenty to life.

The officers asked questions, and Jake answered calmly, keeping his arm around my shoulders. After a few minutes of conversation, he pointed to his leg and grimaced.

"I think I was hit by something, maybe a bullet, maybe shrapnel, but I need some medical attention."

I nodded vigorously as he showed the officer the hole in his jeans. Looking down, I saw the tear in the fabric and quickly turned my head to avoid seeing blood or worse. It must have been bad enough because the officers cleared the way for us to start walking toward the marina. Jake's limp was more pronounced, and he leaned on me, and I started to worry that he wasn't bluffing about going to a hospital. He gave the officer a phone number, and the man let us go toward the parking lot.

"We will have an officer take you to the hospital. He'll meet you at the parking lot. Wait for him there," one of the officers said then barked a command into his radio.

We started walking back up the ramp toward the cars, and Jake leaned in close. "When we get to the car, just get in like nothing's wrong," he said.

He straightened as we rounded a corner, and his limp vanished once we were out of sight of the police officers.

"Are we waiting for the officer?"

"No, we're not."

"Are we going to the hospital?"

"No."

I expected more police in the parking lot, but other than the two officers we saw there was just one other car. About a dozen civilians lined the top of the ramp down to the marina to survey the action and exchange stories about what they saw. Though we were conspicuous in our sopping wet state, nobody stopped us from getting in a small rental car at the edge of the parking lot. I looked around as Jake opened my door for me and saw that Dylan's car was missing. I pointed that out to Jake.

"Who is that guy anyway?"

"Dylan Holland, vice president at Patterson Investment Company, and my former fiancé," I said. Heat rushed up my cheeks.

Jake merely nodded as I climbed into the passenger seat. He drove out of the parking lot at a slow speed, cruising by as if we were tourists who stumbled over a traffic jam. No one looked twice at us as he turned the car onto the busy boulevard.

"How did you find me?"

"Only you would stop for tacos while being pursued by criminals."

"You tracked my credit card?"

"Yes. I got to the hotel just after you and your ex left and just before the cops. I barely had time to grab our bag," he said, glancing in the rear view mirror. "Didn't think we'd be going back there, even if the hotel would allow us back. That door would be hard to explain away."

"Where are we going?"

Jake didn't answer, just focused on the road, putting distance between us and the marina. I looked behind us, but there were no Belize City police racing to stop us from leaving. The marina arming lot was teeming with emergency vehicles, their lights flashing, but no one seemed to notice that the two main witnesses had slipped away. Well, three, considering Dylan had made a hasty retreat, too.

"If you want to change into something dry, your clothes are in the backseat," he said.

I climbed over the center console and into the small back-seat of the car.

"Where did you find a car?" I asked, taking my only other set of clothes out of the duffel bag.

His eyes flickered to the rear view mirror and then back to the road. "I borrowed it."

My eyebrows raised slightly at this. The straight-arrow FBI guy had stolen a car? "Oh?"

He glanced again at me in the mirror.

"I needed it fast," he said. "Because you were in trouble."

"Oh," I said, the word slipping out on a breath. He was worried about me.

While he drove, I quickly changed into my only other set of clothes. It was nice to get out of the wet clothes that smelled like diesel and seaweed. We were traveling south-west, the bay behind us, and the farther we drove, the fewer cars we saw on the road. I spread my wet clothes over the back seat to help them dry and climbed back into the front seat.

Jake didn't speak, and his silence was making me fidgety.

"How's your leg?" I asked.

"Fine," he said.

"You should get it looked at," I said. "That water was pretty gross, and there's no telling what bacteria was floating around in there. Maybe we can stop and get some peroxide..."

I stopped talking as I realized he was turning off a deserted road onto a smaller deserted road. There wasn't going to be a Walgreens nearby.

He turned and looked at me, an eyebrow arched. "I'll be okay."

We headed west, winding through a meadow of tall green grass and toward a dark row of trees in the distance.

"Where are we going?"

The sea was at our back now, and the sun glared off the dusty windshield.

"We're just going to get as far from Belize City as we can," Jake said, glancing at the rear view mirror. I turned, but the road behind us stretched out empty behind the dust the small car threw up. "What happened to the laptop?"

"Dylan took it. He thought it was Bill's," I said.

"You want to fill me in on him?"

No, not particularly. I bit my lip before answering.

"Do you mean today or—"

He shot me a glare. "At the beginning."

"We worked together at Patterson Tinker. We dated. Then we got engaged. When I got arrested, he dumped me."

Jake's expression softened a little, and I bristled.

"Oh, don't pity me," I snapped. "It was for the best. I just found out that he'd been using my name to launder money for some really bad people."

"Jesus," Jake said under his breath. "So all those names we saw, those huge spreadsheets of accounts and businesses, those could be real people?"

"I guess so," I said. The business addresses were clearly fake, but my name was real.

Jake reached over and squeezed my knee, the brief contact intimate and affectionate. "I'm sorry you had to go through all this," he said.

I looked down, blinking away the tears that threatened. "Thanks," I managed to choke out over the lump in my throat.

We continued in silence for a few minutes.

"What happened today?" Jake asked.

I took a breath. Where to start?

"Bill wanted me to go to the bank and transfer money from the account in my name."

"To where?" Jake interrupted.

"I don't know. I guess he had an account," I said. "We never made it to the bank. Dylan and Katrina were near the bank in an alley, and they had guns."

My head throbbed at the memory, my blood pressure rising when I remembered the sight of the gun in Dylan's hand.

"Who's Katrina?"

"She was the receptionist at Patterson Tinker. She's Dylan's fiancée. Or, well, she was. He said she was shot and killed after I escaped the alley."

"Jesus," Jake whispered again.

"He said she had a fake passport in my name, and they were going to the bank, too," I said. "But he wanted me to do it because then it would be better for him and Katrina."

"Because they weren't transferring the money for the clients," Jake said. "They were stealing it."

I nodded. "Yes, I think so."

"Do you know if she's dead?"

I shook my head. "No, I heard gunshots when I ran off. I didn't stick around to investigate." I twisted my fingers together in my lap. "There's something else. I think Bill may be dead, too."

Jake didn't react to the news. "Why? What happened?"

"Dylan said as much on the dock," I said.

He nodded, a grim expression crossing his face. "You didn't see what happened to Bill?"

"No. I ran. There were shots. I didn't look back."

"Well, your former fiancé isn't the most reliable source, so let's not count out Katrina and Bill yet," Jake said.

I didn't respond. What could I do? Argue with that? I didn't doubt Dylan's story, but Jake hadn't heard the flat matter-of-fact way Dylan had announced his fiancée's death. Just the memory of it sent a shiver up my spine.

We didn't speak for a time. The road reached the end of the grassy meadow, and the car entered the edge of the line of trees. Only a few vehicles shared the road with us, most going the opposite direction. Every time another car or truck came into view, I flinched, and Jake gripped the steering wheel so tight I expected it to snap in his hands.

Jake slowed as we approached a signpost with arrows pointing in three directions. The road forked, and a small gravel drive branched off a few yards before. Stopping the car, Jake leaned forward and examined the signs—Sibun Forest Reserve, Santa Marta, and a hand painted sign that was tacked below the official road signs pointing to Gaia Eco-Lodge in twelve kilometers. Below that was another wooden plaque: Closed. Jake threw the car in reverse, backed up several yards, and took the gravel road toward the lodge.

The little car bounced along the rutted road. I put one hand on the roof of the car to brace myself as Jake hit another bump. It was going to be a long twelve kilometers.

"If it's closed, why are we going there?" I asked.

As soon as I asked the question, I knew the answer. Of course, we were going to add breaking and entering to our list of criminal acts.

Jake didn't answer, just focused on the road. It felt like a very long time before we saw the lodge. Two Jeeps were parked in front, the Gaia Eco-Lodge logo painted on the side. We parked next to them, and Jake looked around. I did, too, though I didn't know what I was looking for. Did we want to find people? Or not? I had no idea what Jake's plan was, and he wasn't talking.

He opened the door and climbed out. "Hello?" he yelled. "Is anyone here?"

In the distance, a door slammed, and we both turned in that direction. A blond woman walked around the corner and stopped at the sight of the car. And probably the large, rough-looking man standing next to it. I got out, too, to soften the effect.

"Hi!" I said cheerfully, hoping to show we were no threat.

"Hello there," she said, and I thought I detected a hint of an accent. German, maybe. Or possibly Scandinavian.

Jake came around the car and put his arm around my shoulder. "Hi, sorry to intrude. We saw the sign back at the road, but we were hoping you'd make an exception for us tonight. My wife and I are on our honeymoon and are making our way to Guatemala. Do you think we could rent a room for the night?"

The woman stood straighter and tilted her head slightly. "It's not really tourism season yet," she said. "You're lucky you're not in the middle of a hurricane."

Jake nodded. "Yes, I know. But we always wanted to see Belize and had the time off work, so we decided to risk it."

He took a step forward as she approached, holding out his hand. "I'm Jake Barnes. This is my wife, Miranda."

I flushed at his words even as I berated myself for their effect.

This was fantasy, a lie to get something he wanted. It meant nothing. I smiled and shook the woman's hand.

"Gerta Reichel," she said, taking my hand in a warm grip. Up close I could see she was older than I first thought, fine lines radiating out from her pale blue eyes.

She shook her head with a smile. "Well, it's getting late, and I don't want to send you two back out on the road, so yes, I will open a cabin for you. We're not set to reopen for another month, so it's not going to be in great shape. If you want to get your bags, I'll get the keys, and my husband, Klaus, will show you to your lodge."

As she walked off, Jake packed my still damp clothes into the duffel bag and zipped it closed.

"You gave our real names," I said softly.

"Tell as few lies as possible when you're trying to deceive someone," he said. "Makes it easier to remember your story. Plus, I might have to use a credit card with them. It would be hard to explain the name change, wouldn't it?"

And here I'd been thinking he was a Boy Scout when he had some sort of master's degree in deception.

Gerta returned with a tall, bearded man. She introduced her husband, a bear of a man with a luscious head of red hair and matching beard. His brown eyes were warm and welcoming.

"Honeymooners, eh?" he said with a laugh. "Get too excited to make reservations?"

We laughed with him, and Jake shrugged. "Yeah, we bought the plane tickets on a whim and figured we'd just wing it for lodging. So far, it's worked out well, but this is a more remote area of the country."

Klaus nodded toward a gravel path. "Well, let's get you two settled. I'm afraid the kitchen isn't open, but I'm sure we'll be able to scrape up some food for you."

We followed him down the path, around the corner of the

large main lodge. Gerta opened a door marked "laundry" and then emerged a few seconds later with an armful of towels and bedding. I offered to help, and she put two folded robes in my arms.

"How long have you owned the lodge?" Jake asked.

"We came to Belize ten years ago for our honeymoon," Gerta said. "About five years ago, we returned for a vacation and didn't want to leave. We sold everything we had in Austria and moved the next year."

"It's a beautiful place," I said, taking in the scenery. Besides our footsteps on the gravel, the only sounds were the birds and the breeze rustling through the leaves above.

"We love it here," Gerta said. "You should come back during the tourist season. We offer cave explorations and guided hikes up to the waterfalls. It's quite lovely. Bit less rain, too."

"I'm sure we will," Jake said, keeping his hand at my waist as we walked. I liked the firm feel, guiding me on the trail.

"You can help yourself to the laundry facility, if you'd like," Gerta said. My heart soared at the thought of having clean clothes again. My standards had definitely slipped the last few days.

Klaus let us into the lodge and handed us the key. Gerta followed and started toward the stripped bed with the sheets.

"Oh, don't worry about making the bed. We'll handle that. I feel bad that we've imposed as it is," I said.

She smiled and shrugged. "It's no problem."

Klaus took her by the arm and gave us a wink, then pulled a pen and a narrow form from his shirt pocket and handed it to Jake.

"Fill this out and get it to us after you've settled in," he said. "Take your time."

They shut the door behind us, and I looked around the tiny lodge. It was, without a doubt, the most romantic room I'd ever been in. A stripped-down king-sized bed sat against a wall, mosquito netting draping down tied at the four posters. A small table with two chairs sat at the other side of the room near French doors that led to a balcony. I opened the doors and stepped out on the balcony and gasped. We were deep in a thick canopy of trees, but the fading sunlight provided just enough illumination to view a tree-top view of a luscious jungle. Colorful birds contrasted against the dark green leaves and complemented the scattered bright flowers. The trees opened up just enough to frame a waterfall cascading down a wall of rocks in the distance.

As I watched, everything faded away—the roaring in my head from the stress of the last few days was replaced by the lulling sound of the water against the rocks and the calls of birds. My shoulders relaxed. My stomach unclenched. Nothing bad could happen here, in this beautiful paradise. Right?

I turned to tell Jake to come look but didn't see him in the room. Stepping back inside, I saw the light in the bathroom was on.

"Jake?" I called, my voice echoing in the empty room.

"In here," he said, and I started toward the bathroom. "Wait. How squeamish are you?"

Alarm bells rang in my head.

The bathroom was a gleaming expanse of tile and marble and glass. My gaze swept across the room and rested on the pair of pants on the floor. A few feet beyond the pants, Jake sat on the tile ledge of the bathtub wearing his shirt and boxers. A ribbon of red drifted down his leg, and my breath caught as my mind registered that it was blood flowing down his leg, pooling on the cool marble floor.

CHAPTER NINETEEN

I swayed for a second, my head spinning at the sight of the blood, his blood. Then instincts took over and I rushed toward him, grabbing a towel on my way. I kneeled next to him and pressed it to his thigh.

"How long have you been bleeding like this?"

His face blanched, and his body tensed, so I eased up on the pressure. My hands shook as the red seeped through the thick towel almost instantly.

Jake groaned, and I looked up at him He didn't look well—his eyes were closed and his face was pale. A thin sheen of sweat dotted his forehead, and though the cabin was humid, this was clearly from the injury. He shook his head. "Not long. Walking up the trail seems to have started it again."

"Hold this," I said, taking his hand and putting it on the towel. "Keep the pressure on it."

I wiped my hands on another towel then looked in the cabinet under the sink, hoping to find something else to stop the bleeding. I pulled a small first aid kit from under the sink and opened it, taking a quick inventory. A full box of butterfly bandages would help, as would the nonstick gauze, adhesive tape, and antibacterial gel. A full bottle of hydrogen peroxide sat behind it.

Returning to Jake, I dropped to my knees next to him and poured some peroxide onto a washcloth. I pulled the saturated towel from his leg and saw the blood was flowing, but more slowly. Unsure of the water quality, I rinsed his wound with the peroxide and pressed a fresh corner of the towel against it. Sitting back on my heels, I watched the color return to Jake's face.

"How deep is it, do you think?" I asked.

"Not too deep. If I were home, I'd go to the emergency room for stitches," he said.

"We have butterfly bandages, gauze, and tape. I think we can get you patched up for tonight, go to a hospital in the morning." I rummaged through the kit and found a sample pack of pain reliever and then handed the pills to him.

When the bleeding had slowed enough, I used the wet washcloth to clean his leg. Dylan should burn in hell for many reasons, but not the least was marring what had been a perfect thigh. Even with the scar, it would still rank among the world's best legs—thickly muscled, golden skin. I exhaled slowly and focused on the injury and tried to ignore how intimate the contact felt.

The wound was about three inches in length, but clean. I didn't think it was as shallow as he thought, but between the two of us, we managed to squeeze it closed enough to secure the butterfly bandages over it. I smeared the skin with a generous glop of antibacterial gel and then taped a square of the gauze over the cut.

Jake flexed his leg to check how secure the gauze was, and I wiped the blood from the floor and threw the towels into the bathtub. It still looked like a murder scene, and I hoped that

Gerta and Klaus wouldn't hold it against us. They seemed like nice people, and I hated to make more work for them.

"I'll take the towels to the laundry," Jake said, standing.

I scrambled up off the floor, worried that he was back on his feet so quickly, but he seemed steady as a rock once again. He bent and picked up the jeans from the floor, and a smear of blood remained on the floor. He threw the pants in the bathtub with the towels.

"Take off your clothes," he said.

"Whoa. What?" I said, my head spinning. I wasn't necessarily opposed, but this wasn't the seduction scene I'd been imagining.

"They're covered in my blood," he said, a slight smile at the edge of his eyes.

"Right," I said, nodding toward the door. "I need to take a shower anyway. Then you can have my clothes."

And probably anything else you want, too.

He paused, staring at me in a way that made me wonder if I weren't already naked, then he gave me a quick nod and turned and walked out of the bathroom. I closed the door behind him and hung up one of the plush white bathrobes on the hook near the walk-in shower. I stripped out of my clothes and dropped them in the bathtub with the rest of the laundry, and stepped around the glass-bricked wall into the shower. Under the jets of warm water, the tension that had almost faded away on the balcony finally left my shoulders. I rolled my head and felt the stress melt away and exhaustion creep in.

When had I slept last, really slept? It felt like days or weeks or maybe even nearly two years since I'd had a night where I hadn't woken from a bad dream, only to find I was waking to a nightmare. I closed my eyes and let the hot water run down my scalp, down my body, letting it wash away the nightmares and the tension.

After twenty minutes of sheer bliss, I stepped out of the

shower and wrapped myself in the thick robe. Jake had left the duffel bag on the floor by the bathroom door, and I found the comb and toothbrush and other toiletries. The combination of the warm shower and the fact that I felt safe for the first time in days was lulling me to sleep, even while I stood in the cool bathroom.

While I was in the shower the sun had set, and the main room was lit only by a small lamp by the side of the bed. Jake was gone. So were my clothes—again. The man had no compunction about walking into the bathroom while I was showering. He'd taken the bloody towels and clothes from the tub and the rest of my clothing in the duffel bag, which had reeked of briny diesel. I wasn't going to complain about this theft. Especially since he had made the bed before he left with the laundry.

I lay down on the bed and sank into the soft expanse and closed my eyes. As soon as I was horizontal, a million thoughts, worries, and fears raced through my mind. How were we going to get out of Belize and get home? What if Dylan was setting us up and when we went to the bank tomorrow, he was there? Was he bluffing about the threat to Aunt Marie? What was going on at home? Was everyone I cared for safe?

The adrenaline coursed through my veins, and I fought the impulse to get up and pace the small cabin to burn off the energy. Instead, I forced myself to take a few deep breaths, and keep still, and try and get back to that state of exhaustion that I had felt minutes earlier. Eventually my mind cleared, and the sounds of the jungle filtering through the screened windows lulled me into a light sleep.

A soft click brought me back with a start, and I sat up. I blinked as my eyes adjusted to the dim light. Jake walked through the door with hardly a limp, carrying a tray in his hands. He gave me a smile that made my heart race.

"I stole your clothes," he said with a devilish grin. He was obviously feeling better.

"I'm not surprised." My heart thumped, and my exhaustion faded at the sight of him.

"I threw everything in the washing machine."

"Thank you."

I sat on the edge of the bed, unsure where to go. I was very much aware that under the heavy plush robe, I was completely naked. Jake set the tray down on the table.

"How long was I asleep?" I asked, my head still a little foggy.

He smiled. "Not quite two hours."

"Where were you?"

"Chatting with our hosts. Gerta sent some food and champagne."

Oh, that was going to help me get my hormones under control.

"I'm going to take a shower. You should eat something."

Jake disappeared behind the shuttered doors, and I heard the water run in the shower. My mind flashed on an image of him standing under the water, and my entire body throbbed. God, I had to get ahold of my libido. It had been off on sabbatical for the past year and a half but was back with a vengeance. I fell back on the bed and stared at the canopy and tried unsuccessfully not to imagine what was happening on the other side of the wall.

The water stopped, and the absence of noise shook me out of my daydream. I stood and stretched and then walked to the small table. Gerta's tray was perfect for a honeymooning couple —a bottle of chilled champagne nestled in ice, alongside a bowl of berries and fruit. I popped a piece of melon into my mouth, closed my eyes, and nearly groaned at the sweetness melting on my tongue.

I opened my eyes to see Jake standing in the doorway to

the bathroom, his eyes dark and intensely focused on me. I swallowed as I took in his bare chest and the contrast between his tan skin and the white towel around his waist. *Lord*. The man was built. And confident enough to walk around nearly naked.

He took several long steps toward me, and I stood, frozen in place, unable to take my gaze from his eyes.

"I've never seen anyone more appreciative of good food," he said, reaching past me and picking a berry from the dish.

He tilted his head and moved even closer. My eyes lowered, and I found myself staring at his chest, wide and sculpted in muscle. I took a short breath and glanced up as Jake put the berry in his mouth. As his lips closed over the fruit he licked his bottom lip, and my heart flipped in my chest. The sight was so erotic, my head felt light.

"Champagne?" he asked.

I nodded, unable to speak. Jake pulled the bottle from the ice and unfastened the wire cage, gave the cork a twist, and opened the bottle with a loud pop. While he poured two glasses, I took a step back to catch my breath. I was too close and too exposed to him—in all ways.

He followed, handing me a glass of champagne and a smile that could melt glaciers. The room felt hotter now, as if the warm breeze had stopped and an unseen thermostat was raised. I sipped the bubbly, but it tasted dry in my mouth. I set the glass down and tried to ignore how my hands trembled.

"Can you help me with something?" Jake asked.

"Sure, yeah," I said, turning to him.

"The gauze needs to be replaced," he said.

I nodded, still unsure of my voice.

"I'll get the first-aid kit," he said, turning back to the bathroom. When he returned, he was wearing the white bathrobe that matched mine.

Thank God, I nearly whispered. The sight of so much of his skin was doing terrible things to my self-control.

He pulled out a chair and sat, raising his right leg and resting it on the other chair. I flipped on a lamp near the window to get some light. He drew the fabric up and revealed the butterfly bandages still holding the wound closed. I held the lamp closer and looked for any signs of a growing infection, but the skin was cool to the touch and not swollen.

Bending his knee to allow me to see the wound, he gave me a smile. "Are the bandages still in place?"

I nodded. "Mostly. I'll replace the one that came loose."

He shook the bandages out of the first-aid kit and handed one to me, our fingers brushing. Even that brief contact sent a shot of heat through me. Touching his warm, clean-scented skin wasn't helping either. I quickly fastened the bandage, checked for any bleeding then smoothed a clean square of gauze over the cut, and secured it with the adhesive tape.

Jake poured more champagne. The few sips I'd taken were going to my head. Or it could have been the effect of being close to a half-naked Jake.

"You bounced back from a knife wound pretty quick," I said.

"It wasn't that bad," he said. "I was worried about infection after being in the water, but it bled so much it probably washed itself out."

The thought of his blood on the floor made my stomach flip.

"How are you holding up?" he asked, sitting in one of the upholstered chairs by the French doors.

I perched on the other, still uncomfortable around him, and reassembled the first aid kit to keep my hands busy.

"I'm fine," I said, lying through my teeth.

He stared at me, his eyes boring into mine with a dark intensity that made my nerves jump. "You were kidnapped at gunpoint at breakfast, shot at and kidnapped at lunchtime, and then in the middle of a gun battle at the marina in the afternoon."

All true and it explained my exhaustion. "It was a busy day," I said, trying for a weak laugh.

His lips twitched into a slight smile, and I found my eyes focused there. The tiny amount of alcohol in my system seemed to do away with all my self-control.

"Can I ask you something?"

I dragged my attention from his lips to his eyes, which had turned serious. I nodded, swallowed, and tried to focus.

"How long were you with Dylan?"

A bucket of icy water couldn't have done a better job of extinguishing the mood. I frowned and leaned back in the chair, crossing my arms in front of me. "More than four years. Why?"

I knew I sounded defensive but didn't care. I had no idea Dylan was a sociopath who was using me to launder dirty money. He was well educated, from a good family, had a good job. He had good taste in music and books and movies. There were no signs.

Or were there? I'd been dredging my memory trying to come up with anything that should have warned me away from Dylan. We'd met at work and had similar interests and education, though his was from an Ivy League school paid for by his parents. I'd waited tables and taken out loans to get through a state university. Within a few months of working at Patterson Tinker, we were dating, and then we were both asked to apply for a promotion. Dylan had gotten the job, but was outraged on my behalf.

"It should have gone to you. You do more work than anyone else, and you do it better," he'd insisted.

That was true. At the time I had been upset that I hadn't gotten the recognition, but I wouldn't let Dylan refuse the promotion, which he had offered to do. Eventually, I'd been promoted, too. Now I wondered if that's just how people like him operated. He knew exactly what to say to me to get what he wanted. He'd played me perfectly.

I looked up to see Jake watching me, his face impassive and quiet.

"When was the last time you saw him?"

"Before today? He came to the bakery a few weeks ago, said he'd try to help me find a job," I said. "And before that, when he broke off our engagement. After I was arrested."

I couldn't tell if he believed me, and suddenly it was vital that he did.

"I had no idea he was a sociopath," I said.

"That's how they work," Jake said.

We sat in silence for a few minutes, the only sound the muted jungle noises filtering through the windows.

"Did he tell you how much money is in the accounts?"

Dylan hadn't, but between what Bill had said and the patterns of deposits and transfers, I had a pretty good idea of what was in there.

"Dylan didn't say. Bill thought there was enough money for him to start a new life," I said.

Jake's eyes narrowed slightly. "But he didn't say how much?"

I shook my head. "No. The spreadsheets show just over ten thoussnd dollars."

Was I being deceitful by not telling him what I'd figured out? I was pretty sure of the patterns I'd seen, and if my math was right, there was about ten to twelve million dollars sitting in the account. It wouldn't cover all of the investors' losses, but it might convince them to settle the case. That happened all the time, right? Both sides gave a little to get the matter resolved. The people suing would recover some of their money in return for not dragging out the litigation for years and having some certainty that they'd recover some of their losses.

"You're not telling me everything," he said. His voice wasn't accusatory, just matter-of-fact.

I sighed. "There's a pattern of deposits. It looks automated. But the withdrawals are random, so I think they were done by Bill or someone working with him."

"How much do you think is in the account?"

"Maybe twelve million," I said.

He went silent and leaned back in the chair, studying me intently in the dim light.

"Tell me everything Bill said," he said.

I settled in, tugged the robe around me and recounted everything I could remember Bill said as he drove me around Belize City. Jake sat still and absorbed the story, his face impassive.

"How is your sister going to take the news that Bill's dead?" I asked.

A quick flash of emotion crossed his face—guilt, sorrow. It was gone before I could parse it.

"The divorce wasn't amicable, but they were being civil for the children. They'd reached a pretty good place, I think. It won't be easy for her. Molly cares deeply for him, which is why she wanted me to go find him."

"I'm sure she never thought it would lead to all this," I said, suddenly feeling guilty for dragging him into my mess.

He frowned. "I'm sure you didn't, either."

I looked away, toward the screened window. I should have been home by now, the money safely in my offshore account waiting to get distributed to the victims' lawyers so the lawsuit could be dismissed. My only concern should be explaining to Rob how it was I came to find the stolen funds. Instead, I was deep in the jungle running from Dylan and God knows who else. I wasn't even on the right continent.

Jake shifted, and a slight groan escaped his lips. I stood and headed toward the bathroom. "There's more pain reliever in the first-aid kit. I'll get it."

He stood and shook his head. "It's fine, don't worry about it."

We were standing close to each other, close enough that our bodies were almost touching. The air between us was charged. His eyes were intent on mine, his gaze dark and dangerous. The naked desire there robbed me of breath, and I wondered if it was his emotion or my own being mirrored back to me. I lowered my eyes, bringing my gaze level to Jake's chest. The robe gaped open and exposed a wide, well-muscled chest. My fingers itched to slide beneath the terry cloth and across the warm skin.

A long moment passed, and I exhaled slowly, trying to calm my nerves and my pulse.

"I'm sorry you had to go through all this. I'm sorry for my part in it."

I shook my head. "You couldn't have known that Bill had a gun."

He reached up and smoothed my hair away from my face, and the touch made me shiver all over.

"That's not what I meant," he said, his voice deep. "I mean for all of this. The arrest. The trial. All of it."

I stood still and let the words sink in.

"It's not your fault." I didn't know what else to say. "Dylan set me up. He pulled all these strings. I was engaged to the man, and I never suspected he had a hand in this."

Jake leaned in and kissed the top of my head in a gesture so tender a piece of my heart melted away.

"He's not going to get away with it," he said.

"He threatened my aunt. He said that he'd tell every cartel member where she lived," I said, my voice betraying my panic.

Jake tilted my chin until I looked him in the eye.

"I won't let him hurt you or your aunt."

Standing there, in his arms, even in the middle of a jungle

where we knew no one and could trust no one—and I had never felt safer.

Jake continued smoothing away my tangled hair and then cupped my face in his large hand. He leaned down then stopped, and my heart skipped a beat.

I kept my eyes on his, waiting for him to move in closer. The heat between us grew, and the air seemed heavier. His thumb caressed my cheek, but he didn't lean in closer.

I reached up and ran my fingers up his chest, to his neck, across the scruff on his face. His jaw tensed as my hand brushed against his hair. It was as soft as I had imagined it, the damp strands sliding through my fingers. My breath caught. I pulled him closer, finding little resistance until his lips were inches from mine.

"No," he said, his hoarse voice whispered.

"What?" I blinked.

"You're upset," he said, resting his forehead against mine. "I don't want to—"

Oh, damn it. I had never wanted anything in my life like I wanted him at that moment. And he was going to go and be decent and a gentleman? Not if I had anything to say about it.

"I'm not so upset that I don't know what I want," I whispered.

He inhaled and shifted, and I could feel he wanted me, too. "Miranda," he said after a moment. "I can't take adv—"

"Take advantage of me?" I asked, pulling away just far enough to reach down and tug at the belt of my robe. I shrugged it from my shoulders and felt it fall at my feet. Jake's sharp intake of breath was the only sound in the room. The cool air touched my skin, but the look he gave me made me flush hot. "I want this. I want you. More than anything."

A deep growl, and then he reached for my face again, this time kissing me deeply, our tongues meeting and breath mingling. My body arched as if possessed, and my heart thudded. He lifted me easily, and I was suddenly beneath him on the bed, his weight pinning me to the soft coverlet.

"Your leg," I said, remembering the injury.

His face was buried in my neck, and I felt him smile, and he began kissing a trail down my body igniting a thousand fires on my skin as each nerve reacted to his touch. When he responded, his voice was dark and deep with passion. With promise.

"It doesn't hurt so bad that I don't know what I want."

CHAPTER TWENTY

My skin tingled under Jake's lips, and my heart raced. I closed my eyes as he kissed my collarbone, his hand skimming my side, inching up slowly from my waist. His skin was warm where my hands touched, and I could feel the tension just below the surface.

His lips burned a path up my neck as his hand moved around and spanned my back, hot and solid, pinning me to him. Our lips met again, and my body reacted instinctively, arching and pressing against Jake. I heard him moan at the contact, and the sound was nearly enough to push me over the edge.

"Jesus, Miranda," he whispered, his lips next to my ear. The sound of my name on his lips was an aphrodisiac of its own. The blood pounded in my head, nearly drowning out everything else.

Slowly, it dawned that the pounding sound was external, not internal.

The door to the cabin nearly vibrated with the force of someone pounding on it. Jake leapt off the bed, and the sharp intake of breath that followed indicated he'd forgotten about his injured leg.

"Mr. Barnes," Klaus yelled from the other side of the door and pounded again.

In the darkened room, I could barely make out the outline of Jake at the door. He opened it, and Klaus started to enter, glanced in my direction and saw me clutching the robe around my body, then stepped back out of my view.

"You have to leave."

"What?"

Jake's incredulous and angry tone triggered my brain to go on high alert. I had no idea how long we'd been kissing. Why were we being evicted?

"I brought your clothes. You have to leave. Now."

Jake took a laundry basket from the innkeeper and dropped it on the floor next to him, but made no move toward the pile of clothes. I slipped the bathrobe on and joined Jake at the door.

"What's going on?" I asked.

Even in the dim light, Klaus's blush was apparent.

"Sorry, miss," he said. "Whoever you're running from, they've found you."

Jake swore, and I grabbed the laundry and headed to the bathroom to get dressed. Through the closed door, I could hear Jake and Klaus talking, but their voices were muffled. I splashed some water on my face. The door slammed, and a moment later Jake burst into the bathroom.

He pulled his clothes out of the laundry basket and dropped the robe, standing next to me wearing only his boxers. My mouth went dry at the sight, but I shook myself and kept throwing items into the duffel bag.

"What happened?" I asked, adding the first-aid kit to the duffel bag.

"They heard a call over a radio. Someone saw the car on the road before we turned off to get here," he said, pulling a shirt over his head. "He's going to hide the car."

"How will we get out of here?"

"We're taking their Jeep. I told him we'll leave it at the airport. He can say we stole it, deny seeing us or helping us."

"Why are the police looking for us? Because we didn't go to the hospital like we said?"

Jake paused and shook his head. "It's not the police looking for us. It's probably Bill's clients. I just know that Klaus doesn't want to get on their bad side, and us being here is too risky for them."

I shivered and sat on the edge of the tub and shoved my bare feet into my sneakers. The shoes were still damp from the dive off the pier. Jake shook out a pair of pants and started to put them on, but I stopped him to check the bandage on his leg.

"It's fine," he said. "Do you have everything?"

I nodded. "Where are we going now?"

Jake threw the last of our belongings in the bag and zipped it.

"To the airport and then back to the States," Jake said.

It sounded good. It sounded really good. The thought of seeing Aunt Marie, my tiny apartment, the sweet fragrance of the bakery—it made my heart soar. But I'd be giving up, abandoning my mission. Going home to the same situation, still outcast and unemployed. But even more broke.

"But the money—" I started.

He strode forward and put his hands on my shoulders. "Miranda, it's too dangerous."

He bent down and kissed me briefly. The soft touch of his lips was reassuring, but didn't dull the edge of the disappointment slicing through me.

Jake picked up the bag, and I followed him out of the cabin.

A few minutes later we were driving away in the borrowed hard-topped Jeep—not in the direction we had come, but continuing past the Gaia Lodge with directions from Klaus. He insisted we couldn't go back on the main road in, but we were in for a long, slow drive to meet up with a road that would eventually get us back to Belize City. The road was rutted, but the Jeep handled it better than the small car Jake had stolen. When we left, the sky above the treetops was a deep black as we left, but had slowly turned to a dark grey as we crept along the trail that would lead us to a main road, which would take us back to the city.

As we jostled over tree roots, I studied Jake in the light from the dashboard. His dark hair was as tousled as when he'd jumped out of bed, and the scruff of his two-days growth of beard gave him a dangerous look. He glanced at me and caught me staring and gave me a smile.

"You alright?" he asked, turning his attention back to the path we were driving on.

"Yes, fine." The more removed we were from the encounter in the cabin, the more uncomfortable I became.

"You want to talk about anything?" he asked.

My mind flashed on an image of him, of us, last night. My face flushed hot. Did I want to talk about that? No, not really. But I also didn't want to leave him with the wrong idea about me.

"Yeah, about last night. I just want you to know, that's pretty unusual for me. Very unusual," I blurted out.

"Oh," Jake said. He gave me a quick glance before turning back to the road in front of us.

"I mean, after Dylan broke up with me, I wasn't really in good place to start dating again, you know? And I'd been with Dylan for four years."

"Uh huh," he said, turning the wheel to avoid a broken branch that lay across our path.

"What I'm trying to say is, I'm not usually so, uh, forward," I said.

The Jeep came to a sudden stop, and Jake pulled the brake

up between the seats. He turned to me, his face serious, and reached over, putting his hand on the side of my face, which was growing hotter by the second. My eyes widened at his touch.

"That's too bad," he said. "I liked how forward you were last night."

He pulled me closer and kissed me, slowly and deliberately, igniting a fire within that threatened to consume me. When he pulled away, I was breathless. Jake kept his hand at my neck, his thumb stroking my jaw. A small smile hovered over his lips.

"I don't know what's going to happen when we get back to the States," he said, his dark eyes locked on mine. "But I'd like to have a date that didn't involve guns or car chases. You up for that?"

I nodded, and he kissed me again, sending my head spinning.

"Anything else you want to talk about?"

I shook my head, unable to find my voice, and the slight smile hovering around his lips grew. "Good."

He released the emergency brake and put the car in gear, and we lurched forward on the rutted trail in silence.

We inched along the route for what seemed like hours. The road smoothed out after a while, and by the time the sky turned to a light grey, we turned onto a paved road. Jake reached across me and opened the glove box, taking out a map that he handed to me.

"Klaus traced the route to Belize City," he said.

I opened the map, the kind that tourists would use to get around on vacation, and saw the red ink outlining the roads to take us out of the jungle. I pointed out the next turn and studied the landscape passing the window. The thick, dark green canopy over the road shaded us from the early morning light. It was still cool, probably the coolest part of the day, but the air was humid and heavy with the promise of another hot day.

"When we find a place that's open, we'll get something to eat," Jake said.

My stomach grumbled in agreement, and I realized that the fruit from last night was the last food I'd had.

"Isn't Matt Reese expecting us to transfer the money?" I asked, turning back to Jake. He continued to keep his eyes on the road, but his jaw tensed.

"Yes, but he's going to be disappointed," he said. "Even if we wanted to, we don't have a computer to look at the drive and get the information for the accounts."

"I don't need a computer. The accounts are in my name. I have my passport. I can go in and transfer the funds. That's why Bill kidnapped me. It's why Dylan groomed Katrina to look like me."

Jake was silent for a moment, and I thought he was just going to ignore me. When he spoke, he sounded doubtful.

"Even if we could get access to the money, where would we transfer it to? I've lost that piece of paper with the government's account number."

"To the account I set up in the Caymans. Or the government's account. I remember the number. Whichever one they'll accept for the transfer."

He shook his head.

"You set up an account? Jesus—forget the money, Miranda. It's not worth it."

"We have an opportunity to help the hundreds of people who lost their money and may end a huge money laundering scheme. We can't walk away."

"Yes, we can. If we stay too long here, we're just asking to get shot."

"Then we'll be quick. It won't take me long at all to transfer the money at the bank. We can be there when they open."

"We'll give the information to Matt, and he can open a case. This is what he and the FBI do. Just let them do their jobs."

I sat back in my seat and crossed my arms. By the time the FBI had the information, the money would be gone. We both knew it. The scheme would be dismantled and reassembled under other names, in other banks, and would carry on as usual.

The Jeep rounded a gentle curve and three buildings perched in a row along the side of the road appeared. One had a rusty gas pump in front, and Jake pulled off the road and parked behind the small station.

"Stay here. I'll see if they have anything to eat."

I got out of the Jeep to stretch my cramped legs. Pacing the few feet between the building and the Jeep, I tried to figure out the best course of action now. If we went directly to the airport and Matt was able to get us out of Belize, we'd be in the States by the end of the day. Game over. No money for the Sahara Fund investors. No chance of redemption for me.

But he was right—the odds of getting shot at again were considerably lower. The money would get frozen by the U.S. government, if it could reach Belize accounts through that country's strict bank secrecy laws. Though with the sums I had seen on Bill's spreadsheet, I figured that a well-placed bribe could buy access to the accounts, even without the back-up drive and spreadsheet with account numbers and names.

I was so close to doing what I came here to do. All I needed was to get to the bank. Jake's fears weren't unfounded, but how much delay could it cost us to stop there on the way to the airport? If there was ten million dollars in those accounts, the investors could get about one-quarter of their money back, and that would go a long way to repaying them. Maybe enough to get them to drop the lawsuit. And I would be able to show who was really in charge of the scheme and finally prove that I had nothing to do with it.

I was lost in my thoughts, staring at the lush green landscape beyond the dusty driveway, when Jake walked around the corner, startling me.

"Coffee?" he asked, holding up a paper cup.

I nodded and took it, inhaling the scent of the dark brew. "Just what I need."

He held up a brown paper bag. "Breakfast?"

My stomach rumbled, and my mouth nearly watered at the scent. My resolve to fight to go to the bank wavered as I considered the food in his hand. *Damn.* He certainly knew how to distract me.

We sat in the Jeep with the doors open and ate the tortillas filled with beans and rice without speaking. The dark, smoky coffee lifted my mood slightly, but the rumble of a car passing on the street brought me back to the gravity of our situation. Jake tensed, too, and looked in the direction of the truck, which limped along the empty road and continued past the three buildings without stopping.

I exhaled and lost a bit of my appetite. Jake's cell phone rang from the center console, and I jumped again. I wasn't cut out for life on the run.

"Hey, Matt. We had a complication, so we're heading to the airport early."

I wadded up the paper bag and napkins from breakfast and looked for a garbage can. Seeing none, I tossed the trash into the back of the Jeep while Jake listened to Matt Reese on the other end of the phone call.

"No. Absolutely not. It's too dangerous."

I studied him, his tense jaw, his furrowed brow. His lips tightened, and he turned on the speaker on the phone.

"—If there's a chance to get this wrapped up now, I think we should do it," Matt said.

Jake shook his head. "Matt, listen. We've got trouble

following us now. Just get us on a plane and get us out. Freeze the funds from the States. Send down reinforcements later. But I've got a citizen here who has been targeted. I'm getting her out."

The line was silent, and I froze at the dark tone in Jake's voice. When Matt replied, the tension in his voice carried across the cellular connection.

"That won't work," Matt said.

"Why not?" I asked.

"Uh, Miss Vaughn?" He sounded flustered to hear my voice.

"Yes, it's me. Why won't you be able to freeze the funds from there? I can bring you the flash drive. It has all the information."

"Because this is a narrow window of opportunity. If what Jake has told me is accurate, this is a small crack in the organization. They've screwed up, and that hasn't happened before. If we don't jump on their mistake now, we won't have that chance again."

I glanced at Jake who shook his head slowly.

"Miss Vaughn, how much money is in the accounts?" Matt asked.

"I have no way of knowing for sure, but the spreadsheets indicate that there could be anything from a few thousand dollars to a few million in the two accounts that are in my name," I said. "The information is out of date, though. It's at least three weeks old, and there could be others who have access to the account list. Or they could bribe someone to get access. A lot of money has flowed through the different accounts, and there's a pattern, so some of the transfers might be automatic."

"They've already found you once, at the marina. If they're that desperate to get the drive, they need it," Matt said. "I think there may be more money there than you think."

For the first time, Matt Reese and I were on the same page.

"Look, I can't get a plane to you until early afternoon at the soonest. Maybe one p.m., if we're lucky. You've got time to get to the bank, do this, and then get to the airport. If you run into trouble, call my contact at the embassy."

Jake rubbed his forehead. "I don't like this plan."

"You don't have to like it, but it's your job, Barnes. Miranda, are you okay with this?"

"Yes. As long as the money goes to the Sahara Fund investors."

"It will," he said. "Bring that drive back with you. I need that. If it's what you say it is, it will be crucial to convicting those involved and shutting down the entire network. Can you do that?"

"I've protected it so far," I said, glancing back at the duffel bag on the back seat where I'd tucked it into an inside pocket.

"Jake, take me off speaker."

Jake grabbed the phone, and Matt's side of the conversation was lost to me. Jake made a few monosyllabic responses and disconnected. He stared straight ahead, the hand gripping the phone resting on his knee.

"Does Matt trust me now?" I asked.

He turned to me. "No. Not even a little. But he wants this case under his belt."

"Why did you change your mind about going to the bank?"

"I didn't. This is a stupid idea. But it's not my call now."

He pulled the door shut and reached for his seat belt, so I did the same. He started the Jeep, gripped the steering wheel tightly, and steered us out of the dirt lot and onto the road.

"Can I ask why you called Matt Reese in the first place? Back when we were in Macau, I mean."

He was quiet for a few moments then glanced at me. "I thought you were up to something."

I looked away, the deep green scenery outside my window blurring as my eyes filled with tears. Of course he had assumed that. Hadn't everyone? At least everyone with a gun and a badge. I blinked away the stinging tears and turned back to the road in time to see a sign indicating a turn to Belize City.

Jake navigated the turn, and the road widened. We'd be in the city shortly after the bank opened, I estimated studying the map in my lap. Then I'd do my part to help Jake and Matt take down the scheme.

And then? I really didn't want to think about that. I'd been pinning my hopes on starting over, but was that even possible?

CHAPTER TWENTY-ONE

We pulled up to the bank, and Jake parked the Jeep on the street near a corner. The bank was in the middle of the block. It stood out from the surrounding buildings, a newer and more modern construction amidst its squat stuccoed neighbors.

Jake turned off the engine and leaned toward me.

"You remember the account number?"

I nodded. "I just go in and transfer the money there?"

"That's all. Are you all right?"

"Sure, yeah." My stomach was a jumbled mass of nerves, but I squared my shoulders and swallowed hard. "I can do it."

Just walk into the largest bank in the country and transfer millions of dollars that didn't belong to me.

No problem.

I slid to the door and opened it, stepping out onto the side-walk. Then I leaned back in. "You're going to be here when I come out, right?"

He smiled, and my heart fluttered, ever hopeful.

"I'm not leaving without you."

I shut the door and turned to the bank. The sight of the armed guard in front of the wide double doors nearly caused my heart to stop. Instead, I pasted a smile on my face and walked into the lobby, trying to project confidence, despite the fact that I could still feel my shoes squishing slightly from my impromptu swim yesterday.

The reception desk at the front of the bank was marble and brass, while the woman behind it seemed made of plastic.

"Hello, I need to access my accounts," I said.

The woman, probably in her mid-twenties and yet to see a bad hair day, looked me up and down and then raised her chin several centimeters.

"*Un momento, por favor*," she said.

She walked away, her three-inch heels clicking on the marble floor. Minutes passed in the silent lobby, the only sound was the echo of blood rushing through my veins as my blood pressure skyrocketed. Finally, the receptionist returned with a tall, thin man in a suit.

"*Buenas dias*, I am Hector Tomás, accounts manager. How may I help you?"

"Good afternoon, my name is Miranda Vaughn. I have a couple accounts with the bank. I need to transfer some funds from my accounts."

Señor Tomás tilted his head slightly, regarded me with a guarded expression, and he nodded politely. "Ah, yes, Miss Vaughn. Of course, follow me."

He led me through the bank, which was unlike a community bank. There was no counter where tellers stood to help customers. Instead, there was a long room with seating areas next to dark wooden desks. They were separated by low walls topped with tropical plants. Most of the desks had an employee at them, but only a few had customers in front of them.

"Can I get you something to drink? Coffee? Tea?" he asked with a smile.

"No, thank you."

"I expected to see you yesterday," he said.

My heart pounded so loudly I wouldn't be surprised if he heard it. I made a noncommittal sound and kept my gaze straight ahead. Señor Tomás led me to a desk at the end of the room and pulled out a chair for me. He settled into his chair and leaned forward across the desk.

"You wish to transfer some funds?" he said, his softly accented voice low in the quiet room.

"Yes, from two accounts. I'd like to transfer the balance and then close the accounts," I said, withdrawing my passport, which still felt slightly damp at the center where the pages were bound together. I hoped he didn't notice that as I passed it to him.

"Thank you, Miss Vaughn," he said, turning to the computer and typing in my name. "Yes, yes, I see you have two linked accounts with us. That should make it easier to transfer the funds. We'll only have to do one transfer."

"Will you be able to transfer the funds today?"

He nodded. "Yes, we can do that. Provided you have the account number for the receiving bank account."

I took a piece of paper from the man's desk and the pen he offered and wrote the twenty-two digit code on it. He gave me an unsettled look as he took the paper and then turned back to the computer.

He typed in some additional information and then gave me an odd look.

"I'm afraid this account does not have any funds in it, Miss Vaughn," he said.

My heart skipped a beat, but I nodded, trying to appear calm. "Yes, that's why I want to close it. Can you check the other account, please?"

Señor Tomás turned back to the screen and typed in more commands. My thoughts were a whirled mess of worries. If there weren't any funds to transfer, this adventure to Belize was all for nothing. Maybe we should have gone directly to the airport and jumped on the first flight out of the country.

Señor Tomás looked up, his face stricken. His eyes widened, and his mouth moved without making a sound. The pen slipped from his fingers onto the desk.

"You wish to transfer all of it, Miss Vaughn?" the bank manager asked.

"Yes."

He paled visibly and reached up to his collar as if he were choking.

"All one hundred eighty-six million dollars?"

Did he say one hundred eighty-six million? My instinct was to gasp, but I merely smiled and reminded my body to keep breathing, my heart to keep beating. *A hundred and eighty-six million dollars? That must be a mistake.*

"I mean, when you called a few days ago, I was happy to do the housekeeping you requested on the other accounts," Señor Tomás said, his voice dropping even lower in volume. "But I—I mean, I didn't know you were closing the accounts."

My head spun, but I kept a neutral expression and nodded. "There was a change in plans."

He swallowed. "I see."

His pen trembled in his hand as he copied down the exact figure from his computer screen.

$186,009,886.22, U.S. dollars.

I exhaled slowly and tried to slow my racing pulse. That was far more than I thought there'd be, and it sounded like Katrina had called ahead to make that happen. The thought of that much money was hard to wrap my head around, and I'd worked in finance and had overseen the transfer of huge sums before. But that had been expected at an investment house, and it was just digits on a computer screen or a page. This was different. I was taking this from some really bad people.

Señor Tomás turned back to the computer, and a bead of sweat ran down the right side of his face, despite the air-conditioned climate in the bank. "Where are we transferring this to, ma'am?"

I reached up and retrieved the paper with the government account number on it, then slid the paper back toward me. With a slightly shaky hand, I took a pen from the holder on the desk.

"There's been another slight change in plans," I said.

CHAPTER TWENTY-TWO

I kept my head down as I walked out of the bank, hurrying to the Jeep at the curb. There was no reason to rush, but I couldn't shake the feeling that Señor Tomás might chase after me to get back the money I'd just moved. This was drug money, or it was from the sales of illegal weapons, or lord knows what. And the people who had earned it with their crimes would want it back.

Was Dylan's plan to move it to keep the scheme operating? Bill had said he was taking just enough to get by in his new life, a chance he never got to take. Well, there had been plenty in the accounts to go around—if the cartel or the mob or whoever was laundering the cash under my name was in the mood to share. Which was highly unlikely.

"Everything go all right?" Jake asked as I climbed in and fastened my seatbelt.

"How fast can we get out of Belize?"

He looked over his shoulder for a break in the flow of traffic to pull away from the curb. My gaze followed his and lit on the hulking black SUV pulling up to the bank. There was something sinister about the deep tint of the windows and the way it parked in a fire zone. As we approached the corner, I saw Señor

Tomás hurry out of the bank and talk to a man in the passenger seat. He gestured in an agitated manner, and then the car pulled back into traffic.

"Uh, oh." I whirled back around in my seat.

Jake looked at me. "What?"

The back window of the Jeep exploded, and I screamed, leaning forward as far as the seatbelt would allow me. Jake steered the car around traffic and accelerated, weaving through the heavy morning traffic.

"Are you okay?"

I nodded, but I was definitely not okay. I hadn't had a good night's sleep in many days. I had been shot at far too many times. And I just transferred one hundred eighty-six million dollars that belonged, it seemed, to the angry SUV driver behind us. I was as far from okay as I'd ever been.

Jake reached into the center console and pulled out his cell phone, which he pressed into my hand. "Hit redial."

I did as he asked, and he took the phone back while still driving like a maniac.

"We're coming in!" he yelled into the phone and then took a corner on two wheels. I could do nothing but hang on to the dashboard and the armrest.

The SUV was driving on the shoulder of the highway that Jake pulled onto, gaining on us, sending cars careering off onto the side of the road to get out of the way.

"What the hell happened in there?"

"I transferred the money. I closed the accounts."

Jake swerved to avoid a slow-moving truck, and we found ourselves in the wrong lane, facing oncoming traffic. I put my hand over my eyes.

"Oh God! Oh God!"

Then the car swerved, and we were back in the right lane, speeding past a different Belize City than we'd just been in. This was a dirtier, lower-rent version, basically a strip of salvage yards, auto mechanics, and second-hand tire sales lining the four-lane road.

"Where are we going?"

"We're not messing around anymore," he said, coaxing a little more speed out of the four-cylinder engine. It wasn't going to be enough to outpace the hulking SUV behind us weaving effortlessly through the traffic.

"Are we going to the U.S. Embassy?" I asked. The thought of a phalanx of Marines was very comforting.

"No, the embassy's an hour away in Belmopan."

We zipped around a flatbed truck, passing it on the right-hand shoulder of the road.

"Then where?"

Wind from the shattered back window whipped my hair around my face.

"There's a consulate branch nearby," Jake said, his face grim. "Hold on."

I was already holding on to everything I could, so I just braced myself, unsure what was coming next. Instead of pulling back on the road in front of the flatbed truck, Jake whipped the wheel to the right, sending us through a dirt lot. The Jeep bounced and managed to stay upright, and the wheels connected with pavement on the other side of the lot, sending us jetting forward on a narrow paved road.

Behind us, I could only see a cloud of dust between us and the highway. I kept watch, waiting for the SUV to emerge from the cloud, but the road curved, and we were into the trees, blocking my view of the highway we just left.

Jake took several more turns, and then we were back on a main road, speeding toward a row of concrete buildings. I looked in both directions and saw a black SUV ahead of us and pointed it out to Jake.

He nodded, merging behind a tractor-trailer that kept us hidden from the SUV. We were tailgating the trailer so close that I could see the cobwebs on the dusty bumper dancing in the wind. I gripped the armrest and pressed my foot into the floorboard, as if that could slow us and keep us from plowing into the back of the rig.

We traveled for about a mile, Jake's eyes focused on the truck in front of us while I looked around, trying to keep the SUV in sight whenever the road had a slight curve. Finally, Jake backed off, and I breathed a sigh. He yanked the wheel to the left, sending me into the passenger side door with a thump. The sound of tires squealing filled the air, and I looked up to see a truck bearing down on my side.

Even more alarming was the SUV making an abrupt U-turn behind it.

"Hurry! Hurry!" I screamed at Jake.

The Jeep leapt forward, the sound of an infuriated truck driver's horn fading as we raced down a side street.

"We're close," Jake said. "Keep an eye on them."

I turned and saw a man hanging out of the passenger side, a gun in his hand. A large, semi-automatic gun.

"Gun!"

The spray hit the back of the Jeep and took out the side view mirror near me.

"Get down!" Jake yelled. I ducked and put my arms over my head.

The Jeep swerved again and seemed to be floating as we left the road. I looked up as we landed with a hard jolt, my head jerking back against the headrest. We slid into a parking lot lined with nondescript white vehicles, coming to rest near a gate that opened slowly as we approached.

As soon as it was open the few feet needed, Jake accelerated, guiding the Jeep into a secure parking lot. I leaned back and breathed in, taking in great gulps of air.

"Are you hit?" he asked, turning to me, putting his hand on my shoulder.

I shook my head and felt a few small pieces of glass fall from my hair. He parked the car near the building, and three men ran toward us down a short covered walkway. Two were in fatigues, the other in a suit, his tie flapping as he ran.

Jake came around and helped me out of the car. My knees nearly buckled as I got a good look at the bullet holes in the Jeep and the broken windows and the side-view mirror hanging by a knot of wires. This was no way to repay Klaus and Gerta for their hospitality.

"Special Agent Barnes, I presume," the man in a suit said, hurrying toward us. He ushered us toward the door. "Please come inside. We'll take care of this."

Jake put his arm around me as we walked quickly up the walkway, sliding doors opening as we approached, letting out a blast of air-conditioning into the humid jungle climate. The doors closed behind us with a quiet click, and I started shivering, whether from the cold or the adrenaline, I wasn't sure.

"I'm Chris Jenkins, chief of staff to the ambassador," the man said, shaking Jake's hand, then mine.

"Thank you for your help, Mr. Jenkins," Jake said. "And for the directions. We wouldn't have made it if we stayed on the main roads."

"Call me Chris, please," he said, watching us with concern. "Miss Vaughn, are you all right?"

I tried to smile, but my lips were still trembling.

"Let's get you something to drink. Some tea? Something stronger?"

The ambassador's chief of staff leaned toward me, concerned. He was young for such a responsible position, maybe in his mid-thirties. His light brown hair was thinning, and his wire-rimmed glasses made him look like a professor, rather than a diplomat.

"Tea would be nice," I said, my voice weak.

Jake still kept his arm around me as we walked deeper into the two-story building. It looked like any government office building, but was fortified with thick glass windows and a solid iron fence surrounding the building.

"Where are we?" I asked Jake, and Chris Jenkins turned and smiled.

"It's a small consulate office," he said. "The embassy is in the capitol, Belmopan, which is inland about an hour and a half from here."

He swiped an electronic card past a sensor and then opened a door leading to a wide carpeted hallway.

"Belize City is the largest population center in the country, however, so we have a satellite office here."

He swiped the card again at the elevator, and the doors opened quietly. We got in and took it to the upper floor, where it opened into another identical hall. Chris led us past several doors and into a bright, sunny office. He motioned to a sitting area, and Jake and I sat on a plush settee facing the mahogany desk.

Chris excused himself and went through another door, leaving it ajar and speaking in a low murmur to someone there. He returned and sat in an upholstered chair across a low coffee table from us.

"I've ordered some refreshments," he said, leaning forward in his chair. "Tell me what's going on."

Jake frowned. "We got ambushed outside the bank."

The way Jake jumped to that part of the story made me think they'd spoken before.

"Were you able to transfer the money?"

I looked to Jake. How much had he shared? Jake nodded, taking my hand. "Yes, Miranda moved the funds and closed the accounts."

Chris nodded, looking troubled. "Well, you clearly angered the wrong people."

"Cartel?" Jake asked.

Chris nodded again. "The bank manager probably alerted them that their money was leaving the country."

There was a soft knock on the door, and Chris stood and let in a young woman bearing a tray. We were silent as she set it up on the coffee table and then left, closing the door behind her. Once she was gone, Chris poured the tea and began talking again.

"Belize is a safe country, comparatively," he said, offering me sugar, which I declined. "Unfortunately, the cartels don't respect borders in their own clashes. We get some spillover violence from the traffickers."

I sipped my tea and tried to stop my hands from shaking.

"I can assure you, the ambassador has been notified of what's going on," Chris said, giving me a gentle smile. "You're safe here."

Nodding, I tried another smile with a little more success.

"We're arranging your transportation back to the States," he said.

"Thank you," Jake said. He sat next to me, and I could feel the tension roll off his body in waves.

Chris stood and walked back to the phone. As I watched him cross in front of the large wooden desk, my gaze fell on the nameplate perched on the desk.

Christopher A. Jenkins, Chief of Staff.

Seeing his full name written out jogged my memory, and my mouth went dry. The tea suddenly tasted like diesel. I had seen that name. It was on several of the accounts listed on the spreadsheet.

My teacup clacked noisily as I tried to set it back on the saucer. I choked, and Jake patted my back. Through watering eyes, I looked back at the man at the desk. Was he a victim of identity theft, like me? Or was he involved in the money-laundering scheme, too?

Chris looked concerned as I caught my breath, but I smiled and waved to indicate I was okay. I was anything but okay. My heart was pounding, and my palms started to sweat.

"What's wrong?" Jake asked, but I just shook my head. I couldn't say anything, not with him standing just feet away.

Chris picked up the phone and punched in a few numbers. "Yes, I have them in my office. They're safe."

He smiled as he hung up the phone.

"Are you hungry? Do you wish to change clothes? What can we do to make you comfortable while you're waiting? I can have an officer bring your bags in," he said.

His tone was friendly and sincere, and I wondered if it was merely a coincidence. Christopher Jenkins wasn't an uncommon name. Or maybe he didn't know his name was on accounts being used by the cartels. I tried to tell myself that I was being paranoid, but it wasn't working. The hair on the back of my neck was on end.

There was another knock, this time at the door that Chris had used earlier when he'd ordered the tea.

"Come in," Chris said.

The door opened, and Dylan Holland walked in. His crisp white shirt was now smudged and wrinkled as if he'd slept in it, and his normally perfect hair fell over his sunburnt forehead. His eyes held all the hate in the world. My stomach dropped at the sight.

"Hello, Miranda," he said. "You little bitch."

Jake started to stand. He stopped when Chris Jenkins withdrew a handgun from a shoulder holster.

"Stay seated, please," he said in the same tone he'd used to offer us tea.

Chris reached into his pocket and tossed Dylan something, and I recognized the flash drive as it arced through the air and into Dylan's fist.

"Found this in the duffel bag. Is that going to help you get this resolved?" he asked Dylan.

Dylan smiled, and my blood ran cold. He held in his fist the only evidence of the scope of Patterson's scheme. It was the only way for me to clear my name. Without it, I'd remain in that grey area of not guilty, but not cleared.

And Dylan's worldwide criminal enterprise was going to go on as before. Everything we'd just gone through had been in vain.

"That will get us back in business," Dylan said, turning to me. "There's just the small matter of the money that Miranda transferred."

CHAPTER TWENTY-THREE

Dylan and Chris conferred by the door that led to the hallway, eyeing Jake and me as they spoke in low tones.

Jake poured some tea for himself, the delicate porcelain cup dwarfed in his large hands. Unlike mine, his hands weren't shaking and sloshing tea all over.

"I am really starting to hate that guy," he said quietly, glancing toward the two men at the door.

I followed his gaze and silently agreed with him. What had I ever seen in that bastard?

The door opened, and a man in fatigues handed Dylan a bag, and I recognized the tan fabric of my trusted computer tote. Dylan took the bag, shut the door, and turned back to me, his eyes narrowed.

"She says it's not Bill's computer," Dylan said to Chris.

"Did you look at it?"

"It's locked." Dylan walked over to the sitting area and stopped a few feet in front of me. He threw the bag at me, and I caught it awkwardly. "If it's yours, then what's the password?"

I glared at him. "It's 'Dylan's a fucking asshole.' All lower-case, no spaces."

Dylan's face flushed even pinker all the way to the tops of his ears. His eyes narrowed. How had I ever been attracted to him? How had I not seen the pure evil below the highly polished exterior? My stomach turned at the thought that I could have been so completely deceived, ready to commit myself to this man for life.

"Doesn't matter. I have the backup and the files," he said. "If it were Bill's computer, it just would have saved me some trouble."

Chris put his hand on Dylan's arm. "We've got a tech downstairs who can crack that."

He took the bag from my lap and turned to Dylan.

"Give me the flash drive, I'll have them open that, too."

Dylan hesitated, but reached into his pocket and retrieved the drive and handed it to Chris, who looked at it with interest. "Will this do you any good without Bill?"

Dylan nodded. "Yeah, I can make the transfers. It won't be a problem."

"It better not be," Chris said. His voice was neutral, but his eyes were cold and flat. "I'll get these unlocked, but then you have to get out of here. And get them out of here."

He nodded toward us as if we were a couple pieces of unwanted furniture.

Dylan frowned. "What am I supposed to do with him?"

I glanced at Jake, his face a mask of glowering rage.

"That's your problem. You take care of it," Chris said.

The two of them walked out of the room, leaving by the door that led to the hallway. As soon as the door clicked shut, Jake was on his feet and across the room, trying the other door, which remained stubbornly locked in place.

I moved to the hall door that Dylan and Chris had just used and found it locked as well.

"Now what?" I asked.

"I need to reach Matt, but my cell phone is in the car," he said. "Check the windows, see if they'll open."

He went to one end of the office, and I went to the other, and we checked all the windows. Most were plate glass with no latches, but one overlooked the fire escape.

"Here," I said, reaching for the top of the frame.

"Wait." Jake hurried to me and examined the window carefully, then flipped the latch open. He looked down at the courtyard below, and I followed his gaze. Our now-battered Jeep was at the edge of the parking lot, near the secured gate. Guards patrolled the perimeter of the fence.

How were we going to get out of here?

Jake put a hand on my shoulder, and I looked up at him. "We're going to have to climb down there. Are you okay with heights?"

God, I hated heights. Just the thought of climbing down the flimsy-looking metal steps made my stomach do somersaults. I took a deep breath and shook my head. "Not really, but I'll get over it."

He took my hand and squeezed it. "I'll go first and catch you if you fall."

I squeezed his hand and nodded, my mouth dry with fear.

Outside the door, I heard a muffled sound in the hall. Jake dropped my hand and moved across the room, standing a few feet behind the door.

I remained at the window, unsure what to do. Jake motioned to me to move toward the couch, but before I could take a step I heard the beep of the electronic key pass.

Dylan opened the door, saw me standing by the open window and rushed forward into the room.

"Where the hell are you go—"

Jake's fist cut off Dylan's angry words, smashing into his jaw and knocking him to his knees. He fell to the carpet, and Jake followed him down, struggling to keep Dylan pinned to the ground. As they struggled, my paralysis vanished, and I glanced around for some sort of weapon, my gaze falling on a bronze bust on Chris Jenkins's desk. I ran to the desk and grabbed it with both hands, swung, and felt the satisfying thunk as it connected with the side of Dylan's head. His eyes rolled back, and his body went slack. Jake pushed Dylan's dead weight off his leg.

"Find something to tie his hands with," Jake said, rolling Dylan over and searching his pockets. He pulled out the white plastic key pass, the silver handgun, and Dylan's cell phone.

I yanked the cord out of the telephone and then helped Jake use it to tie Dylan's hands tight behind his back. Standing up, I had to fight the urge to give the unconscious man another hard kick, just for karma's sake.

"Come on, let's go," Jake said, pulling me away from Dylan's prone body.

"Did he have the drive on him?" I asked, looking back at the trussed-up figure of my former fiancé.

"No," Jake said, passing the card in front of the sensor to unlock the door. "It's probably in their computer lab. Which is probably even more secure than this room."

"But this pass might get us in there," I said. My instincts were to flee, save ourselves, get as far from the consulate as possible. But in the back of my mind there was a small stubborn voice urging me to get the drive, bring it back to the States, if there was a chance to recover it.

Jake's lips tightened, and he nodded. "I know you want it, but we have to get out of here."

He opened the door a fraction of an inch, looked out, and pulled it open. He grabbed my hand, leading me into the hallway. It was empty and quiet, but I doubted it would stay that way. The building had security like a high-tech fortress, and I was sure that included security cameras in the halls.

As we reached the end of the hall, Jake peered around the corner and then pulled me with him down the stairs. The staircase was at the rear of the building, at the opposite side from where we had entered.

"Look for an exit," he said. His voice was low, but echoed off the concrete walls.

A door slammed in the distance and I froze. Jake tugged at my arm, urging me forward. My heart pounded, and my knees were shaky as we took the last few steps to the first floor. The stairs opened to a hall lined with closed doors on one side and a windowless wall on the other. Jake looked in both directions, then headed toward to the right, still pulling me behind him, Dylan's gun in the other hand at his side.

The sound of running footsteps above our heads echoed down the stairwell. Jake swiped the white plastic security card against a sensor, and the door unlocked. He opened it slowly, then yanked me around and slammed the door. I leaned against the wall in the darkened room, listening to the chaos outside. The only light in the room came from the crack under the door.

As my eyes adjusted, I could see that we were in an empty office.

Jake moved through the room while I stayed against the wall. A shrieking alarm pierced the air, and I put my hands over my ears as a red light started flashing over the door, illuminating the room in blood red. Jake whirled toward the door, the gun steady and aimed at the still-closed door.

"Get behind me," he said, and I jumped to comply.

The screeching continued as Jake pushed me behind him. Through the noise of the alarm, I could hear running and shouting past the door. Jake moved closer and listened. I followed, staying behind him, his t-shirt gripped in my fist, as if that would keep us from getting separated.

"It's not us," he said, his head tilted toward the door. "There's something else going on."

Behind the alarm, voices rose, and the panic was unmistakable. Jake turned and tackled me, throwing both of us behind a desk. There was, at the same time, a roar—the sound of a high velocity projectile meeting tons of steel-reinforced concrete, followed closely by a concussion of an explosion that reverberated through my body. The alarm stuttered and stopped. The red light went out, and the light under the door was extinguished. And in the blackness, I detected the acrid smell of smoke.

I tried to breathe, but my nose was filled with dust and smoke, and I felt the panic rising in my chest.

"Are you okay? Miranda, look at me!" Jake's voice came to me muffled through a thick layer of cotton in my head. I opened my eyes, blinking away grit.

"Are you hurt?" he yelled.

Jake took my face in his hands, and I focused on his eyes, an anchor in the chaos. "Are you okay? Where are you hurt?"

I shook my head again, the picture coming into focus finally. An explosion. A fire.

"Fire? What—" I asked, barely hearing my own voice over the chaos, and the static, and buzzing in my ears.

"The building, probably an RPG," Jake said.

I shook my head and did a mental inventory. My head was throbbing. My ears were ringing, and though my body felt like it had been dropped off a cliff, nothing seemed broken. Jake pulled me to my feet, and we felt our way to the door.

He yanked at the door, which stuck until he put his foot against the wall for leverage. The explosion had rocked the building so hard that the doorframe had shifted, but he was able to get an opening wide enough to squeeze through. Outside the hall was empty except for an orange and brown smoke that was billowing from the front of the compound.

We hurried toward an open door at the end of the hall. Bright sunlight streamed in, mingling with the dust particles in the air, creating a beacon for us. Jake covered his mouth, and I followed suit, though it didn't help filter out the grit in the air. As we stepped out of the building and into the bright sun, we were greeted with a ghostly sight—a half-dozen people staggering in the sunlight, covered in white dust, some bleeding. I realized Jake and I were also coated in the same grime—his dark hair was grey with dust, the same grit that turned my navy t-shirt nearly white.

I turned back to the building and saw the smoke pouring from the upper floors.

Dylan was in there, I thought, with a pang of something that felt like guilt. Guilt over the man who had tried to kill me, who had destroyed my life. What was wrong with me? Maybe I was mourning the man I thought I had loved, that person who never even existed.

"We need to get out of here," Jake said, grabbing my hand and leading me toward the side of the building.

A wave of people stumbled through the opening that Jake and I had just come through, helping each other step over the broken masonry in their path. One of the camouflage-uniformed men carried a body over his shoulder like a sack and I saw the hands tied behind the back. He set the body on the ground and reached down to untie Dylan's hands, and I exhaled a long breath.

"You know he just tried to kill us both, right?" Jake asked. At the angry tone, I turned toward him. His eyes were cold and his jaw set.

"Of course I do! Just because I didn't want him to die doesn't mean I don't want him brought to justice. I want him humiliated, publicly. I want him to have to live through it—everyone knowing what he did, how he did it, what a horrible sociopath he really is. I want him alive to suffer. I want him to live a long life—in prison."

Jake paused and gave me a long stare that I couldn't interpret then nodded. "Okay, that I can live with."

He pulled me around the huge metal trash bin and crouched low. I knelt on the ground next to him.

"Stay close to me," he said, his voice low.

Crouching, we skirted the official vehicles in the parking lot, staying between the front of the row of SUVs and the concrete block wall of the first floor of the consulate office. Several times, Jake hissed at me to stay still, and I heard footsteps on gravel. In the distance, I could hear shouting. Nearby, the crackling of flames in the building. I held my breath until the footsteps faded and then followed Jake as we crept along the edge of the parking lot.

When we reached the last car, Jake nodded toward the Gaia Lodge Jeep a few feet away. "Stay here," he whispered, and snuck closer to the Jeep and peered in the window.

He looked back and nodded at me to join him. I hurried to the side of the Jeep as Jake opened the passenger door. I was half in the Jeep when I heard the crack of a shot. Jake's body slammed me into the vehicle. I turned as best I could, pinned against the seat by Jake.

"Stay down," he said.

Over his shoulder, I saw Dylan standing at the corner of the building, raising his arm to fire again.

"No!" I shouted, trying to push Jake down, get him out of the path of the bullet, somehow get him to safety.

CHAPTER TWENTY-FOUR

We hit the gravel and rolled under the Jeep, Jake's arms tight around me.

"Miranda!"

Dylan's voice filtered through my damaged eardrums. Jake urged me away from that voice, and we crawled out on the other side of the Jeep, staying low.

"You're going to have to drive," Jake hissed.

He held his hand over his left shoulder, and I could see the blood seeping through his fingers. I nodded, unable to speak.

"Keys are in the ignition," he said.

He grasped the door handle and tugged, opening the driver-side door. He crawled in, staying low, and I followed. The Jeep was riddled with bullets, but the engine started right up.

I looked to my right and saw Dylan break into a run toward us. I threw the Jeep in gear, spun the wheel and accelerated forward, spraying gravel in Dylan's direction. The Jeep fishtailed through the parking lot, the passenger door flying open before Jake grabbed it and slammed it shut. When he released his injured shoulder, I could see the red stain spreading across his chest.

"Oh my God," I managed to get out before I was forced to focus on aiming the Jeep at the only opening in the fence—a narrow gap in the chain-link fence that looked like it was blown out, the edges ragged and torn as if it were made of silk.

Our exit from the compound was greeted by a hail of bullets, but I pressed the accelerator into the floor and said a quick prayer as the Jeep sailed through the fence, over a shallow ditch and bounced sideways into the field. The car skidded across rutted ground, not staying on any road, and each contact with the ground jarred my body and pushed shards of glass into my skin. I corrected and aimed for the main road in the distance.

I looked away from the road to see how Jake was doing. His jaw was tight, and he was again holding his left shoulder with his right hand. The Jeep's tires hit the pavement, and the road smoothed out. I swerved to pass a slow-moving pickup truck and brushed my hair out of my face.

"Are you okay?"

"I'll be fine," Jake said, but winced when the Jeep hit a pothole. "Head to the airport."

The scenery sped by, none of it familiar. "I don't know where the airport is. I don't know where we are!"

He pulled the map from the console and unfolded it awkwardly with his left hand, keeping his right hand over the wound in his shoulder. "Stay on this road until we hit the highway, then head north."

I checked the rearview mirror, but didn't see anyone behind us with guns blazing.

"Is my phone still here?" Jake asked. His voice sounded fainter, and I rummaged in the center console until I found the device.

"Look for recent numbers, Matt's office is on the list," he said.

I was still speeding through the outskirts of Belize City, but traffic was lighter, so I glanced down and found the number, hitting the call button as soon as I saw Matt's name.

"Tell him what happened. Tell him to get a plane to the airport now." Jake's voice was softer and his jaw was set. He closed his eyes and leaned back, still gripping his shoulder.

"Jake!" I yelled, juggling the phone and the steering wheel.

He opened his eyes and gave me a slight grin. "It's okay. Just get us to the airport."

Matt answered, and I just started unloading information on him.

"There was an explosion at the consulate. Dylan shot Jake. We need a plane now."

"Jesus! Is Jake all right?"

"No! He's been shot. He's bleeding. It's his shoulder."

"Okay, okay. The plane's in the air. It will be at the airport in thirty minutes. Can you make that?"

"I think so."

"I can call my friend at the embassy for help—hell, I don't know if I can reach him if there was a blast there. Did you see if Chris Jenkins is alive?"

I nearly swerved off the road at the mention of Jenkins's name. "He just tried to kill us, Matt!"

"What?" Matt's voice betrayed his suspicions of me.

"Chris Jenkins is working with Dylan Holland. They're moving the money for Patterson."

There was a long pause, and I exhaled. I didn't know how to make him believe me.

"Give me the phone," Jake said, raising his left hand. I put the phone in his hand and gauged the size of the bloodstain on his shirt. There was so much blood. So much more blood than when Dylan stabbed him in the leg yesterday.

"Matt, it's Jake. Jenkins is dirty. He's working with Dylan Holland."

There was another pause.

"If Jenkins helped arrange the rendezvous at the airport, we can't go there."

He handed the phone back to me as I was negotiating a gentle turn in the road. I put the phone between my ear and shoulder and listened to Matt sputtering. "—If you can't go to the airport, how are you going to get home? Just go to the airport!"

I grabbed the map from Jake's lap and unfolded it, looking for the symbols I'd seen earlier.

"Matt, who arranged for the plane?"

"I did."

He said the words with emphasis, and I had to make a decision.

"Okay. We'll be there in thirty minutes."

I disconnected the phone before he could argue with me and gunned the Jeep, cutting off two other cars to take the exit north of the city, and speeding past the exit that led to the Belize City International Airport. I fumbled with Jake's cell phone while trying to keep the Jeep on the road, managing to punch in the familiar number into the keypad.

"Sarah Girard."

The breath left my lungs at the sound of her voice. If there was anyone in my small circle of friends who could pull off the impossible task I was requesting, it was Sarah. She also wouldn't ask any unnecessary questions. For now.

"Thank God. I need your help."

"Miranda?"

"I need a plane from San Pedro airport, Belize. To the nearest U.S. city with a hospital."

"What?"

It appeared I had stunned even the unflappable Sarah with this request.

"It's a long story. I promise to explain later. Can you do it?"

"You know I can."

"Use this credit card," I said, fumbling with my small purse, then read her the numbers. "We'll be there as soon as we can. Call me back on this number if there are problems."

"Who's flying?"

"Me and Jake Barnes."

"FBI Special Agent Jake Barnes?"

"It's a long story."

I heard faint clicking on a keyboard as Sarah got to work. "And you'll be telling me every detail," she muttered.

I said a quick goodbye, disconnected the call, yanked the wheel to the right and pulled into a familiar gravel driveway— the marina where Dylan had chased us yesterday. I drove as close to the docks as I could get, driving onto the lawn to park the Jeep in the shade beneath a small copse of trees.

"Are you going to be okay if I leave you for five minutes?" I asked Jake. He nodded and exhaled. His face was pale, and his skin looked clammy.

"I'm fine," he said, but his eyes were closed, and his breathing was labored. "What's the plan?"

He turned his head and opened his eyes, and my chest constricted at the pain etched on his face.

"We can't trust Matt. I know he's a friend of yours, but he knew what happened at the marina before we talked to him this morning. I think he's connected to all this."

Jake closed he eyes and exhaled slowly. "Okay."

My heart hammered in my chest. *Was I making the right decision? What if I was wrong, and Matt was our best hope of getting Jake to a hospital quickly?*

"You going to sit there, or are you going to get us a boat?" he asked.

His faith in me spurred me on, but his voice, fainter and slower, alarmed me. "I'll be right back."

I jumped out of the Jeep and looked in both directions, my eyes settling on a target—a fishing boat with two men standing on the deck. I ran toward them, my heart pounding.

"¡Ayúdame!"

Their heads snapped, and one man, the younger of the two, took a step forward as I approached.

"San Pedro? The airport? Can you get me there?"

The two men looked at each other, confusion crossing their faces.

"I can pay you." I reached into the purse at my hip and pulled out a wad of hundred dollar bills that I'd withdrawn at the bank. "I have to get to the airport at San Pedro. Can you do it?"

They looked at me, at the money in my hands, then at each other. The older man nodded, and the younger one turned to me.

"How long will it take?"

"About ninety minutes," he said, a faint trace of an accent in his voice.

"Can you make it faster?"

"Maybe a little more than an hour," he said.

"Great, I'll be right back." I stuffed the bills into my purse and ran back up the pier to the parking lot.

Jake was pale, his breathing shallow, and his skin damp when I returned. I started the Jeep and drove a dozen yards, parking it behind a large hedge that shielded the parking lot from the marina. I left the keys in the center console, making a mental note to square up with Klaus and Gerta once I was back in the U.S.

I helped Jake out of the Jeep and grabbed his duffel bag from the backseat. He leaned heavily on me as we made our way back to the boat.

"Miranda," he said, his voice in my ear. He was practically draped over me as we negotiated the ramp.

"Don't try to talk, it's okay. We're going to get out of Belize City, get home. We just have to get to the San Pedro airport."

"When I said..." His voice trailed, and my heart stopped as he took a breath, then continued. "When I said that I thought you were up to something..."

My eyes stung. "Jake, please, don't."

"No, I want you to know..."

"Jake, don't talk, please."

The drone of a helicopter overhead drew my attention overhead, and I saw the aircraft heading south, following the highway we'd just been on. I pulled Jake into the shadow of a large yacht tied off on the dock. It wasn't much cover, but I hoped that it was enough for the helicopter to continue searching the roads and not the water.

Jake's grip around my body tightened. "Miranda, I don't think that anymore. I trust you."

The air left my lungs in a rush. I wasn't sure I deserved that trust. "Oh."

We walked forward, and the two men waiting at the end of the pier at the fishing boat leapt forward to help me get Jake onto the boat. They looked around in each direction and then pulled me onto the boat quickly.

"Get down," the young man said. "Over here."

He helped me get Jake to the front of the boat and lower him to the deck.

"What kind of trouble are you in?" he asked.

I gave him a shake of my head. "Better you not know."

He nodded. "Raphael," he said, extending his hand.

I shook it. "Miranda."

"My father and I, we'll get you to the airport in San Pedro. Just stay out of sight here."

I tried to give him a smile. He handed me a bottle of water, ran back, and cast off the ropes fastening the boat to the dock.

I knelt next to Jake, running a hand along his face. In the mid-day temperatures, he was cold. I sat next to him, and he moaned, falling over into my lap. I pulled the duffel bag closer and unzipped it, finding the first-aid kit and a clean t-shirt.

The boat pulled away from the dock, and the warm breeze caressed my face and ruffled Jake's hair. As we motored out of the harbor, I tore his blood-soaked t-shirt away from his body and splashed some water on his flesh to see how much damage the bullet had done. It was impossible to clean away all the blood, so I pressed a clean shirt to his wound and hoped that he could hold out until we reached the airport.

I looked back toward the harbor and saw two helicopters now hovering over the coast. I swallowed hard and tightened my grip on Jake. As long as the helicopters kept searching the roads, we'd be okay. I kept them in my sights as long as I could, until the boat shifted course and headed for open water.

As the boat picked up speed, the warm wind dried the tears on my face.

"Just don't die," I whispered to Jake's still body, cradling him in my arms. "Please, please, don't die."

CHAPTER TWENTY-FIVE

The light green walls of the hospital made everyone look sick. It was one of the little details I noticed while I waited in the small family area for a nurse to let me know I could go back in and sit with Jake. If he wasn't in my sight, my body tensed, and my breathing grew shallow. I had already thumbed through all the worn magazines, my eyes skimming prose about maintaining tropical plants while my mind relived the horror of the last few days, always coming back to rest on Jake.

Always back to him. What was going on in there? Why wouldn't anyone tell me? Was he going to be okay?

What would I do without him?

That last one was selfish, but there it was—even if he survived, and the doctors and nurses had assured me he would, he would go back to being an FBI agent. I would go back to California, still "not guilty" but not exonerated of my crimes. Jake was not mine to keep.

That kiss, those small touches, the time we'd shared. That would fade into his memory.

But for me, it was seared into my being. Moments when I'd had genuine hope for the future, for the first time in a long time.

Hope that someone like Jake would look at me, really see me, really want me. That my feelings would be returned.

I moved from the too-firm sofa to pace the hall again, feeling hllow inside. The drive was destroyed in the fire along with the computer that contained all the evidence from my trial and the hard work culling out the documents that just might have proven my innocence. All of the time I'd spent, all of the work I did, all of the money spent that I didn't even have—it was all for nothing.

Worse, I'd almost gotten a good man killed.

My eyes ached from holding back tears. Hell, everything ached. My body from running and from the explosion. My jaw from when Dylan smacked me. Mostly my heart, though.

What was I thinking? I shouldn't have done any of this. Shouldn't have gone to Macau. Shouldn't have dragged Jake into my mess. Shouldn't have pressed him to let me go to the bank. If I hadn't, the bullet Dylan fired would have hit me, not Jake. Of that, I had no doubt. Dylan was trying to kill me, not Jake, with that shot.

"Miss Vaughn?"

I whirled around at the sound of my name. A nurse in pink scrubs walked toward me, a smile on her face. "You can go back in."

I thanked her and hurried back to the room, taking my seat by the edge of the bed. My eyes swept over his body, covered by the thin blanket. He looked exactly as he had thirty minutes earlier—still, pale.

"Is he getting better?" I whispered to the nurse.

"He's resting. He suffered a big trauma to his body, and it's now trying to heal. That takes a lot of energy, so it's good that he's sleeping." She patted my shoulder. "I left you a blanket. Try and get some sleep."

"Thank you," I said, taking my seat in the chair next to Jake's bed. I wrapped the thin blanket around me and tried to get comfortable in a chair that was as tired as I was. I still hadn't slept since landing some twenty hours earlier, just a few hours ahead of Rob and Sarah who had jumped on the first flight to Miami. While Jake underwent surgery to repair the damage from the bullet, I fielded questions from a bewildered local FBI agent with Rob at my side, his eyes growing wider at each revelation. When this was over, I hoped that he was still willing to hire me. If not, that at least he'd be willing to defend me against what I imagined would be charges of felony stupidity.

I had just closed my eyes when I heard someone cough softly. My eyes flew open, and I leaned toward Jake, the blanket falling away. But he was still asleep.

"Miss Vaughn?"

Donna Grayson, the assistant United States attorney who had worked alongside Matt Reese in prosecuting me, stood in the doorway. During the trial, her dark hair had been pulled back in a tight bun, never a hair out of place. Rob had told me that she had been a federal prosecutor for twenty years and had a reputation for never getting rattled.

As she stood in the door, that polish was gone. Her hair was loose and messy. She wore no make-up and was wearing a casual pair of khakis and a simple t-shirt featuring the logo of a local bike shop. Her demeanor was even more of a contrast— she definitely looked rattled. Her face was pale and her lips tight. Throughout the trial, she had barely looked at me, and when she had, it was with a cold detachment. Her anger now was apparent and something new.

I stood, unsure what to do and looked toward the door. This would be a good time for Rob and Sarah to return from the cafeteria. When they didn't appear, I faced the prosecutor with dread.

"Ms. Grayson," I said. Did she still think I was responsible for the fraud scheme? If she did, was she going to indict me? Was I going to have to relive that hell again?

She paused awkwardly in the door, waiting for me to invite her in, as if I had some claim on Jake's space. After a few long seconds, I motioned to the chair in the corner of the room. She nodded and entered the room, then dragged the chair closer to me. I scooted back in response.

But Donna Grayson slumped in the chair, and she couldn't look less threatening. She rubbed her face and took off her wire-rimmed glasses.

"How's he doing?" she asked, sliding the glasses back on her face.

"The doctors say he's going to recover," I said, looking at Jake's body.

He hadn't regained consciousness since a brief moment on the plane from San Pedro Island to Miami. He had grabbed my hand, whispered, "Are you safe?" Then he slipped away from me again. When we landed in Miami, we'd been whisked to the hospital where Jake went directly to surgery, and I was given a thorough once-over by a doctor. That felt like eons ago, and I was still waiting for him to wake up and give me a grin like the one he'd flashed in the Mexican restaurant just a month earlier. Sweet and sexy and smart.

"What are his injuries?" Donna asked, leaning forward and resting her arms on her knees.

"The bullet entered his back and exited his shoulder, narrowly missing his heart. That's what led to the blood loss," I said, keeping my voice low, as if I'd wake him if I spoke too loud. I wished it were that simple to wake him. "A half-dozen stitches in his leg, where he was stabbed. No infection, so that was good news."

Donna nodded. "I heard what happened, how you got him out of Belize."

I glanced back at her, cautious. Her tone was conciliatory, but I wasn't sure why.

"I talked to the agent who met you at the airport. He said you got Jake to San Pedro Island by renting a boat, that you probably saved his life," she said.

I shrugged. I'd gotten him into the life-threatening mess in the first place. It didn't feel at all heroic that I'd done my damnedest to get him out of it.

"I want to assure you that I had no idea that Matt Reese was involved in this...this scheme. I knew Matt from when he first was hired and worked closely with him. I trusted him," she said. "I regret that. I'm very sorry."

I nodded. "I lost the drive. Dylan and Chris took it."

Donna put a hand on my arm in a surprisingly warm gesture. "Don't worry about it. We'll work to reconstruct what you know, we'll go back over all the discovery in your case that led you to uncover this operation. Please, don't worry about the drive."

The prosecutor's change in attitude unsettled me.

"What happened to Dylan?" I asked.

Donna sighed, running a hand over her slightly frizzy fair. She barely resembled the uptight woman who had prosecuted me just months ago.

"Dylan Holland left the consulate compound and was caught trying to cross the border into Guatemala. He's currently in prison in Belize, and his attorney informs me that he'll be fighting extradition."

I breathed a little easier knowing that he was behind bars.

"And what about Chris Jenkins?"

"He's in jail, also, but is on his way back to the U.S. I think he knew the conditions of jails there well enough to know that he'd be more comfortable back here."

A slight movement in the bed caught my eye, and I leaned

forward to study Jake. His eyes fluttered and then opened slightly. He blinked, and his eyes scanned the room, coming to rest on my face. He started to reach out but groaned, and I jumped up.

"Don't move, that's your bad arm," I said, taking his hand in mine.

He squeezed my hand and licked his lips. "Thirsty."

I smiled. "I'll check with a nurse."

"I'll get her," Donna said behind me, hurrying to the door.

Jake's eyes, which had seemed so unfocused when he first woke, now honed in on mine. "You're okay?"

I nodded, feeling the tears fall and not even caring.

"Stop that," Jake said, his voice low and gravelly.

"I'm just so sorry. This is all my fault."

"No," he said, squeezing my hand again.

The nurse appeared at my side, and I stepped away to let her do her work, wiping my face as I did.

"Mr. Barnes, nice of you to join us," she said, turning to Donna and me. "You two can wait in the hall for a few minutes."

I left reluctantly and then stood awkwardly in the hall with Donna Grayson, waiting to be allowed back in.

"Miss Vaughn, I am very sorry," she said.

My head snapped around, and I stared at her, my mouth partially open. "For what?"

"I trusted Matt Reese. I mean, I trusted him to do his job. He reviewed the evidence in your case and assured me that the only irregularities in Patterson Tinker's records were related to the Sahara Fund investigation," she said. "It appears that he was paid off to look the other way regarding the money laundering."

Finally, the last piece of the puzzle snapped into place. That's why no one else had seen the money trail that I had found.

"I can assure you that there will be a full investigation of how your case was handled," Donna said. She closed her eyes and ran a hand over her hair. "Including my role in the prosecution."

"Oh, well, that's good, I guess," I said, not sure what I was supposed to feel. She had been the enemy for so long, but she seemed genuine in her remorse for what Matt Reese had done.

"I can't help but think that had I supervised him better, none of this would have happened. And an FBI agent wouldn't be lying here with a bullet wound."

"No, it's my fault."

She tilted her head. "How so?"

"I wanted to go to the bank, and Jake didn't. I convinced him to let me do it before we left for the airport. I told him it would just take a few minutes," I said, the words rushing out as my chest tightened. "If we'd left when he wanted to—"

"You would have been killed at the airport." Donna's tone was flat and her expression grave. "Chris Jenkins knew that you were going there, that Matt was arranging to get you and Jake out of the country. One of them would have had you two taken from the airport, probably turned over to Dylan or someone worse."

I couldn't think of anyone worse, but I didn't know anyone in a cartel.

"The cartel was tracking Dylan. They learned that he was in Belize to try and get the money moved, and with their reach, they would have found him, and you."

Her words sent a chill up my spine, and I rubbed my arms.

The door opened, and the nurse walked out and smiled. "He's all yours," she said with a laugh. "And make sure you keep him in bed. He's feisty and anxious to get out of here."

Donna and I went back to the room and found Jake sitting up. He had a paper cup in his right hand, his left arm still wrapped and secured to his chest.

"How are you feeling?" I asked, standing at his side.

He gave me that grin I'd been missing, and I nearly started crying again. "I'll be fine. Are you hurt?"

I shook my head, and he drained the water and set the cup on the tray that was half over his bed. Then he reached over and took my hand in his.

"Are you sure?"

I nodded and tried to smile.

"Donna, what are you doing here?" Jake's eyes flickered past me, and I turned to see the prosecutor standing at the foot of the bed.

"Checking on you," Donna said.

"What happened?" Jake asked, his brow furrowed. "I remember being in the Jeep, then nothing."

"Miranda got you to San Pedro, where the plane brought you to Miami."

"San Pedro? You mean San Pedro Island?"

"It was the nearest airport and it got us off the roads. They were looking for us on the highway," I said.

"How did we get there?"

"By boat."

He leaned back on the pillows and stared at me. "By boat? Did you steal a boat?"

I laughed and shook my head. "I rented it."

"With what?"

"I had withdrawn some cash at the bank. I thought it might help us, you know, if things went bad and we couldn't use credit cards," I said.

"Miranda applied direct pressure to your wound, stemming the blood loss, for the entire trip to San Pedro. There was a paramedic on the plane, but she probably saved your life."

My skin prickled as Jake looked at me. I didn't like getting praise for doing the right thing, especially from Donna. Her voice indicated she was maybe a little shocked that I'd not left

Jake to die, given my past. Plus, the whole mess was on my head anyway. I shouldn't get the praise without the blame, too.

"I'm just glad you're going to be all right," I said, finally finding my voice.

"What happened to Jenkins? Dylan?" Jake asked.

Donna filled him in while I stood next to Jake, still gripping his hand.

"I got word an hour ago that a body washed ashore and authorities in Belize believe it's Katrina Lore," Donna said. "It looks like she was shot and dumped offshore."

I expelled a long breath. I hadn't wanted to believe that Dylan had actually killed Katrina, even though he had admitted it to me.

"What about Bill Macias?" Jake asked.

Donna shook her head. "Nothing yet about your brother-in-law, but they're still looking."

"The accounts? Were you able to get any more information from Jenkins?"

"Yeah, some. He's going to cooperate, try and get a better deal. Dylan's not talking," Donna said. "But I'm hopeful that with Miranda's help, we'll be able to reconstruct the evidence and build a case against him that will convince him otherwise. Or at least convict him at trial."

Jake squeezed my hand, and I looked down at him. His face was still pale, but a more natural color than when we were on the fishing boat. His hair was disheveled. My instincts were to reach up and smooth it, but I kept my hand in his.

"Did she tell you that she's good with numbers?" He smiled weakly, and my heart skipped.

"Uh, no, but I'm not surprised," Donna said. "We were able to find a number of accounts, which we've frozen. The funds that were transferred will go to repay the Sahara Fund investors, as we agreed. The rest will be held until the outcome of the case."

The prosecutor let out a long sigh and looked between me and Jake.

"I just want to thank both of you, but especially you, Miranda. You certainly didn't have to help the government, but we couldn't have gotten Jenkins and Holland into custody without your help."

I nodded. "I just wanted to clear my name and help those investors harmed by Ralph and Tim."

Donna nodded. "I'm going to leave you two alone now. See you back in California."

She started toward the hall, paused, and turned back.

"I know you two have been through a lot in the past week, but I do need to ask you both to not discuss the case with each other. We've taken Miranda's statement, but I imagine we'll have more questions. And I'll need to get your statement, Jake. Then I imagine you'll both be key witnesses against Holland and the others. I may not be the one prosecuting it, but I really don't want this case to be compromised."

Jake nodded. "Of course."

Her gaze moved to me, a hesitant expression on her face. "And I hate to be so personal, but are you two, uh, involved? I mean, romantically."

"No," Jake said. His voice seemed suddenly stronger, and my stomach plummeted at his terse response.

I pulled my hand from his and tried to keep a poker face. We weren't involved. We'd shared a couple of kisses. I'd tried to throw myself at him, and we got interrupted, and then I nearly got him killed. That was no one's definition of romance.

So why did my heart crumble at the sound of his quick denial?

Donna left, and Jake reached up for my hand again. He

leaned back on the pillow, his expression relaxed and his eyes starting to droop.

"I think my nurse doped me up again." His voice slowed, and his eyes were starting to glaze over.

As much as I wanted to hang on to him, I gave his hand a slight squeeze and pulled away.

"I should let you get some rest," I said.

His eyes closed, his breathing deepened, and I thought he was sleeping.

"When are you going home?" he asked. He opened his eyes, but it looked like it took effort.

"I have a flight out in a couple hours," I said. As comforting as it sounded to be going home, I wasn't looking forward to facing Aunt Marie. When I called and told her where I was and gave her a brief, sanitized summary of what happened, she had promptly grounded me.

Jake nodded, and his eyes closed. His face relaxed. Whatever the nurse had given him had taken effect. I watched him for a minute, then reached out and smoothed his hair from his face, as he'd done to me. A slight smile flickered on his lips, but he didn't wake.

This was for the best, I told myself. Once he recovered, he'd get back to work, making sure Dylan and his coconspirators didn't get away. With some luck and Rob's forgiveness for stealing the discovery from my case, I'd go to work at the law firm and begin rebuilding my life. I might see Jake around since we were both going to be testifying at Dylan's trial. But we were not on the same path.

"I'm sorry," I whispered to his still form. Leaning in, I kissed his forehead, his skin as hot as the tears that seeped out of my eyes.

Then I left.

CHAPTER TWENTY-SIX

Three months later

The scent of pine trees and moist soil lingered in the air after the previous night's rainstorm. Underfoot, my boots crunched on small patches of snow and ice and occasionally slid on wet leaves as I approached the steps that led up to a wide deck.

"As you can see, the roof is new. So is the siding."

Sheila Aaron, my real estate agent, pointed to the metal roof with the copper trim and at the clapboard siding that sported a fresh coat of paint. The hand-turned railings and front door were also new. Sheila herself was new to real estate, she had told me when I called earlier that day. I chose her by her fortunate placement in the phone book that I'd found in the hotel night-stand the night before. She had no idea that I was going to be the single easiest client she would ever have.

"The deck was constructed about a year and a half ago, and if you know anything about Lake Tahoe permitting, you know what a miracle that was," Sheila said, brushing a few drops of water off her fleece jacket.

I ascended the few steps to enjoy the breathtaking view of

pine trees, the green boughs washed clean of snow last night, and the tiny sliver of blue water that lay in the distance. With its new coat of paint and expanded deck, I almost didn't recognize the cabin that I had sold nearly two years earlier, but the view was familiar.

"Why are they selling it?"

Sheila sighed and shook her head. "They were from the city. They thought it would be fun to have a cabin at Tahoe. This was affordable, so they bought it without realizing that this was an actual cabin—not a summer home on the lake within walking distance of the casinos."

She took out a ring of keys and unlocked the solid wood door. "Anyway, the first weekend, they put the trash out in a regular trash can."

"Oh, rookie mistake," I said, knowing what was coming.

"Yeah. They got bears that night."

Bears could smell garbage and would tear apart anything in their way to get to it. Including cars. A trashcan posed no barrier to a black bear.

"So they had a custom-made 'bear-proof' trash receptacle built," Sheila said, making finger quotes to emphasize her disgust. She pointed toward a pile of kindling near the corner of the cabin. "There it is."

"It's wooden."

"It *was* wooden. Some artist in Berkeley made it out of reclaimed hardwood, and it was just lovely. The bears tore it apart in about a minute."

She opened the door and let me enter. They may not have liked rustic living, but they sure had good taste in the renovations they made to the Vaughn family cabin.

"It's empty, but it's clean," she said.

I walked in and smiled. The small kitchen now had granite counters, and the cabinet doors had been updated. The hardwood floors were the same but had been refinished, and it gave the living area a new life. The single-pane windows were gone, replaced by winter-proof storm windows. Some of them were larger, letting in more of the view of the pine trees. The rebuilt deck was accessible through the new sliding glass door.

"How's the wiring?"

"Completely redone," Sheila said. "I doubt it had ever been updated since the cabin was built in the 1930s. But now it's up to code and shouldn't give you any troubles. There's also new insulation and new plumbing."

I walked around the small interior, taking in the changes big and small. All the things that should have been done over the years the Vaughn family had owned it and then the chores that I had always meant to do after I inherited the cabin—all of them were done. New paint. New carpet in the bedroom. A spiffed up bathroom. It was like seeing a familiar old friend who had blossomed out of her awkward phase with a complete makeover.

"The fireplace had some cracks, but it's been repaired. The chimney was cleaned when we put it on the market," Sheila said, her eyes roaming over the list in her hands. "And the new wood-burning stove is much more efficient than the old open fireplace, so you could even come up in the winter and not freeze to death."

I smiled and nodded, picturing my things in the cabin, once again. My family photos on the walls, my books on the shelves, not to mention my friends on the deck. Sarah was already planning our weekend ski trips in the winter and our summer cookouts under the trees. She said I owed her for putting her through hell when I called from Belize, and I happily agreed. It was a debt I'd never be able to repay.

Despite everything I'd done for the government, I wasn't getting my old life back. There was nothing the federal government could do to replace the two years spent fighting for my freedom, or the loss of my reputation and my career. But this was a start.

The last few months hadn't been easy. Rob had negotiated a "whistleblower" reward for me. Basically, I got to keep some of the money I transferred from Patterson's illegal operation to myself. After taxes, repaying Aunt Marie for my legal fees, and the costs of my travel to Asia and Central America, I had enough left to start rebuilding my life. The money was nice, but it certainly wasn't a windfall, so I was back working at Rob's office, though this time for a small but steady salary.

Since the Sahara Fund investors got all their money back, no one seemed too upset by this. Well, maybe Dylan, Matt Reese, and Chris Jenkins would be upset, but I hadn't heard from any of them. Matt and Chris had quickly pleaded guilty to conspiracy charges. Dylan was preparing for trial, charged with attempted murder of me and Jake, the murders of Katrina and Bill, and too many money laundering charges to count. The thought of testifying at Dylan's trial made me slightly ill, so I pushed it to the back of my mind.

Sheila left me alone in the empty cabin, and I wandered down the hall, my footsteps echoing off the bare walls. It was exactly as I'd imagined it would be someday—cozy, rustic. After I checked the tiny bedroom, I returned to the living room and climbed the ladder to see the loft, which smelled of new carpet.

Satisfied, I found Sheila on the deck checking her email on her phone.

"So, what do you think? Is this what you had in mind? If not, I have several others that are closer to the water," she said, reaching for a folder in her giant black bag.

"No, I'm good. I like this one. I'd like to submit an offer."

Her eyes widened and she smiled. "That's fast, are you sure?"

I nodded. "I'm sure."

"Well, why don't we go back to my office, and I'll get the paperwork together for the offer," she said.

She locked the door, and I stood on the deck, my hands resting on the cool damp railing, and stared into the trees.

"I'm going to take a walk around, but I'll meet you at the office shortly," I said.

Sheila gave me a wide smile.

"Sure, take your time," she said, then practically skipped down the steps to her small SUV.

I brushed some wet pine needles from the picnic table and sat on it, my feet resting on the bench seats. It was peaceful here, just as I remembered. I'd inherited the cabin nearly twelve years ago when my father died, and Aunt Marie and I had spent a lot of summer weekends hiking around the forest and over to a small mountain lake a few miles away. The cabin wasn't fancy, and I liked that about it. Even with all the upgrades the sellers had put into it, it was still a one-bedroom, one-bath cabin in the woods. It was a world away from everything.

And that's where I needed to be right now—away from everything. While I liked working for Rob, much of my energy was still spent on what I considered my case. Technically, it was the case against Dylan. Because I would be testifying against him, I'd met regularly with the FBI agents and Donna Grayson. Even though Rob was always at my side during those meetings, and he assured me that I was the government's star witness, it was hard not to feel defensive when being questioned by my former prosecutor. The thought of facing Dylan in court made me ready to head for a mountain hideaway.

The sound of car wheels crunching on gravel brought me out of my thoughts, and I stood, expecting to see Sheila returning, probably to double-check my quick decision or bring me the completed contract she'd whipped up in record-time.

Instead, a black truck pulled in behind my car and parked.

The door opened and my breath caught in my throat as Jake Barnes stepped out. The sun burnished his dark hair, and when he took off his sunglasses, I could see his deep brown eyes locked on me. I exhaled slowly as he walked toward the steps to the deck.

"You're not easy to track down," he said, resting his foot on the bottom step and leaning against the handrail.

He paused there, waiting to be invited up. My heart seized at the sight of him. Though I hadn't seen him in three months, not a day passed when I didn't think of him. I had spent so much time going over what happened, showing his FBI colleagues the trail of money transfers that had tipped me to Bill Macias's involvement, how we had followed Bill to Belize. And each time, hearing his name spoken out loud turned my insides into a tight fist of delicious tension. Ms. Grayson was adamant that I not discuss the case with other witnesses, and that would be Jake, so I hadn't attempted to reach out to him. Not that I would anyway. The guilt I felt at his injuries was overwhelming. Seeing him in front of me, I struggled to find my voice.

"Hi," I said, showing off my stellar conversational skills. "How did you find me?"

"Your aunt told me."

I raised an eyebrow. That didn't sound like something Aunt Marie would do.

"Rob Fogg vouched for me, so she told me where I might find you," he said, leaning on the railing. "How are you?"

I thought about that as I studied him. He seemed fully recovered now, strong as ever. I had suffered sunburn and a few bumps and bruises. Nothing compared to what he'd been through.

I shrugged. "I'm okay."

"I heard you're working for Rob now," he said.

"Yeah, he put me to work doing discovery review and clerical work," I said and motioned toward the deck. "You want to come up?"

I backed up as he came up the stairs, as if I didn't dare be too close to him. The back of my legs hit the picnic table bench, and I sat down hard and tried to look like I'd done it on purpose.

Jake's eyes crinkled at the corners, and I could tell he was suppressing a smile.

"This is nice," he said, sitting next to me on the bench and surveying the view.

"Thanks," I said, trying not to think about how close he was.

"Are you buying it?" He nodded toward the freshly planted "for sale" sign.

I nodded, and he raised an eyebrow. "I heard you got a whistleblower reward."

"You hear a lot of things," I said. "This was my family's cabin before I sold it to pay for my defense."

He smiled, and my stomach flipped. "Hey, I don't begrudge you the reward. You earned it."

I wondered what he got out of the experience. Other than a bullet wound.

"How are you?" I asked.

"All healed up and back to work," he said, tilting his head and smiling at me.

I bit my lip at the memory of him, barely conscious and bleeding. "Yeah, about that. I really need to apologize to you. I'm sorry you were hurt."

He smiled and shook his head. "Don't worry about it. I survived."

"No, it was my fault you got shot. Dylan was trying to shoot me. And you were only there because of me and—"

Jake turned and took my hand in his, the warmth enveloping my cold fingers and sending a zing of electricity up my spine.

"Miranda, I'm fine. I'm a law-enforcement professional. I

didn't walk in blind." He squeezed my hand. "And none of this was your fault."

I didn't believe that, but it was nice to hear. And it was nice to touch him.

"How's your sister?"

Jake frowned and looked down at the deck. "It was quite a shock to find out what Bill was up to, but she and the kids are doing pretty well. Lily's too young to really know what's going on. Molly told Henry that his dad died, but nothing about the circumstances."

"Of course," I said. "Oh, damn, I just remembered. I'm not supposed to be talking to you about the case. Donna Grayson is going to kill me."

He smiled. "She knows I'm here."

I shot him a suspicious look. "Why are you here?"

He kept my hand in his. "Thought you should know that Dylan has agreed to plead guilty. There's not going to be a trial."

My breath escaped in a rush of relief. No trial meant not having to publicly relive my betrayal by my former fiancé, the chaos of Macau, and the disaster that followed in Belize. It meant that I could move forward and stop living in the past.

I looked up at Jake. "Really?"

He nodded and his lips quirked up. "Yeah, really. He's looking at a forty-year sentence, but that means he could possibly get out of prison when he's a very old man. Otherwise, he was facing at least life in prison, if not the death penalty."

I tried to wrap my mind around that. For three months, I'd been focused on some unknown date in the future when I'd have to return to the courtroom. Now the future was wide open.

"Is he pleading guilty to everything?"

Jake shook his head. "No, they're dropping one murder charge. Without Bill's body, that would have been a difficult case to prove. But he'll plead guilty to the money laundering and attempted murder counts, and to the murder of his fiancée."

I let the news sink in. "Wow, so that's it? The case is over?"

Jake nodded. "Yes, it's done. They might ask you to give a statement at sentencing, but that's up to you."

I should have been relieved, but it almost seemed too good to be true. It was eerily similar to what I'd felt when the jury found me not guilty, like teetering on the edge of a cliff. I was free to go.

To go where?

I had a new job, new friends, and now, nothing tying me to my old life.

"Looks like you're getting back on your feet," Jake said. He looked down at my hand, still wrapped in his. "Buying the cabin, will that help give you your old life back?"

I shook my head. "I don't want it back. It was all lies."

"Not all of it," he said gently and raised his eyes to mine.

"Yeah, the true parts stayed around," I said, thinking of Aunt Marie, Rob, and Sarah.

"Are you going to look for a job in finance again?" he asked.

I shook my head and shrugged. "No, it appears that I'm still not considered a good employment risk."

"You helped bring down a world-wide money laundering scheme."

"The government hasn't exactly touted my role in that," I said. Donna Grayson hadn't so much as breathed my name in public. While Dylan's lawyers were aware of my statements, there had been no public exoneration for me. Jake had gotten more credit than I had, at least in the newspapers. Not that I was upset at that. He took the bullet. He got to be the hero.

"Donna should correct that," Jake said, releasing my hand and leaning forward to rest his arms on his knees.

I shrugged again. "I don't seem to care as much anymore. I

don't want to go back to work at Patterson or one of the other banks."

A long silence followed, and the only sound was the water dripping off the roof onto the deck.

"You were gone when I woke up," Jake said.

"Well, you were recovering from surgery, and I had to get back to California," I said, shifting on the cold wooden slats and focusing on the trees to avoid looking at him.

"But I didn't get a chance to thank you," he said.

I turned and looked at him. "Thank me? For what?"

"From what I heard, you saved my life by not taking us to the airport."

I shrugged. "I got you shot in the first place, so it doesn't seem proper to take credit for getting you to a hospital."

He gave me that smile I'd been missing, and my stomach clenched.

"That wasn't your fault," he said. "I was starting to think you were avoiding me."

"I had my orders to avoid you," I said. "Ms. Grayson said not to talk to you. It might jeopardize the case against Dylan."

"Well, you don't have to worry about that now."

I bit my lip at that thought.

"Like you said, we weren't involved. I didn't see a need for a drawn-out goodbye," I said, hoping the words sounded lighter than they felt.

He lowered his eyes to the deck and gave a curt nod.

"When Donna asked if we were involved, it caught me off-guard," he said, and I could tell he was choosing his words carefully. "If I'd said yes, it would have been more difficult for you. There would be more scrutiny. More suspicion of your motives. And of my objectivity."

I opened my mouth to respond, but Jake turned, and his serious expression stopped the flippant reply I'd readied.

Instead, I closed my mouth and looked away. He reached over and took my hand again, and the touch sent a flood of warmth through me.

He pulled me to my feet, and we stood facing each other inches apart, my hand still enveloped in his.

"I guess I'll see you around the courthouse," he said.

Struggling to find my voice, I nodded and took a shaky breath. "Maybe so. I'm helping Rob in a trial in January."

"Yeah, I know. I'm the case agent on it."

"Does that mean you'll testify?"

He nodded, a slow smile crossing his face. "And I'll be working with the prosecutor at the trial. So I'll see you every day."

Well, crap. I was no legal ethicist, but I was pretty sure it would be bad form for Rob's assistant to have an inconvenient crush on the FBI agent sitting at the prosecution's table.

He grinned and winked, giving my hand a squeeze before releasing it.

"Behave yourself, Miranda," he said and then turned and walked down the steps.

I watched him get into his truck and back out of the driveway, then drive down the road away from the cabin. I rested my hands on the railing, closed my eyes, and shook my head. It was going to be a long trial, sitting a dozen feet from Jake and trying not to show how that affected me.

Fate had a weird sense of humor, throwing Jake and me back in each other's orbits, yet conspiring to keep us apart. But maybe this time, I thought, maybe now we could figure out how to navigate that conflict.

I pushed off from the railing and walked to my car, ready to move forward and find out.

ABOUT THE AUTHOR

USA Today bestselling author Ellie Ashe has always been drawn to jobs where she can tell stories—journalist, lawyer, and now writer. Writing fun, action-packed mysteries is how she gets the "happily ever after" that so often is lacking in her day job.

When not writing, you can find her with her nose in a good book, watching far too much TV, or trying out new recipes on unsuspecting friends and family. She lives in Northern California with her husband and two cats, all of whom worry when she starts browsing the puppy listings on petfinder.com.

For more information, check out Ellie's website at http://ellieashe.com/.